Radio Joan

Kevin Davey

Radio Joan

Kevin Davey

AAAARGH! PRESS

Published in Great Britain in 2020 by
Aaaargh! Press
119 Woodbridge Road
Ipswich
Suffolk
IP4 2NJ
United Kingdom
Copyright © Kevin Davey 2020

ISBN: 978-0-9573635-9-5

Typesetting and design by Paul Anderson.

incline your ear for I am sated with evils and
my life reached the brink of Sheol

as waves coming from more than one transmitter
I then heard
fused voices, and with broken phrases,
and many birds making counterpoint

Inform. Educate. Entertain.

All at once? A tall order. At the very least, entertain.

– I was twenty-three years old when the troubling of my life began.

– Tell me.

Ears gloved in phones, I bend to the microphone's bud.

– She was all snares. Nets her heart, fetters her arms.

Foldz buzzzz in tracheal breeeze, jawsome cavity ampso cheeeeeeky. Paddle tongue tollolloll I tip I teethe I nase I nip my lips. Mylar's shaking coil's a quaking current's swell oscso I wave.

The first fifteen seconds, life or death in the radio game.

Britain's master spook speaks, pre-recorded, plum.

– Joan Cade was an English Amazon. Mosley's whore they sneered but I say democracy is in her debt.

Over the cans, song.

– Beset the slumberer's bed.

Pit of strings accelerato animato.

– Wake up and reflect!

Red light flashing red on green.

– Here we go counting her in two one fade up.

> *it's all over for me I won't last much longer now I used to want to make the hundred get the gram but I don't anymore I've made it into the nineties I'm past ninety myself I've seen wars revolutions the miracle of radio no regrets no not me this is my finale the last test and willament of Joan Cade ha I've lasted longer than my teeth my friends are gone I heard the Soviet Union croak I'm ready to shake my maker's hand ready*

to follow Willy and Tom so her maj the kween kaydoubleyou
that's how Willy spelt it oh he did used to make me laugh haha
tin Lizzie the Fritz can strike me off her birthday list

– Preserve a high moral tone.

– It's of paramount importance.

Joan's room in the private care home has a picture window running the length of her single bed. She always sits with her back to me. From the brow of the hill we look down at the town and over the bay beyond. She measures Whitstable with the pin of a brooch.

I'm stationed behind her, notebook in my lap. The mic's between us. From outside we look as if we're sitting in a glass-fronted booth. Watchers view us from the tree line, others sit in parked cars. The sun rises, the sun sets, to its place it glides, there it rises.

– Stick to what you can see.

Control's curt reminder.

The smelter on the quay, a storm-beaten watchtower. Emphysemic sea breeze, sprays of tar-drift, steaming whelk-mist. Ridgetiles. Saltcrust walls. Floodtide natives. Sodden floors. Halfway down the hill a tree half-green, full-leaf, half-glittering flame.

The window is flanked with curtains, twin falls of fabric lanced by a large wooden needle. On the drapes red poppies large as plates, buttoned black to grey stalks. On our left, basking in the estuary, the Isle of Sheppey. To her right Joan can see the sprawl called Tankerton. Essex grins from the horizon, chip teef Sarfend. Round and round goes the wind, on its rounds the wind returns.

– Don't push it.

– So whisper me sound advice.

– Creeeeaaaaaahkagruppttertupsk

Tumult in the air. Below my sight line a waste truck wheezing. Lift, eeeeg. Eeeegont upending eeeechgeechgeehg the champ, returning eeeg. Joan looks down at the confiscation. I'm too far back to see the action. Castors resonate in tubs on slabs. Outsourced gloves drag empty bins back to a recess.

– fallen in love with someone you shouldn't have fallen in

A radio in the cab pesters the cul de sac.

– Good morning pop pickers apple pickers nose no a step too far for the beeby sea guten morg pickled peckers here's a pick-me-up broadcasting the best that's right that's right that's right that's right in every department of human knowledge, endeavour and achievement.

Joan's words haze the pane.

> *we get very good reception up here that's a boon for me I'd be lost without my wireless and my radio for company they're my comforters these two*

A wooden valve wireless occupies a table at the foot of the bed. A plastic transistor perches on the cupboard by her pillow.

Eeeeg eeeeg. Another bin. Eeeegeegeeg eeeg bock-bock-bock-bock-bock-bock.

> *recycling that's the preferred way these days isn't it not landfill I always hoped to be landfill haha but it will be incineration for my bones human smoke*

Framed and braced on the cupboard, beside the bedside tran, there's a grey photograph. It's the reason I'm here. I pick it up. The scar, William Joyce's second smile, is unmistakeable. Curving from his mouth to the lobe of the right ear, the weal sags to the jaw.

– Put a prop under that washing line Willie.

Young Joan's a-teasing. He pouts. Lipsin they sipkiss, kissip they nuzz. The stripe stiffens. Her lips venerate the rut.

A man in a vest sups gel from a glass. Smooching a raised arm, the underside, slurpily he slops.

Viceroy of India, purrs Joan. She laps sud from Joyce's seam. My Curzon.

– Balls. Hung out to dry by the Bleeder, that's me.

– We'll make him regret it.

My Joan my Joan Willy mumbles from his twofold maw.

When the portrait was taken, in 1937, Joyce was director of propaganda for the British Union of Fascists.

– Honey and milk under your tongue.

- Lips lilies, scent of breath like apples.

- Oh that I were young again and held him in my arms!

  *our last good time that was Willy was on the back foot soon
  after he was sidelined by the movement didn't know which
  way to jump Britain or Berlin the rattle or the Reich it was
  our last good time full sixty years ago when we'd both been
  sacked by Oswald Mosley hahahaha*

Her wizened hand stirs the atmospherics. Sherwoooosh shoosh sherwoop.

The intricacies of wireless reception. The philistine obtrusion of the apparatus itself.

- Channel-hopping aller time she was.

- A wave-hunter.

Joan and Willy smooch shupshoo. They beak they breast their temples eave. And the correct answer is necking says the host of a quiz show. Haha hilarity, for two seconds set free. That's necking, the host continues, as in heavy kissing of the neck and of course it can also mean stretching, deforming under tension.

Must we have that on, he asks?

We must she murmurs.

- Judicial bloody murder, a lynching by the state.

- What Haw Haw? Joyce deserved it. Most hated man in Britain.

- Hush now, the signal's weak as it is.

- Hitler's bliddy mouthpiece. Gave comfort to the enemy.

- Shup an' lissen.

Crowds have gathered outside the prison gate, as crowds always will, the announcer says.

- The shrubs lining the path are frosty today and the pond in the park has frozen over.

Standard English, received pronunceeay, no sham or push for ratings.

- A young girl is stamping her feet to ward off the cold.

The plaint she's makin' to her muvver – am atch longer? – ain't erd, to the detriment of the vigour and varied beauty of the English language.

– They are waiting for the announcement to be posted up.

The tools of the executioner are laid out, ready to hand. A pair of rubber shoes, a small door in a frame. A sock for my hand – once on it stays put. An axe handle, oiled, in a vice. A cupboard face-down over trestles, doors secured by a walking stick. A heavy rope tethered to a post, coiled hose, washboard, striker, celery.

We've rehearsed the routine scores of times. It takes six seconds.

Tripod to red.

Footsteps, a door closing.

– I think we'd better have this on you know.

Creaksquee-clat. Tug. Carotid collap. Severtebrae. Skup skup snap.

At 9am on the morning of 3 January 1946, Willy two-grins swings in Wandsworth jail.

I part jelly with my fingers.

The buccal rip recurs, lip to lobe agape.

I wedge a pencil's rubber tip between four buttons of my keyboard. Rotating it one way then the other I sham the sound of rope, heavily weighted, swaying.

An infant screams. A mother mourns. A scar spawns. Redout.

A blue clock over the prison gate, the large hand falling. A dying salute for the full quarter. The hour, slow riser, slably unbedding.

– In our proper motion we ascend.

Climbing back up, that's the difficulty, that the labour.

Awaken. Find the beginning.

An old lady from behind, framed in skyglaze. She has driftwood arms.

– Say something please Mrs Cade, to check the volume's right, anything.

some for the levels dear that's what you mean I'll sing of
arms of a man fated to be an exile who is it sifts my voice
from dust what am I to you ancestor muse that'd make a
nice change moooze I'm your source press firmly for more
sauce will that do

I fumble with the recorder. Morse horse? The set-up's all wrong.

– A little more please.

you unseal my tomb with a view underworld on the peak of a
hill whose bright idea was that I wonder grace this chamber
in which I'm beset a radio at my back a receiver at my feet
I'm a rectifier resister ready to go with my brekfarce show
it's what I was put on this big bead for I'm Radio Joan my
mojo's workin work my mojoan won't you mister DJ please

– She's a live one. Joan is zo funkisch!

– The distortion's bounce from the window.

– A tad more, we're nearly there.

I'm a tower of power I'm a mill I'm a steeple look inside there's
audio people I'm your eyeful a mast from the past blowing in
the wind Daventry Shukhov Fernsehturm can you hear the
wind dear we'll be asking this morning can man heerda wind
I wan-na know can an-nyone herd the wind

– Thanks Mrs Cade, that'll do nicely.

this is what I call a ball this is Joan Cade Radio Joan of
Kent reporting on the century coming to a close from Century
Close Whitstable

BADOOM BADUM

Two clouts to the door. Joan has enemies in the care home, neighbours with
stouter cartilage and memories of the war. They know we're recording. They
really don't like it.

BADAM

Come along now, the dayshift drover calls.

– Back to the lounge, tea's waiting.

- Blackshirt bitch!

- Come along now.

- Lies an' Nazi propaganda.

- Tea that's lovely ta.

- You want the truth ask us what suffered!

- There's balance and there's bollocks.

- Are there biscuits?

The daily spite of this unmannerly town.

Joan's nape ignores the interruption. She may not have heard it.

- You're a pro Mrs Cade I can tell.

She replies over her left shoulder.

> *there's plenty more where that came from dear I'm ready*
> *when you are*

Glorious view up here I say. Enter a ship with a merry song.

A steam cruiser appears in the estuary. Joan places a hand on the window, a hand wrinkled like the foot of a goose. The ship enlarges. From the upper deck, young girls in summer dresses point at us, waving. A gent doffs his boater, bowing. They're gathered round a wireless set. A woman waltzes alone, hand on nobody's shoulder, the other in his palm. Red hoops of skirt swirl astatic.

- They complete their toilette while listening to foxtrots.

- They read newspapers to the sound of tangos.

- They take their meals accompanied by rumbas.

The deterioration of listening.

Quick quick quick steps the tinny headboard transistor. Quick quick quick. How do you do Mrs Cade who's the date? A josh from the gent replacing his straw. His sonorant query hurdles the footboard.

> *local historian would you believe*

- My dear how wonderful! Do say it as you saw it.

the truth as I recall it yes I will

A flurry of steam condenses on the glass. The dancer dissolves, a mosaic of crimson scales that drip, merging, to the sill. The gent is washed away. The ship shimmers and shrinks. It is further away than it used to be. I am looking at a long scratch in the stern, for it is especially the scratch which is further away. The prow pierces curtain poppy crop, the stern departs damp flag fraying. The window clears, the bay is empty. Another steam cruiser noses the wake of the first. Joan raises her hand.

– I'm ready now Mrs Cade.

my life is looking out from here it's all I have it's marvellous

Don't expect me to describe her, I can't.

The recordings took place more than twenty years ago. She rarely turns from the window. I interrogate the nape of an antique neck.

cycling dancing whistling looking out into the world feeling young to know I'm free that's what I long for but those dancing days are gone all that silk and satin gear just look at me now puh this body's nearly done wise decrepitude don't make me laugh

I'm greeted by her left profile, fleeting, never more. Joan's back is her welcome, hulloey! or hi! pitched from a blouse, morning muttered from a blanket shawl, that time already grunts a sluggish nightie, late again the dressing gown's dressing down. On summer Sundays – satin, scented, elegant – hi hi it's such a lovely day! Those were our best.

Nape natter framed by the bay. Her vertebrae knuckle a nose, jut a chin.

– How are we today? Ready to cough?

if you're ready to catch

I grill a thorax boxed between bony blades.

– How does the cone of the individual gyre with that of the world?

The skate ripples its fins, Joan's back laughing on tiptail.

not that old chestnut pass ask another

Before I can it booms:

> ***the beginning of eternity the end of time and space the start
> of every end what am I hahaha***

A laughing kite, blowy, button-tail frisking in backsway. Her neck rises swan, unusually long, slender antenna soaring. I open my notebook, click my pen.

Upright it locks.

– That straight back and arrogant head.

She vases by the window. Now and then, to examine me, the stalk rotates.

– The left-looker?

– That's the one. Her eye gauges my thoughts. I never see the full dial.

– Come, fix upon me that accusing eye.

– Cyclop Cade.

– Copepod Cade!

– Sometimes she scared me, seriously.

> ***tell me about yourself what's your interest in fascism?***

– Not now Joan when there's time I will.

The stem wilts the wispy dome dips the eye sets to the floor. Mrs Cade sprouts a thorn.

> ***if it's a one way street you're after forget it kid you can think
> again pass me the radio pages I've better things to do***

– Let's press on.

Barber, I clip history from her nape.

> ***first time I met Willy was Chelsea town hull a speech about
> women***

I'm a pastmonger trimming skate.

> ***we went to Berlin in thirty-three we stayed at the Excelsior***

Shadow behind her shade.

we had forty thousand members by 1934 but why do you ask

Know the enemy, I should have said. Know the enemy never fear battle again.

– For the record Mrs Cade, the historical record.

I sit behind her, slightly to the left, not far from the bedside cabinet to which I move the microphone. Its foam tip gorges our words. The nape, a baffle, nips the top notes from Joan's answers, flatting the tone.

buh whe duh yuh won to knoh dea cun wuh tock abow ewe?

I was sired by an Oswald, I could have replied. A Suffolk's hurrah for the blackshirts. I should have shown willing, made something up.

but he doesn't does he he's a dull emitter

– Not now Mrs Cade there's no time for that.

I'd prefer you more chatsome bear that in mind

Sometimes I vary the setup, placing the recorder on the bed. Sheets slink, the quilt peaks and plodes. My mic's a skittle to her elbow. It flops when she shrugs and swoons when she sighs. Clouts of bedding stifle her testimony. F/X clump a paddling pool. I'm unable to make out her words. Mics are delicate petals. Why can't they be turned, like wooden bowls, and gape? Why aren't they funnels?

Occasionally I sit in a gap between the drawers and the door. My elbow does the damage there, jolting the cupboard, bludgeoning Joan's trill.

British Union berwhooomp after the meeting at olbrummmp
berbbbbdom Jews Tom said he knew it was a lie

As for the balance, that's awful whatever I do. My questions are inaudible, feeble bassoon. Joan's replies are often indistinct. We're fenindinc, too fen, the both of us. We're going to need enhancement.

– No budget for that.

– Not now but in development.

You studied where which subjects under whom she asks. Which texts what topics did you vote? Tell me how, tell me why, what do you hope for, what do you dream? I keep my answers brief. What do you care about who do you care for what are you going to do with your life.

have you ever killed

Electrodrone spiky bristling deep persistent from the phonic workshop team.

well have you go on

Brzzz ozzz uzzz rising mains hum erzzz ozzzberuzzzz ozzz.

She starts to laugh. I play along. I've got no choice.

let's hear it what have you got

– Nothing not really.

go on tell me

Zing zing zing zing.

– Chimes from the kitchen, a brush sweeping cymbals. I thought maybe I'd left the radio on but it came from the cooker. A mouse trapped in an oily wok, frantic, clawing concavo, slipping then scuttling. I try to pitch it in the garden but the mus bails on the backswing, lands on the lino and shoots to the wall. Stretched out flat I can see it, a throbbing seam of fur.

then what go on then what

– I cut it in half with a bread knife.

Clinical, she says.

– No, desperate, what else could I do? My partner would have flipped.

tell me about the others

– What others no there weren't.

Have I ever betrayed anyone?

– I'd rather call it whistleblowing Mrs Cade.

can you

– What?

whistle a tune

– Yes.

let's hear it go on

I purse my lips I shrill the national anthem. I stop after one verse.

13

— I forget the rest.

Go on she says go on. She croaks along.

> *scatter her enemies da da da da confound their politics
> frustrate their knavish what an anode you are not knowing
> the end you are English aren't you pah you should be
> ashamed of yourself*

Have you ever abandoned anyone? Crophoghak! she coughs crophhog!
When did you last make someone cry? Croph!

> *are you a selfish man*

Finally the skate takes the bait. The nape agrees to interviews, two mornings
a week until we're done. It kites for hours. Her years in the Labour Party.
Mosley's solution to unemployment. How it was blocked. Launch of the New
Party. His conversion to fascism. Her affair with William Joyce. The war, the
trial, his execution.

> ***Willy was the love of my life I begged him not to go to Berlin***

When I lob, the nape blocks.

When I laugh it objects. And then she starts to share. A tale some names
a date. Tom this, Willy that. Memory release, the slow unwinding of Joan.

A strand appears at her left shoulder. Yes Willy owned a gun, she says,
many men did. I pull gently, passing the thread back across the bed. Did
you see it yourself? The nape takes it up. He shows me how to fire it as if I
didn't know! A strand, a pass, a gentle tethering. Too risky to keep it he says.
I wouldn't I said, so he buried it in Midhurst.

Little sedentary stitches as though we are making lace. And do you know
where? I am the needle's eye. Yes I do, says the nape, but why should I tell
you. Inside, she was singing and weaving with a shuttle made of gold. At
Ethel Scrimgeour's place. Where, exactly? By an elm in the fruit garden,
wrapped in an oilcloth. I wind the rope and sing. It's probably still there she
says. Taps at the door add punctuation.

> ***clear off I've a man in here we're not presentable***

— Don't give me no mind you finish him off.

As it opens, a dressing gown falls from the back of the door. It bags my head, lights out. Soapiness, softener, funk. It slips to the floor. Leaning forward to pick it up I clat my skull on the handle.

Rim of a spoon, hard to a breadboard.

hopeless isn't he just look at him

– Good morning to you too Joan.

Nylon nurse, wafting floral disinfectant, meds on a tray.

what's good about it

– Anything you need today?

yes let me be loved as though still young

– Fancy it true like the rest of us do. Time for your pill.

I loop the dressing gown back to a hook clogged with bag strap and coat. Again the gown drops. Stooping I knock off the bag. The nurse turns towards me. She mimes a rebuke. Her voice spings, tinning and thin at my elbow. She's skirling from the plastic radio.

– Be more considerate with Mrs Cade and her things.

don't rip the unsewn stitch you tell him Vera

– Thread of your untold tale.

the song of us together hahaha

Should I look at the radio or the nurse when Vera's speaking? Which is the most polite? Nape Joan hugs her shoulders, kissing air, hips awaggle.

I'm feeling hot tot tot

– Age gracefully Joan give it a go for me.

sorry matron carry on sergeant matron major

I pick up the zista. I slide the volume down to zero. Nurse Vera tos and fros and tuts in dumbshow, dappling the room, a bustle of sunblock. I ease the sound back up.

– feel like a gooseberry in here.

you're hairy enough hahahu

The double act riffs on, ding dong. I put the zista back on the cupboard. Can we get on I say. The nape calms, the nurse turns. I nudge the tone.

– I'm only allowed till lunch.

Vera Hairberry looks from the bed to me then back to Joan.

– Behave yourself missus. And you – don't tire her out.

Next door a Foley picks up a tray. It's stacked with plastic tubs. He shakes it a little, he shakes it gently. Four steps by a boxing glove follow, two on a carpet, two on tiles. Swish the nylon florets, shut a door.

– Tad of ech too, issa corridor door.

Our mornings dawn a method.

> *I remember how we argued at the Excelsior we argue because Willy's overexcited he knows Hitler's methods won't wash in England not really not on the scale needed he realises the impetus will have to come from outside and that idea frightens him he can't cope with it that's how it seems to me looking back I'm telling you things I've told no one before I know there are holes and gaps in my story I can't explain I can't help that nobody can dear when you play it back later you must pull my memories apart not lump them together like I do unpick me take nothing on trust don't defer or be polite that's not the way to the bottom of things*

– I hear you Mrs Cade.

Joan's strictly nuchal, never face to face. She bestows her left elevation like an honour: lofty chin and drawstring lip, crocodentals, one adjustable lens. A sniffit snoot above the town powd snitch of eagle. Zygomatic quaking. She's a one-eyed sky god, rapid occipit eclipse.

Her view of me is equally constrained.

– I do sometimes wonder.

> *what do you wonder dear*

– Would we recognise each other in the street?

> *it's easier to talk this way*

– We'd be strangers wouldn't we?

16

I'm more comfortable like this.

– Sfine by me Mrs Cade, whatever suits.

I'm not shy it's not that

– Of course not Mrs Cade.

I'm not confessing neither nor ashamed and call me Joan

– No I mean yes Joan.

alright it's confession but it's not a consultation this cot's no couch I'm not a nutjob and I'm certain you're no shrink if I face this way it's because I remember more with the town in front of me

– You're comfortable, Mrs Cade, that's the main thing. Joan.

Freckled shingle, sunset blush between her stooped shoulders.

if you was looking at my face you wouldn't hear me the same

– I suppose not.

I've a touch of deathness in my right ear I hear you better when I sit this way

– It works for me Joan.

The ask, the return. The buzz the flow the loading at the gap – a spark – twists and obstructions a wall and a piling. Arc back helter hinder retroskelter waves of recollection. Morning broadcast Radio Joan.

Between oscillations I flick through the listings. I listen to the radios. I track barges tilling the bay and squint at remote sea forts. A sallow chimney pot, a duckling swell. I pan the skyline broken by the nape. Dancing silver birch and distant sails. I put a question. When Joyce left what was his plan? As the nape deliberates, I scale a gable and remove my shoes. I pad slate pitching, leaning to the ridge. I trip on a cable and slide. I soil my socks in a gutter. I don't believe he had a plan she says. Just fewer and fewer options and a fear of jail. Angus paved the way, she says, he sounded out Berlin. Sometimes I let the tape do the listening. Hand over hand I swing from branch to bough hand over hand. Leaves twigs Joan's tattle flick at my ears. On slow days I schlep the labyrinth at the foot of the hill, lowering myself to the pavement, finding ginnels and byways I've not used before.

a short cut to the beach not safe but short cuts never are

Her footboard is a palisade over which the wireless watches.

you see the thing with Willy is he longs to be a soldier no an officer at least he was a general in his dreams he craves battle longs to lead men as a child he'd idolised the black and tans then the Royal Worcesters turf him out

Tell me something I don't know.

he's paid by the secret service he supplies them with information all through the thirties he was a snob he cheats at chess he only pretends to like Wagner how's that for starters

She's reading my thoughts. But how? I'm not sure what I do know now.

I let her skirting board show me round the room. Copper slots, a rocker, a plug in a wig of dust leeching plastic. The tail meanders in grey flats past a disc specked with plaster, a button perhaps, a coin. I don't believe we've met before, indeed we've not, so when did you arrive? An interrupted circuit. The cable pipes past fabric poppies heaped in shade by sheepskin slippers. Past varicose socks on marbled pillars. Entering the shadow of the old receiver, the flex snakes between the tablelegs, vaulting to the set.

— What do I miss? What was she saying?

Willy gave me the wireless I don't think he'd like the tran he hated imports when he hears that Union Jacks are being shipped to London from Japan my what a fiery night that was such fireworks I thought his scar would burst he blamed Jewry of course he always did alien financial domination Jewish banks and intrigue bringing Britain down forcing governments to let cheap tat through ports butter boots blouses balaclavas louses refugees Jewfugees Haile Selassies same night on the wireless there's a Jewish violinist playing Eli Eli the psalm about suffering on the cross well Willy explodes at the wireless old faithless over there it's a racial war cry by the Jews he yells he didn't turn it off though did he cos he likes shouting back so red he is they're accusing us of wrongness Joannie us it's about us being the persecutors when the real crimes are theirs bloody Reith shouldn't bloody allow it he roared things will be

different when we run the BBC he discusses that with Tom
a lot Lord Reith of the BBC has a scar too his left cheek was
torn badly in the war he was a mirror for Willy

Now we're getting somewhere.

– And that's roughly how it went.

– Horse's mouth, backside to cart. She never turns around, not properly?

– That's how it was.

– Ashamed, I suppose. I imagine she was lonely?

I'd indexed that. I find it quickly, know what he is driving at.

every year that passes is cruel to women most men are too
women are the record of that cruelty men lie about loving
you needing you then they leave men slice in and out of your
life none of them stay no staying power loyal as sparrows
dependable as the weather with their sorries and betrayals
and their thoughtlessness Willy upped and went in thirty-
nine my Joe was always leaving too not by choice didn't
come back the last time poor man the convoys were Russian
roulette after Joe others came and went men diminuendo
they come less often I get no nods no winks my way these
days I'm lucky to have your company dear I like you here
even though you don't say much what do you have to say
for yourself today any feelings insights you'd like to share
eh no I didn't think so I'd have preferred someone a little
more affably inclined I must say not just questions and more
questions then the foolish conclusions you draw

That's not fair Mrs Cade a faint bassoon objects I'm just.

try harder not to interrupt you always interrupt I'll teach
you to stop interrupting if it's the last thing I do

Listening's live puzzling. Sounds to the cochlear, soft loud clear, patterned
unpredictably. Sounds you hear indifferent, or deferent, hovering, alert.
Alien sounds familiar embodied sounds recorded. Beat and breath subvocal,
inner speech contrapunting – questions, connectives, associations, imag-
inings. We comprehend part or nothing of most we hear, our frames failing.
But now and then, now past now, the future crystallises, meaningful.

19

– Okay Joan but

you're doing it again stop crashing in on me do let me finish it really matters when you're listening that you think of me as I was then as Joannie young and pretty keen to learn not Eva Braun decaying in room eight hear me as the Joannie I was then as I do myself what I say will make more sense

Her crumpled hands clasp her nape.

She rubs her atlas, shield hand wary, finger to the axis. A threat to the rear, sensed not seen. Lidless eyes of Trackers. How will it come? Blade or blow of retribution, pillow, needle, gun? A razor mowing wisps, round in the chamber, cosh falling. A clawhammer, icepick, shattering the cervical?

– Tissue decay. Mind pox. The melanomic mole.

Scur hair on end, nape wired and edgy.

the tag in this blouse chaffs my neck I'm itching to death

It's me of course, the threat. I'm all that's here.

Sticking my neck out, closing on Joan, beak wide.

– You were a smasher Mrs Cade.

what do you mean were

– Still are.

I was wasn't I

– Mosley thought so too I bet.

of course he did

– Go on.

Dark web, nape in my bill. Cnaep, the top of a hill.

It's evening on the Thames.

The young man admiring gives Joan the eye. His sleeves are wet. She knows he's looking. The punt is illuminated by a Chinese lamp, a swell of orange hanging pumpkin from a pole. MODERN WIRELESS. There are cushions fore and aft in black and orange chequered slips. One shilling. He has a thumbprint on his shoulder. June 1924, Vol III. Joan lounges, propped on a forearm, looking into the horn of a wireless set. UNUSUAL FAULTS. She smiles on the silent void. There's a kite-shaped aerial on the mahogany till, wiring webbed to dowel struts. AN ST100 SET WITH TWO H.F VALVES. Caps on orange, bold and black. The paper lamp, Joan's inkless gown, his stock shirt, reflect in static ripples. HIGH TENSION CIRCUITS EXPLAINED. Orange the sail above

– A punt you said, a punt.

Orange banner overhead, another on the riverbed, weighted with black rules. The glowing ink gilds Joan's hair. Orange pools in the lip of the horn, rims the aerial, blots his crown.

The late train railing over Kent. Joan's alone, her back to London. The hurtling locomotive fugs gardens, smuts trees, soots utility poles. Trackside chimneys morse signal from the moon, a frenetic, indecipherable strobing.

Joan trails her fingers in a wireless magazine.

Electro-oceanic waves sweep over the country to local radio receptors. Radiating currents become letter signals on the screens of enormous books erected in public squares, higher than houses, books turning their own pages. Expanding libraries of the street, dielectric codices of radia.

– Wireless is disrupting the world.

– Wireless civilises.

– Many people imagining opera to be dull and dreary are converted in a single evening.

Grzzzooot. Father strikes a match but fails to light his pipe. His hair's standing on end, he's going to burn his fingers. He stares at the daughter who has just switched on the wireless.

Joan's semi-respectable: elegant heels, a pleat skirt. Radio's tendrils deform her head. She's modern art burlesque, Anglo-cubist Bracasso, jugsaw pirate with a patch. Not at all the landscape on the wall.

Her blouse has a high-frequency collar. Her left arm's shortwave. Electrons sideslip from her boho frizz, fracking the mirror.

A hand appears. A fingernail engraves a footnote on the carpet. It's a

warning: *curious effect of a piece of modern music on a very receptive listener.*
Father's face grows pale.

– Clashing discords loss of equilibrium!

Ma drops her knitting.

– Principles overthrown, unexpected drumbeats.

The wool mimes Miro.

– Great questionings. Apparently purposeless strivings.

The infant sister looking up.

– Stress and longing, chains and fetters broken.

Her brother gaping.

– Opposites, contradictions.

Cat arc back fur static.

– This is our harmony.

– Allus fishing for signal were Joan.

– Hungry ears, she couldn't help herself.

Sherwoooosh sherwoo. Interminable manipulations and adjustments.

Eight years later, the train reversing. Joan, her back to London, looking from the compartment window. The high street low the bridge, river vista river derci. Beach barges saltmarsh shrinking. Hop gardens rush the carriage, blur and wane. The Medway bridge retracts to Rochester.

Rasping handsaw ripping plank.

– Don't go.

Suspended between two trees, a taut rectangle of wire frames hills and hedges. Each corner is tethered to the nearest trunk with an adjustable strap. Two leads run from the lower edge of the copper rim to a suitcase wireless resting in the grass.

– A loop aerial is fixed in position and incapable of rotation.

– What does Joan see through its window?

A squad of radio towers, six, advancing on a village. Divine whistlings. The foremost is cropped. The spire of a church pimples at its foot. Bliss of sound. Mesh masts hatch the carriage window in their own image. Scored signal shreds clouds. The train slows and stops. Neglected monochrome fields await their fate.

A cheerful announcer calls on every cottage.

– And now you are all going to 'ear Sid 'Ambone singing Tripe and Onions.

I still have it.

The tape of our first wrangle. It's embarrassing. I was so green.

– You joined the British Union of Fascists right at the start, didn't you?

speak up dear I won't hear you if you mumble yes in 1932 lots of socialists and suffragettes joined the Union well where else could we go Labour had stiffed Tom they scuppered his plan to end unemployment something new was needed Tom Mosley was the man to do it

– Why did you join a fascist party Mrs Cade?

I wanted paid work for everyone well paid jobs a better Britain equal rights for women no more war no Moscow communism either it was time to push the bankers back we all knew that the usurers too the ones who caused the crash

– Wasn't it also about attacking Jews?

not at all the Union wasn't antisemitic well not to start with Tom definitely wasn't no man will be persecuted because he is a Jew Tom said lots of members weren't I wasn't that's the kind of hand me down received idea which will stop you understanding anything about the Union at all we had Jewish members it was there of course it was everywhere but it wasn't the policy at all not at the start you haven't done much in the way of homework have you that was all much later years later it wasn't why I joined

– But you did support Hitler?

Mussolini mattered more Italy was the window to the future

23

you'd know that if you'd prepared properly everyone knew Germany deserved a better deal I didn't support Hitler but I certainly didn't want to go to war with the German people that's not the same thing at all they were being bled dry and they wanted to reunite their people everyone understood that at the time where are these questions heading I'm not sure you really know what you're asking me about do you

— We're getting off on the wrong foot Mrs Cade I'm sorry

if anyone's at fault it's you just tell me what it is you want to know that's if you know yourself my programmes come on at eleven I want to listen to them

If bad contact develops at either end of the wire, there is quite a possibility that one effect of the resistance introduced will be to couple up the two circuits sufficiently to cause trouble.

— I was hoping we'd have more time

you live just down the hill I'm going nowhere there are things I like to do in the mornings so I'll fit you in when I can dear my time's precious you know it's not for squandering you were late this morning don't forget and then you took forever miking

— But, um, what was it like? Working for fascists, Mosley and Joyce?

what was it like he asks a job that's what it was like doing the typing the telephone calls running errands smiling for visitors telling white lies making tea you do it they pay you that's what work was for women like me so don't you judge me with hindsight a lazy view from your arse

— I'm sorry but I do think it's

what was it like they are men vain men ambitious foolish too like all men are pththhh but Tom and Willy were visionaries too men of action we called them men of action in terrible times for our country they do their best opposing unemployment resisting the war calling out the banks when parliament wouldn't who else was standing up to it all the communists Moscow's pups I don't think so Labour had chucked in the towel as they always do Tom and Willy weren't perfect none of us are I do know they weren't but building a party is about aligning wills not ideas try and see it that way I thought you told me you'd prepared for this are you sure you're ready it's nearly eleven now

With a new and unstable receiver stabilisation requires the removal of stray couplings responsible for the unwanted feedback.

— I'm sorry Mrs Cade I didn't mean to

sorry's what you should be time's short especially mine I don't have days to fritter perhaps you'd like to start again in fact why don't you work up some proper questions go away and do the deskwork read Skidelsky visit Colindale look at Action read Tom when you're good to go let reception know

— I will Mrs Cade. Thank you.

Six weeks later I thought I was ready.

The skate drips butter.

Brown studs fasten the back of Joan's polka dress.

the clouds are workers in white the workers wrath condenses into clouds they go their own way on strike against the sky wrath condensed into clouds do you see it

— Britain between the wars, the bigger picture Joan. That's what we said we'd talk about today. If that's OK?

have I lost you already on strike against the sky is Mayakovsky do keep up the big picture was ugly wasn't it longer hours lower wages Black Friday nine days' wonder the slump national government Tory government same blasted thing unemployment anger massing like these clouds then thin as mist it wasn't so bad here in the south for some when jobs come back it's the rush to war the frying pan face down on flames and nowhere to jump between the wars was a pause for breath that's all a trough between two crests war is long wave never ending I couldn't abide Ramsay MacDonald he cut the lifeline what did it matter if Baldwin was One Nation Baldwin was Tory nobody took Lansbury seriously he was weak living on his laurels Labour was a spent force dear a bit like me full of want without a way Pollitt was poison Russia first barbarians in the gate Cripps wasn't much better should I have stuck with Maxton maybe I should have Jimmy visits Tom in prison you know two of a kind Jimmy's lot bully me into snitching cocks all of them men my undoing I'm hoping you might undo me dear

The nape wriggles her shoulders. A stud pops. I think she knew it would.

no leave it just leave it I like it you're so single minded a disappointment really let me read you something by Tom

Mosley's voice parades from the wireless.

– When the government elected by the people is incapable of rapid and effective action private and vested interests assume the real power

Popper and seam flap to the speech.

– not by vote or permission of the people

Nape bobbing agreement.

– but by power of money dubiously acquired.

he's right about that I think you'll agree clouds gather the human herd changes drovers Joannie that's all that parliamentary politics amounts to Tom says to me one day duh as if I didn't know that the condescending Bleeder a stronger kind of state is needed he says one that can resist the banks

The road to socialism, whispers a waning voice, is paved with nothing, fading and so faint, but thunderous, then almost inaudible, defeats.

– New batteries for the transistor, quickly.

– Coming.

– Hurry.

I remember Willy in Hoxton sounding off about the mean employer of labour who

Thumbs press the cells home, click the flap shut.

> *sees conservatism as a way of holding onto his wealth the*
> *crowd was huge*

Revived the tranny rages.

– The mean narrow souled pig eyed comfortable employer of labour who
sees in conservatism the hope of conserving the wealth he has amassed.

I turn it off.

> *is that right-wing I ask you or just right*

– It was antisemitic wasn't it? Pig eyed?

> *he didn't mean that*

– Yes Joan, he did

> *you're clutching at straws*

– No, not in those Jewish streets.

> *everyone talked like that you know well yes I do see your*
> *point you're right in a way I suppose but so am I today*
> *they say jokes about pork and noses abuse Jews but they*
> *were challenges to the high and mighty back then I know*
> *they weren't all high and mighty no so yes you're right but*
> *anyway it's how people talked*

– I am old and you are young, and I speak a barbarous tongue.

An alternating current in the primary will induce a similar alternating
current in the secondary in the opposite direction.

I suppose it was far from his worst, I say.

– Submen with prehensile toes. Oleaginous parasites from the East. Hang
them from the lamp posts. That's how he usually put it. But pig has
always been applied very broadly as a term of abuse.

> *I won't defend his words William Joyce was a fascist driven*
> *by hatred of the Jews no question about that the question*
> *is why did people follow Tom and Willy join the Union the*
> *answer is the blackshirts stepped up when Labour stepped*
> *aside that's how it felt when MacDonald was suckered into*
> *national government and slashed the dole Labour was*
> *numbers without purpose words without meaning no one*

said that about the Union I can tell you

– So there was Labour, with National Labour outside it and Independent Labour inside?

the rump was divided yes a socialist rump flabby like my rear dear that's the doctor arriving I know you look at my bum I feel your eyes when I lean forward to look out the window enjoy the show ha it's nice you show an interest

– I do not. What are you like, Mrs Cade.

don't be embarrassed I bet you're blushing now yes I'm sure you are he'll be up in a tick for my check up such bad timing it was just getting interesting we'll have to leave it there today

I press play, I tune my ears.

I like it up here by the black windmill the sails are like the wings of an angel it's a timber moth a raven black wasp I can see the whole town from here yes I do like it the higher the hylle be the nerer it is to heven

Her cadence returns.

I'm safe up here I wake to the morgenrote and at night the stars hang over the bay like fairy lights you can lose yourself in them ride waves of light and radio waves tides of voices passage of peoples

An electromagnetic intimacy.

– She sounds a bit batty.

– I like it. Who talks that way now? Thinks like that now?

– Precisely. Could be a problem.

– It's the attraction.

Tremble the cone, confound the grave. Listening in to the past.

truncheons rising and falling batons conducting the music of history

- One of the last, her generation's gone.

- A few stick it out. In anecdotes, in archives, footnotes of a journal, mentions mentioned in a book that's browsed.

- Precisely. They're all gone. Run an audience test.

  the reasons for joining were the same as now the views of plain people ignored no voice no way forward rubbish jobs unhomely homes so much hope so little change then a leader puts it into words says it's possible makes it possible songs of protest today they're songs you shop to buy it wear it throw it away people too thrown away shifting sands of England dissolved by radio gone in the consumer flow nation class gender place waste and litter on the wavelengths no borders for finance or for foreigners be anything you want to be a freak show a driftwood nation all at sea scattered by the broadcast storm it's obvious who benefits the banks they always do

- Zat fash? She on a big picture that girl.

- She's just a sort of bigoted woman. Says she used to vote Labour.

- Da Nazis was white boy murder massive man, genocide for slow down Babylon an da Hebrew dat is evil man.

- Globalisation and the markets, you can't defy them.

- Reaction with a logic framework. Gas chambers with a business model. Ovens with corporate oversight. Budget lines for mass burial.

- And it's not over! Fascist white supremacism in our schools. Goebbels in the safe space gallery! Feminazis in bed with red fascists. The Islamo-fascist tide! Christofascist reaction, ecofascists everywhere!

- Fascism has no meaning today except in so far as it signifies something not desirable.

- Like that old lady!

- Pig.

- Using fascism as a casual insult, that insults the dead.

- The word's a sign of impotence. It's used by losers.

- It's infantile.

- Fuck the hive mind. Judgment, leadership, order, efficiency, they are all fascist? That's crap.

- The extreme right's a real threat. Wake up, fascism's coming back. Broadcasters mustn't encourage them. Look at the alt-Right, Charlottesville, Le Pen, Golden Dawn in Greece, the Freedom Party in Austria, Britain First. Just for starters.

- I'd rather not bruv.

- She's a muddled old lady who doesn't make sense to me.

- We need more shows that promote British values, respect and tolerance those things, democracy. We did it at college.

- Somadem are nats not fash they're neo-con, blue collar populisers not solid Nazi. She minds me adem.

- End the great replacement! You will not replace us! Remigration now!

- Their supporters have good cause for complaint. No homes of their own, no mortgage offers, low wages, insecure employment, poor services.

- The country needs orderly, efficient government to fix that. A new kind of leader.

- I like these voices. We could run with these. There's a programme here. Why bother with Joan?

- She's a better way in.

The Bleeder closed us down.

- Mosley axed the women's section?

    I was furious Tom hobbles us but he still wants us to canvas and knock people up oh yes three hundred houses each can you believe that get out on the doorstep stick to the script we soon put a stop to that pah Mary Richardson the suffragette dug her heels in she spoke for us all a brave woman she demanded equal pay at HQ argued with Tom said you can't afford to lose us without the women you'd have nothing just infighting straight out she told Tom to his face so they drove her out expelled her I wanted to quit too but it wasn't straightforward for me never was Willy persuades me to stay he said we'd get things straight in the end I should give Tom a chance he mustn't be made to look weak the leader will come round I knew he wouldn't of course but I gave in

Were women in the British Union of Fascists picking up signal from the suffragettes?

– They thought so.

how could he treat us like that we stood for King Country Empire for work and getting the job done not the collapse the Bolsheviks wanted that a bit of me still wanted too we knew a national emergency would encourage people towards us Cripps and Pollitt in Whitehall would be chaos by breakfast collapse and arrests and uproar then us on white horses tidying up the King conferred with Tom about that

Were men and women in the British Union of Fascists picking up signal from an older, silenced left?

– Many of them thought so.

I was a socialist I'd been in the Independent Labour Party lots of us had Tom John Beckett McNab Raven Thompson he started as a socialist Richard Forgan too and Bill Risdon that's how I met Tom and Cimmie his first wife poor woman visiting mining villages mills on short time something should be done the future King said he backed us you know I wanted class privilege to end I'd read Berkman and Goldman and Souvarine I knew for certain class hadn't disappeared in Russia the tups of the Comintern weren't turning the world upside down the Union it was a volcano it was uncontainable we held on to what we'd stood for in Labour and the ILP we stood up for our people for peace against unemployment the bankers caused the crisis so we were going to do something about them we had Blairs and Browns and Murdochs they were called MacDonald, Snowden Beaverbrook but we didn't sit on our hands complaining we stepped up a new kind of Englishman

If any government or party undertake this work it will need force, marching men. It will not promise this or that measure but a discipline, a way of life.

> *when you stop listening to traditional Labour voters you make them invisible you prepare the ground for a man of action another Mosley when you stop listening and turn your back on plain folk putting the needy second to banks and spivs swelling their ranks with strangers I say if you take them for granted they will find someone less compromising to speak for them someone like Tom or Willy*

Larus Marinus gliding estuary pink.

Black back red tip alar salt air spearing.

Gizzard loaded, sailfeather flexing, course set.

Back muscle contracting pector compress rarefy ompress arefy ress fy es beat over sparkle, shore nearing, glide the spreading shore, beat ah ress, the shore mounding.

Rib silt and shingle, rim of the town, wall.

Gullarum call of familiars. Rooves hotholes roost cable crap furrows scran.

Beat ah beat a way.

Car bus bench. Bread chip bin.

Scran an grounders scran an claws n barks n biters.

Exhaust plume scud, nox of crankcase blowby. Monox diox hydro carburn.

Hill swell turnpike bostal scar, air mill.

Five span five pound missiling momentum.

Scope tower passover, grey resemblers on a rampart, flight path trackers.

Perches poles dipoles wavetraps. Partitions of partitions. Colour coded lofts. Kinked magnetic field, tilescales pitching, greentop signal flash.

Drawn bow below, flicking, fragging, balconied, gabling.

Granary holt down. Semblers sousleaf squeal for chow.

Lock to the block on the brow. Sky chock summit block.

Eyes on target blurwhite, no beak, no beak wide.

Instant impact second redtip hurtling to.

Chlobkt mandib coring the skull, brainblur sllup, sep sep sternum gizzard riving. Rib rake. Tusks bust to stub, wingsplay on the window, flap frac frac pink toes scratting. Fowl fall leaving:

– A daystar in the glass.

– A phantom print in powder down.

– Joan screaming.

> *it flew as though it would have torn me with its beak blinded me smiting with that great wing as though it would have torn me*

– Really?

You let yourself be gulled like that?

Keys jangling.

Stacks of echo, rubber boot reverb. Gate of the landing metal clang langling. Brass peals of prized tumblers. Wandsworth prison nineteen-forty-six. The full-on jailhouse atmo.

– Kid's stuff for a good effects team.

A woman, the scar, both seated. A table between them, guard at the door.

– You and I are one Joan.

That's Joyce. Clairaudient, that's me.

– Where'e're I go, my Soul shall stay with thee: Tis but my shadow I take away.

And that's Dryden. Willy's last words to Joan before returning to his cell.

– Don't go.

Her last to him.

– Can't stop now don't you know I ain't never going to let you go don't go.

Electropop funnelling along the care home corridor.

A cleaner lumbers past Joan's door, transistor on her trolley.

Frustrators were frequently deployed to prevent our conversations. Sometimes they were successful. During those moments I drew daggers in my notebook, clusters of daggers with triangular blades.

– Can you talk about that day at Dover?

one day he got into a boat

Slops from a bucket on an outside wall. Waves slap the harbour arm. A handheld klaxon, field recording overdub. The ferry foghorn startles gulls.

In 1939, when war with Germany is certain, Joyce catches a steamboat from Dover. He's headed for Berlin. The harbour's on high alert, silting with munitions, spiked with heavy artillery. Platform Joan spots Joyce twixt coach and berth. Willy! A metal grille separates them. Margaret, frowning, turns away. Two young men engage her, young men in pale raincoats, men in matching hats, travellers without luggage. The wife's distracted. Joan hands Willy sandwiches, he trades an envelope. Wheeling gulls monitor the parting paramours, screeching code to listening posts. Stenographers decrypt the skrawk. A typed report is filed below the swell.

– I'll be back Joan, don't you worry.

– Don't go.

– In a couple of years, tops.

– Don't go Willy.

– I'll see you in a new Britain.

– Don't go.

These were her pleas. But no griefs moved him. He heard but did not heed her words.

– You're determined to go and leave poor Dido?

The helmsman won't look back. Steer straight, that's his credo.

– Will the same wind carry your sail and your promise away?

His mind remains unmoved.

– Don't go.

The tears rolled in vain.

– He wasn't interested. The thrill had gone. He'd married Margaret.

Men desert for some trivial affair or noisy insolent sport beauty that we have won from bitterest hours.

> *Willy shouldn't have gone he shouldn't have left us he shouldn't have*

– He comes from the people but no longer loves them.

– He tends towards an aristocracy of thought and heroic will.

– He's not that smart.

I feel the reactionary growing in him, his violent and agitated temperament full of Napoleonic authoritarianism, of growing aristocratic contempt for the masses.

Telemachus commands his companions to take hold of the rigging. They do. They raise the mast of pine inside the rounded block.

He casts crust from the step. Beaks wing beaks bicker beaks claw. Butter, ham. Castanets. The blast of a vast horn, prolonged. The horn woke me, says Dido.

– I was seated on a rocky shore. I knew straight away he had betrayed me. The wind was fair. His ship is on the open sea, distant and disappearing. My nightdress is open. My breast yearns. Cupid weeps at my feet, his bow thrown aside. I raise my arms. Oh oh oh radio-oh-oh. It was a pointless gesture yet I have to make it.

Dido expires. Penelope pines.

– More substance in his enmity than in our love.

> *I couldn't imagine life without Willy life without him gone*

– Don't go.

She looks out from the pebbly weed, her eyes despairing. She wavers neath great waves of fear. Radio-oh-oh. Don't go-oh-oh.

I made a spectacle of myself, she tells me.

I hand him the sandwiches then they all walk on he doesn't
look back he's gone ooooo all the liking of life out of land
wendes I languish left leve ye forever I bawl

All walk on? That's more than two.

– So the Joyces were accompanied to Dover?

At the window, dribs flush her corrugate cheek. Palms mop the sockets.

young men chatting up Meg is all I saw I can't be sure

I go. I come back again.

ha you have been doing your homework

It's three in the afternoon. Nape Joan is laying on her side, facing the bay.
Poems tickle her toes. Now the leaves, the wireless reads, are falling fast.
Nurse's flowers that won't last. She chafes one foot with the other. The zista
trickles *Gardeners' Question Time* to her left ear.

– Cut back anything throwing shade such as shrubbery overhanging
branches get rid of nearby sheds or fencing this one doesn't like to be
overlooked rotate the mulch a couple of times a year.

– Everything necessary to the modern man a radio a gramophone a car a
frigidaire

– Let her spread a little don't prune try not to prune and I'm afraid that's
all there's time for this week.

– Proper opinions for the time of the year.

The room resonates to the orotund voice of the elderly wireless receiver. It
has an underbelly known in the trade as brown. Tan eloquence debarks the
transducer, deploying phoneme by phoneme, taking full possession of the
bister chamber. Joan is hazel, the view dun.

The Shrub A34 is a vintage British wireless, patrician, a prized prewar set.
Close inspection reveals it's walnut. Closer sham nut, mostly veneer. The
hunch shoulders and low brow of the cabinet triarch symmetric, a grave-
stone. Its backlit roster of European cities is called a magic eye.

Rome Trieste Turin Madrid Toulouse Strasbourg Berlin.

- Hamburger!

- Liverwurst!

- Twerpenburg!

Ten-fifty, Paris market fish prices from the Eiffel Tower. Twelve-fifteen announcement of the time. On Sundays concerts from the Hague at three. Lectures from Berlin six-thirty – not daily – news and concert eight-fifteen. Spain, irregular trials eleven-to-one. Haw Haw takes the air at nine-fifteen.

- People's music for the people's receiver.

- Volkische classics keine Juden.

- That's how it was.

Joan sits up and turns towards the wireless set. Rising, she reconfigures on all fours. All sixes next, on knees and toes and elbows on the bed.

She slices through the *Brains Trust*. She scissors Scarlatti, rolls over Beethoven. The aluminium blades of the ganging condenser close on Hamburg's broken nose. William Joyce whines.

- It is an unforgettable experience to watch the entrance to a London theatre in the evening. Prewar, of course. Limousine after limousine with extravagantly clad women and their male companions, stepping out of cars like condescending gods and goddesses, whilst the dull and silent crowd composed of the members of the lower nation looks at this brazen display of wealth and leisure. The sight almost reminds one of conditions in the declining Roman Empire, and one is at a loss to say whether the impudence of the upper classes or the meek tractability of the lower is the more astonishing. The upper nation of the Mayfair type of snob feeds on the lower nation whom it robs. How long is this going to last?

I marvel at her left footsole, a circuit diagram in folds of crumpled parchment. I admire the smooth pivot of the ulna on her left casing, branching antennae of fingers extending. I watch the red veins warm in her variable vacuum tubes. Beneath the cotton coupling there are sheaves of blue wiring in her translucent calf, ceramic egg ankles, spade terminals ten.

I turn away. I do. She notices.

It's not a bunion, she laughs, I cross my toes for luck.

A superhet receiver depends for its efficiency upon the accurate lining up of as many as twenty circuits. The slightest maladjustment in one of these may make all the difference in performance.

It's helluva project, restoring a vintage set.

– Trace the faults

– Check the connections.

– Energise the windings.

> *permanent and cultural vibration I saw that on a wall once it was a slogan permanent and cultural vibration the walls of cities are always worth reading adolescent angels sing on walls vibration permanente et culturelle it was Paris bliss that dawn*

Radio Joan spins the dial on the tombstone. She palps the set softly with her right forefinger. She hooks a wave.

– age only matters if you're cheese or wine it takes two radio two

Twisting she tones, her other hand ladles my way for the transistor. Pass it me please, she says. I hand it over. With her left thumb she shunts through a torrent of crackle krishtoskoskoskdokdroootsch chat in a storm steam scorching from a spout the whistle stutters steadying. The greatest danger of all would be to do nothing, the path we have chosen for the present. Joan ups the volume, passing the tranny back my way. Kneeling between the two receivers she claps her heterodyning hands she slaps buttery hips she's raising the hem of her nightie in oscillous mayhem.

– Joan don't

– One path two radio two we shall never choose two radio two surrender or submission a family favourite

Binary voicing pitch displacement fifty-one-hundred parcels waving, packs of fifty-one-hundred parcels thrown in radial batches, waving hunnerds of batches twice per sec of parcels current with notes. Package electrons popping and streaming coiling and doubling, cut demod to mags clicketilick ickick to voycesing joycesing pitch.

– Jairmany calling Jairmany calling

> *double bubble it's always happy hour here christmas mayday memory lane all year round yes I knew it was Willy*

She turns back to the window.

Exterior: snow, a concrete portico, a lattice mast in blue. A steel stook rakes an isoscelic shade leaking from a shadow. A solitary wavequaker. Clouds stacked on sky racks. A wall of glass, a pane tilting open. Interior: a chest cabinet, BBC faux Tudor, plank grid nutbrunette. Raised eye dials, binnacle rows lit ohs – not I not I – hands jazzing over handwheels. The masthead sliding down a wall. Sixpence.

A Christmas issue of the *Radio Times* trembles on the bedside table. Tea rippling. Tremors from a Hoxton sweatshop, a passing tram, the crashing pound. Wall Street racket for another year. Labour in office, it isn't by August, and Joan's jobless too. She dances with the Tailor and Garment Workers Union. He was on the stump, she says, a kind man I don't recall his name. Boom biddy biddy boom biddy biddy. They wear crepe paper crowns. Hers is blue, it beards his smile. Tall, he was tall, she says, my kind of man. They've tossed their shoes and socks aside. He had nice feet, she says, like creatures undersea all pale and squiddy, toes like razor clams.

– What year is this Joan?

No idea she says I don't recall.

– Jarman plains fline oer East Anglier taday are reporten ousewives waven to em from dare gartens shells soaring he's hit he's coming down peace is cumin ginger turmeric will be needed for this rather spicy Indian national dish so let's play just a minute

Superhet Joan fuses separate waves, unequal, to a single heterodyne beat. Her glowing nape is the glass pinch of a memory valve.

They don't make sets like this anymore.

Protest grows in the care home.

Ten residents have handed in a petition calling for a halt to the recording sessions. A woman in the room below Joan complains that marching songs, Hitler recordings and bursts of loud clapping keep her from sleeping at night. Someone puts salt in Joan's morning tea. No stopping me now, she says, not after that.

A news item appears in the local paper. It quotes Century Close resident

Reuben Reznick.

– The BBC must not let the barbaric story of the holocaust be white-washed by its perpetrators. Hath not a Jew eyes, hath he not ears? The producers should focus on the atrocities inflicted on Jewish people, along with the protests and sacrifices of those who resisted fascism, not the self serving anecdotes of Mrs Cade, a former Hitlerite.

A flyer saying 'No Platform for Nazis' slides beneath each door in the care home. It also drops through the fifteen nearest letterboxes. Posters appear in shops and cafes in the town. Fifty people gather outside the bank one morning. Fascist Granny Lies, the placards say.

The director of the care home calls for a risk assessment. As the case review team assembles, at an undisclosed venue, Joan readies her radios.

– Velvet revolution that regime came tumbling down a year later

– Reissued it went straight to the top of the charts how did you feel

Pinching the walnut's fine aerial wire with her left hand, the chrome antenna of the zista with the other, she studies the town. You too, she says, come on.

> *take one in each hand finger and thumb only stand behind*
> *me we mustn't be touching so not too close*

With one knee on the bed I stand behind her, clipped to each set with my arms outstretched. My limbs parallel Joan's. We're analogue.

– Let's use the hairbrush as a spreader?

The parallel wires used in an aerial are usually separated by a pole or a hoop. That might help, she says. I drop the wire and place the head of the wooden hairbush between Joan's shoulder blades. Leaning forward, I lodge the tip of the handle below my ribs. Hurry, she says. I pick the wire back up and spread my arms again. Joan swivels her head slowly, turning from the right jamb of the window to the centre of the pane then back again.

– Her hair a flock of goats moving down the slopes of Gilead.

– Her nose the tower of Lebanon which looks towards Damascus.

> *you take that half I'll go this way do it the same as me point*
> *your nose to the frame then don't rush it meet in the middle*
> *then back come on they'll be there by now*

We snuff, we snift, we proach and part. My nostrils prick with Joanscent. Hair spray soap powder. I think she's sucked an orange. The radios bluster and whistle, billowing fuzz.

– What are we doing Joan?

– Hush an lissen.

Breakfast fry up, full sizzle English. I can smell it through the wall.

this way the harbour we've got them they're at the health centre

Gasping parasites gobble mush. Suddenly they stop.

– often listens to a pair of radio sets at the same time

yay told you me and you we make a damn good aerial hold still now absolutely still

Grey hairs spring erect in the bristle of the brush between us. Charged, a filament emits a spark, then a tuft a scattering. Soon fiery pyros race to the nape in circuit bursts of tracer.

– she seems to hear each broadcast quite distinctly she enjoys the refraction and appears to thrive on dissonance and contradictory stimulation no harm is apparent quite the contrary

that's my doc you tell them dear

– as the lead doctor I've no objection radio boosts the physiological and emotional response of its listeners raising heart rate body temperature and electrodermal activity now together as we know these indicate higher levels of cognitive processing and emotional arousal.

– I had no idea.

– The heart rate rises by two beats a minute body temperature goes up two degrees.

– Mrs Cade's doubling of stimulus doubles the benefits?

– The parallel feed may strengthen her memory.

– Are we sure that's desirable [hahaaher].

who's that I don't know that voice

- I think Joan would call it cohering.

- Fat chance of that [hahaha].

- Hippy dippy Nazi [hahaha].

nasty man I'd report him if I could

- She's a harmless old lady she's nice show her more respect.

thank you Vera recognise her voice you tell them

- Are there any side effects?

- Introspection, some loss of selectivity, occasional overexcitement.

- She may throw off her sheets [hahaha].

- Nothing detrimental to her wellbeing.

- She's sleeping better and I also see she's more engaged with staff.

- So no clinical reason for concern?

- Not as far as I can see.

- And she keeps the volume down.

- But number six says

- I've put my own ear to the wall. You can't hear a thing.

- So the complaints are malicious?

- I think so, possibly.

- What's the view of the service?

- No action. We're here on a watching brief. We do have some concerns about the research interviews. Twenty-five hours are logged to date.

I'll tell you about him one day

- We've referred the broadcast up the line.

up up you need to keep still or we'll lose them

- It's done her no end of good. She's bright as a button these days.

- She's ninety and frail. We've a duty of care

- To the others as well but I won't join a witch hunt.

- Do we deny him entry? We can cite medical grounds.

- There's no need for that.

- We're monitoring the situation.

   two of them well I'm flattered I must say

- Anyone else? No? So we're agreed. Radios remain in situ and the interviews continue.

   anything less they'd have a fight on their hands I know my rights

- And what about the publicity, the impact on our reputation?

- Your leaker's the risk. Deal with him

   we've chalked up a win you and me let's have a bit of chocolate

We unclip from the wire and chrome. The matted brush drops to the bed.

Naked sitting on a wooden chair.

Palms on his knees, right hand pinching a cigar.

- Not quite naked he's got glasses on.

   and a headset hahaha

It's 1929. He's what, forty years of age?

- Who was he?

She remembers the bells of passing trams. Horns above his hearing cups.

   a bull of a man no hair on his chest

Feeder wires merge at his collarbone. Skirting the left nipple, they drop to the brass terminals of a small wireless on a low stool.

- The painting gives no indication what the listener-in is listening to.

- He's returning our look.

- His bush, the root above the left wrist, compete for our attention.

- Hence the cigar?

- As does the teat of glass swelling from the receiver.

- Coil recumbent for reception.

- O it's so orific!

- RadiO!

The floor's exposed, bare plank. The front legs of the chair are turned and grooved, splayed and fret the stool. He's lit from the front, a window perhaps.

- The apparatus restores his flesh.

- How so?

- Heightened awareness. Disembodied voices do that.

- Is that lipstick? Who is he?

- Mann mit Radio, that's all I know.

A young woman answers the questions, a young woman possibly Joan, from the far side of the room. Over there the boards are dressed with rug. She's in her twenties, in a cardigan, in an armchair, a headset, in some kind of trance. She stares middle-distant, watching the empty, seeing intensely.

> *I wasn't looking at anything I was listening in I wasn't interested in a middle-aged man in his birthday suit not back then I wasn't*

Her right hand rests on a wooden box on a wicker table. A finger is raised, the wave chaser, agile agent of the dial. In both canals the poet tympanic, double you be.

- You would be listening in twos and threes. I would be myself alone speaking to something like a visiting card on a pole. Before me floats an image, man or shade.

We don't call them up, she says.

> *I don't call them up*

- We make the right conditions and they come.

> *they come when I get the settings right*

Joan drops a shoulder, then the other, then the first again. The nape swings slowly from left to right and back across the calibrated window, this way that, the arrow headed needle of a test meter. Tick toc ick tock a spring creaking, gentle ululation, switch of station, scraping no-no tremor gathering speed gong bong ul oh oh flailing.

– The upward kick of the meter needle indicates that distortion is occurring through anode bend rectification.

– When the needle kicks downwards the valve is passing current on the positive peaks of the signal.

Swaying sawsee faster deeper fitlike calling louder louder alto trilling drilling buzzer sounding elbows shoulders head rebounding from the care home trampomatty wooo and wheeeeee.

I grab her from behind and lock my hands.

– Joan stop you'll

> *spoilsport radio was my first love it liberates it lifts it lasts radio carries me away from here and time passing not passing don't worry bout me boy I'm in good hands I'm in yorn now ooh I got me a hug at last didden I*

Back, back they come.

Tracking finger raised, elbow to wicker, she's listening in. I watch her from the chair in headphones, holding a cigar. In your specs too hahaha she laughs oh do get dressed she says.

– It's not true I'd nothing on I had the radio on.

Over the cans I hear trams, rough rolling squeal tones, jolts and airflow, damped bells. Control discussing budget with the FX team. Fruit wax sticks my lips. The young woman has Joan's profile.

Polished, her teak set gleams. Two knobs are visible on the dash, two labels of instruction, two sets of brass stumps. A glass tube bloats beside them. Short rubber cables connect one pair of terminals to stubs on a glass battery the size of a shoebox. Acid sulfs sheet lead within. Also wired to the box are two large cartons branded RED SEAL DRY BATTERY. The wraps promote A BATTERY SUITABLE FOR EVERY USE. Inside, carbon rods smoulder in zinc pots of paste. Joan taps both flows of moto-electro go, one tense, one less. Cords serp from jacks and tangle on the wicker, weaving a knot at her throat. Parting at her chin, they feed cups pressed to her ears by adjustable shafts. Pointed rods project above her head. The headphones clam. An arc is forming between the magnets, her wireless smile.

passing not passing don't worry bout me boy

Whitstable Motor Engineering Works 14-16 Canterbury Road. Wireless Department. ACCUMULATOR CHARGING We invite you to inspect our up to date charging plant and see for yourselves how your batteries are charged. We have the largest and the most efficient equipment in the town. We collect and deliver your batteries Free of Charge. We solicit a trial, and guarantee to give you satisfaction.

– There was a trial alright.

– An we knew the verdict fore it start.

Willy wanted a trial he wanted to speak to explain it would have been a rant it would have done no good for Margaret's sake he drops it so a deal is struck

Let us convert that old set for you. Phone 68.

Willy was relaxed in the dock composed but I could see the strain he was under

Large stocks are kept of all High and Low Tension Batteries, also other wireless accessories.

I sit between the silent couple – Mann mit maybe Joan – typing with a radio on, half listening to a book slot.

– Eliminate the audience he said the audience has always had a damaging deforming influence on books I must say I think that's ridiculous how so I say give them your best shot what they should like and will come to like as the supply of good things will create the demand for more

He and she and me fish ether fathoms. I'm an accumulator. I'm a linear amplifier.

– We have it on for company.

– It gives the home a new centre around which to fix.

– As necessary to home life as the singing of a kettle to the hob.

– No place is home without a radio.

Look at the poor lad. A few weeks ago he bought a kit of parts for a wireless set, including a diagram and elaborate instructions. He said it was inexpensive, it could be built in a couple of hours and it would save him pounds. After two days of worry and hard work the set was practically finished – and so was he! He had to buy batteries, aerial equipment and a loudspeaker before he could test it!

- I told him to get a Fellows Little Giant Set like mine.

- Fellows Little Giant Sets are cheap.

- Fellows Little Giant Sets are complete.

Entering through a cylindrical lead-in insulator set in the window frame, eighty feet of copper fetter the chimney to a wireless pole. Pure twelve strand, twenty-eight gauge, at half a crown a hundred feet.

- Since it is somewhat inconvenient to keep one's receiver at the bottom of the garden, it is necessary to take the signals picked up by the aerial to the receiver without interference being picked up en route. This is done by means of the step-down transformer and screened low impedance cable. The latter can usually be readily disposed inconspicuously by burying it or cleating it to the garden gate.

- Try a class 7 Met-Vick Elastic Aerial. This unit enables you to vary your aerial backwards and forward to any desired length from maximum to zero. It's as though you had a thousand aerials!

No eye contact. No words pass between them. Millions are listening. Each listens alone.

- We are termini.

- Of the Bossy Boys Club.

Get up everybody and sing. Yes we are termini.

- Of the Band Behind the Cupboard. The Big Bloody Crowd.

Get up everybody let's sing.

- To Bloody Baptist Cant!

Yes we are termini. Come on let's hear you!

Accumulations of anti-vaccinationists and Esperantists and propogandists on every subject. Advertisement-mongers and Members of Parliament, pacifist organisations, women's organisations, Empire Marketing Boards and Channel Tunnel promoters, A J Cook and Lord Ronaldshay and Indian musicians and infant welfarers.

– A practical unity of the human race. Of which we have never had a fore-shadowing.

– Except in the Gospel of Christ.

A little overwhelming in the mass, admits the director of talks.

– I went to the BBC for a voice test. I was taken into a small room they call a studio. It seemed to be hermetically sealed. I sat at a desk. You are taken into a studio, which is a large and luxuriously appointed room. There is a desk, heavily padded, and over it hangs a little white box. The official testing me sat in a corner with a headphone on his ears. There was a box hanging above the desk. It was the microphone receiver. The only thing in the room was a red lamp.

– I began to feel artificial as if my voice did not belong to me at all. When the red light is on you are speaking to the civilised world. When it goes out your voice is inaudible. At the end of five minutes I was eight lines behind.

– There are lots of menacing notices.

DON'T COUGH

you will deafen millions of people

DON'T RUSTLE YOUR PAPERS

popping a paper bag would blow every fuse you had to be careful in those studios it didn't suit every temperament I'm amazed that Willy managed it so well

– One has never talked to so few people or so many.

– It's very queer.

– It is strange to think that someone with a very powerful wireless set could hear me talking in Boston.

Radia the life of every sound infinite variety expanding agency of a people of noises.

Diva holler, Deutsch, over strings in Bayreuth.

Joan squats on the bed, calves for cushions. She matches the lead for six
bars, note for note. Swiveling, she tugs the duvet over her knees. Dover, she
says, facing the window, yes Willy boarded the ferry at Dover.

> westwards the gaze wanders
> eastward skims the ship
> fresh the wind blows
> towards
> home

– Toopahnds fora tanner.

– Getchor anges freshor anges.

Baskets bustle banting barter. Oil givyer anuvver fer arf the ask. Weights
lunk scales, parsnips shudder. Chalk butts squeal prices 4d 3d 1/- chalk
butts scrawl slogans NO BUF and MOSLEY OUT! Temperance hall, tea
and tonic. Hair brooms, two bunch a penny primroses, rabbit fat rabbit!
Black gloves stick bills to wall tiles, MOSLEY WILL WIN and GET YOUR
COPY OF ACTION TODAY. Caulies biggist collyedds in 'oxton.

– Degenerate race!

A street warbler shrills from the bedside zista. There's a slurp of applause
from the pie and mash stall.

– Unworthy of your ancestors!

The busking Jew has switched to the walnut set. She hawks her discount
arias by the graveyard.

– A hypocrite shuts the gate on love.

Her sidekick scuffs a fiddle. Stunned coins, tossed at the cemetery wall, fall
at their feet.

Twenty yards on, at spouters' corner, Willy's scored cheek pumps like a
concertina. The yap – two lips that slap – mocks democracy, jibes at Jewsury,
slams the banks. Black shirts fence the platform, a decorator's ladder by a
van topped with wooden speakers.

– She enjoys open air meetings. Recording what Joyce says in public is
somebody else's job.

– Does she know who?

Joan observes the barrage drill. Prime the thumpline, an intake of breath. Throat and cavity elevate, lock. A few seconds of measured release – the half fact, a telling stat – as the chin reconnoitres the crowd. Thundermaw Willy mortars the mob. The burning torch of the spoken word hurtles to the masses. Followers return his fire with cheers HEIL MOSLEY!

A halfpint fuhrer, Joyce's heels jut from the fifth rung.

– The Mighty Atom!

During reload he wobbles. A muscular aide steadies the steps. A second intake of breath, the catapult scar draws tight. Convulsing it salvoes the length of the street.

– Britain, colony of Palestine!

Willy's wisecracks rouse the teeming park.

– You're a right bastard!

– Thankyou mother!

His warnings pock the wall of the Temperance Hall.

– Elimination of small traders by the Hebrew system.

– Creeping Judah, state within a state!

– Democracy is the road to oblivion.

A mouthful of wind.

– You knocking me, red?

A small square pugnacious man, drinking constantly.

– Taking the piss?

I felt as though I had seen something unclean. He comes closer.

– We know where you sleep.

Fear and trembling came over me and made all my bones shake. His face deep scars of thunder had intrenched. In a loud voice, to keep him at bay, I chanted Of Man's first disobedience and the fruit of that forbidden tree, the nearest to a prayer I could remember.

- I'm trying to portray you Mr Joyce. In context.

- Accurately, you think?

- I'm against what you stand for.

- You could explain that I was a child soldier, a Galway boy brutalised by black and tans, you could say I saw a policeman's brain puddling a road at a very impressionable age, you could acknowledge that terrorists conspired to kill me. That Jewsury rules. That this country bred me.

- I choose not to.

- Some of these men wear trade union badges.

- So?

- Take this as a warning.

I was in Accident and Emergency for seven hours. Concussion and stitches.

- Toopahnds fora tanner. Freshor anges.

Joyce showed himself to be a very able speaker, an unknown Watcher reports in KV 2/245/1a.

- Some of his remarks were rather insulting and provocative, but he managed to transform the subsequent heckling of his opponents into support for his own proposals.

- Within ten minutes of this twenty-eight-year-old taking the platform, I knew that here was one of the dozen finest orators in the country.

- His voice and delivery were excellent; his manner was entertaining and often plausible. His imitations of Mr Churchill were masterly fooling.

Pinky, porky, persuasive, the scar wins respect. The Lambeth Honour, so-called, is the Flanders trench old troopers never forget, a ranker's stripe, a gangster's crest, tomorrow's forward line, last ditch for a stand, a brightly lit corridor in the Black House, Mosley's headquarters, filling with new recruits.

Who cut this crowded rut?

- It weren't me. Don't you look my way. I takes great care to slash down a face, never sideways, never up, no, I always ever do the cut down. No skid or snag to an artery that way. Chivving sends a message, a strong one, but arteries, bloody arteries is murder an murder ain't for me. Who done Haw Haw took a 'uge risk an they mayer meant worse.

– Joyce is a fascist and an antisemite. We slit the throat of Amalek in self defence.

– I did it. He ruined me. Lecherous beast. I did it!

– A channel from the mouth, the fount of human speech, to the auditory canal. A scribing of radio's expanded space, a liberation of voices. You're looking for a wireless engineer.

– Step back now step back he informed for the Bratish he had to pay the price. Another mouth we gave him for his mouthing off.

– Bog off yer Berlin bogtrotter!

From sidestreets, the hidden hands of Hoxton lob cobs, the auld confetti. Women drop slop from high windows. Bluebottles swarm, truncheons for wings. The crowdie legs it, flooding alleys, chasing trams, taking sanctuary at the Nag's Head and St Anne's. Joyce leaps from the ladder, it's whanged in the van. Get in professor! The engine cusses, the bonnet spirals crackling along the snagged groove of an acetate disc in the studio. They're heading for Old Street. The combust fades. The boneyard lament resumes.

vengeance for the treachery
easement for the heart's distress

A sharp penny, honed for a fascist cheek, chips brick and – ting – drops to top the take. The fiddle brays. The bed groans as Joan turns and leans to the wireless. Sherwooosherwuppppp

– You'll need a strong umbrella later storms are coming we'll have the weather forecast in five but first a feetwarmer from just what is a gastropub we will be asking the chef behind the Eagle the first of its kind in Britain a new direction for Britpop big flavours and rough edges.

The rubbish truck has left the close. The care home cleaner has moved on. My recorder is ready. The nape's at the window.

– Let us shut off the radio and listen to the past.

> ***give me a minute or two dear I need to give my head a shake to wake up properly get my thoughts together they're like butter eggs this morning just a moment I'll be ready soon***

Spade of nape, the shaft in pearls.

I've been looking forward to talking today I'm nothing when you've gone dear at evening one beds down weeping in the morning glad song as I know you're on the way but why do you come

– You interest me Joan.

I'm interested in you too come closer why don't you

Satin nightdress, smoking. The pudges of her upper arms sag, soft cheese swaying in bags. A pocket radio newses on the pillow. That one doesn't disturb the neighbours, she says, it starts and ends the day.

– What was Joyce like to wake beside? Was he a morning person?

Willy was a cuddler most men aren't not really spooning's not the same often a sore head hangovers all the time guilt and grumps too an awkwardness after marrying Mag at first anyway he was always in a rush to get off sometimes he'd be gone before I woke but usually he'd give me a shake his second coming he called it but now and then not nearly enough we'd walk in a park or along the beach before he caught the train we had to be careful I never knew when someone might lunge for him or cuss at me it was horrid it happened all the time

The shaft shakes the head. The pearls shill, clicking like billiard balls.

Neck like the tower of David whereon there hang a thousand bucklers, shields of warriors and mighty men.

– Did he tell you how he got the scar?

the Lambeth Honour he called it his second smile it's how people recognised him he was a steward at an election meeting back in the twenties in those days parties had to protect their speakers with fists Willy is hired by a Conservative MP a Jew as it happens Lazarus was the name oh the irony it was before Tom set up the Union Willy was one of Orsman's fascisti Britain's first fascists they were mostly ex-soldiers they steward meetings for the Conservatives this one was in Lambeth Baths as it ends the reds rush the platform trying to snatch the flag everyone did that it was a ritual the Union did it too but that night it was especially bad a red with a razor a Hebrew Willy said well he would this goon jumps him going for his throat he opens Willy's cheek right up poor boy he was only eighteen that's what he told me afterwards but other versions do the rounds

Suddenly there was a rush down one of the gangways, a scuffle with the stewards, and in the middle of it, the flash of a razor.

Th'ethereal substance clos'd not long divisible, and from the gash a stream of nectarous humor issuing flowe'd sanguine.

– Read orler bahtit ither Stanard!

some said it was afterwards in an alley on the way home a chase he pushed his luck too far they held him down sneered in Yiddish sliced him through it might have happened that way I can see why he wouldn't brag about it if it had someone told me it was an Irish lass with a grudge who did it payback for dobbing to the Tans anyway it was a lifechanger as they say twenty-six stitches our living martyr we called Tom the Bleeder but it was Willy who bled wasn't it all those stitches I visit him in the hospital his head is a football of bandages just his eyes showing where the laces go eyes with fight in them mind eyes with a question to me in them you can see someone's soul in their eyes I saw his my heart went out to him there is blood in the windings blood of the lamb the Lambeth sacrifice I kiss his wound

The rocking of the spade at the window slows. Rhapso, her neck watches over the bay. One stitch two stitch three stitch four. Prick and push and make do mend. Hem swab push swab, tack and pull swab, poppy splash, spiral binder needlecraft for twenty-six turns. Two drop phases short of the moon reel Joan, why?

– One up from square, one short of cube?

– No.

– Iron?

– Possibly.

– Yehovah, gematric, that's it!

Bavarian toffs graduate with duel scars. Willy is elite. Gloria in excelcis nobilis. Gangsters pick up trading scars. Willy is street. Gloria in excelcis victor. Damage attracts the ladies, daring draws the boys. Willy's a man of action. Gloria in excelsis heros.

– The old fruit salad, me Lambeth Honour.

– It has no bearing at all, none.

– A permanent humiliation.

The wound is withheld from the lens, lit for effect, airbrushed till faint, is flaunted, is him not him. It entices Joan, opens to Joan, engulfs Joan. Why should the faithful heart most love the bitter sweetness of false faces?

– Love is ever slow to expose.

– Always eager to believe the best!

– Always hopeful. Always patient.

> *Willy taught me things I'll never forget take a small potato he says one that sits snug in your hand you pinch the razor blade push it in the top till there's a quarter inch showing you put it there so you can grip the bottom when you throw it two blades are better than one its best to go for the face aim well throw it with force he trained my hands for battle my fingers for the fray we used to practice spudding in Blean wood we hung balloons on trees for targets when Willy wed Mag I felt like spudding her well you do don't you I asked him why why Willie he said because I love her more than I love you that emptied me I let myself go for a bit*

Women like me, she says, the violent hour passed over she says, we get flung into some corner, she says, like old nut shells, she tells me, that's what happens to women like me.

> *for a few weeks seeing them together was like blades to me blades under my skin but at least I knew where I stood he came back to my door quite often and did I make him pay I did ha he was just like you dear he couldn't keep away*

It was blunt, the memo from upstairs.

Mrs Cade claims that she visited Joyce in hospital in 1924. How can this be? The profile you have provided states that she was living in Whitstable at the time, and that she had no contact of any kind with fascist circles until 1932. This is further confirmation that Mrs Cade is a highly unreliable source. At best, she is a fantasist with confused recollections. In our opinion, in all likelihood she is a fraud. The viability of the series is listed for review at the next meeting of the commissioning panel.

Humming sands.

Pub on the beach, the Old Neptune, plank-lined pocket of the sea wall.

I stagger left as I step in.

– Extreme low frequencies scupper your balance.

– A hint of how you'll leave.

I grab the mantelpiece.

– It's the boards, the floor's not flat!

Wings thrum overhead, flapimba beat, toucans pluming three on blue, one fat two flat, a threecan. Migrant barclaws bearing beer, two glasses each, ginger beaking trays of stout. Ramphastos refugees, Columbian curates. Nice day for a Guinness someone shouts in red. The bar is busy.

– Toucans'd ship cans

– Yeh not glasses.

– You need ta watch that floor.

I spot Joan and Willy by the flaking waterline, nebulous dabs of grey and brown. Without moving they approach the Neptune.

– Toucans Willy look.

– You know they're not.

I didn't expect to cross their path today. I didn't want to. I'm out for lunch, a break with a book and a beer.

– They've been here for fifteen years.

– Waiting on you.

– I never noticed them before, not once.

A five plank moment. A shock I won't forget, Joan and Willy at that water's edge. I look away.

I take a table by the window where the musicians play. Ninety years ago, when the publican installed a wireless set, cottagers complained. Disturbing our peace, infernal racket, can't hear usself think they dinned at the door. They'd no rest for dancing at the bloody Savoy. Knob it off or we will. Now they're back, objecting to the local cover bands.

– Nothing changes

but nowt stays the same

I wait for Joan and Willy to enter. I wait for more than an hour, but they don't show. I look for them when I leave. They haven't moved.

– Water the clay while I roll up my sleeves.

– I'm on it.

– Pass the bucket.

Waves slop. Sandals splot silt suck. Seaside sounds soil my shirt. A woman's laughter, crawkern incur of gulls.

– Welter you wave, swirl!

– Who's that singing?

– A mermaid Willy, a mermaid riding a dolphin.

The fiend is in love. I wait for my cue by a bucket in the studio.

– Dulcet and harmonious breath.

– The sea grows civil at her song.

POLUNK.

Joan casts a peb in the seep. I cast it. Then Willy's ask, unsure.

– Will I stay sweet Joannie, or do I get the train?

– The lecherous rogue!

– Let's teach him a lesson!

A slop, a slap, palm wet to my thigh. A rebuff.

– Don't, not here.

– So do I get the train?

– No need for that.

I tuck in my shirt and fasten my belt. A few minutes later I spot them again, pat grey dab brown on the postcard high street. I follow them into a tea shop. Willy's techsplaining. I ope my journal. They sit in the window.

– Try to visualise a magnetic field by thinking of the whirlpool created in a cup when tea is rapidly stirred.

– Oh I understand that alright. The strain in the coil is comparable to the unnatural condition of the tea when it's forming the whirlpool. Radio wouldn't be possible without that.

I like me tea I'm the better of a cup of tea me

– Two lumps or three?

– Galena's sweeter.

A native lead sulphide used as a detector, sensitive, irregular and easily upset. I drop my pen. It rolls under their table. Keeping my eyes fixed on Joan, I bend to retrieve it from beneath the bed. Her nape, a counterweight, spikes a passing cloud. The crystal tip of Joan's vertebral stack radiates roundels of enlarging rings rings rings.

– forever blowin bubbles pretty bubbles in the air

I'll be ready for you soon give us a min

– You alright Mrs Cade?

She shrugs. Her waveform – shoulder domo shouldo – modulates the contour of the walnut wireless case.

I'm dreaming dreams I'm scheming schemes do you know why I've put on silk today I'm wearing it because it's an insulator that's the reason I'm in silk hachahachehee

Her mic-blasting cackle rinses round the room, draining with a guggle down the transy grille. The pierced cloud seeps across the window, leaking rain. An ambulance swings into the cul de sac.

– eeeeeeeeeeenowowowoweeeeeeeeeeeeeenowowowoweeeeeeeeeeenouw

The driver shuts the shrieker off.

it's grab and go Jim don't let him in I'm not done yet

Blue light spurts the walls, swabbing the nape. Joan, a vivid vintage filament, fluoresces.

how all things were how all things are I know how all things will be I see

She shimmers in the blumination‚ scratching a shouldazure.

Gas in a valve will act as a conductor, creating a blue glow. This radiance is seldom caused to any appreciable extent in today's components.

all things that are end

Her Prussian nails rake the cobweb, her bouffe beats bright cyan. Her thumbs-up isn't intentional.

a thief at night be ready

Blue snap to dusk. Thynne it lay by colpons on and on. The glory of grey hair.

I'll be with you soon

– In your own time Mrs Cade.

I glance at the desk. My producer gawps both palms, fingers splaying question marks. We don't do talkback anymore. I know her brow's revising budget.

Control points past me jabbing frantic.

Sharp to my jaw, slicing to my ear.

– She's a very old lady.

The nurse's fingernail, lifting my headphone.

I didn't hear the door.

– Almost a centenarian.

– Yes.

– Be patient. Give her time.

The cushion snaps back to my ear.

Vera's a wily one. The siren was a distraction to cover her entry. Smart. She hands Joan a beaker, a pill and a napkin. More downtime. I scribble a note.

Photography is overrated, my fledgling hand opines. Joan Cade's photo of William Joyce hides from view the fascist thug who hated Jews and championed Hitler. The real Haw Haw was never captured by a camera. Her smiling portrait masks the man: it does not record his contempt for democracy, disdain for all parties, and hatred of Jews. His counter-insurrectionary fantasies and wifebeating absent themselves. Mrs Cade's bedside snap is a silver-framed lie, I write, a disavowal of the brutality of Oswald Mosley's blackshirt crusade.

listen to you with the open mind think you know it all you do but you know nix

Later – weeks or months later – I amend the note with a different pen. Photographs have no meaning, I add.

what time is it I'm still here you know

Shot with an impulse one forgets, they are developed in a solution of memory and nostalgia. A hand-drawn line swoops across the facing page, lassoo to six more words.

We fix images in conjecture.

– Predigital. Past its use-by. Dump it.

things to do places to be that's me you know how it is I've a window but it's closing

– You can ask too much of a photograph.

– Too little too but you're right.

– This is the BBC. It is now a quarter past nine and time for schlurwioo schlurwioollingoo Jairmany calling.

Hamburg o'clock? I'm sure I flicked the footstone off.

– The brave bomber crews of the Luftwaffe are on their way.

you heard him don't just sit there make yourself useful

I swaddle the window with blackout. Control confronts me, miming no, shaking her head. She throws her cans at the console. I tuck Joan up in a utility bed. Churchill winks from a Winnie print above the headboard.

– Pin her hair in curlers.

– On it.

– Hide the radiator with a dressing table.

– Make the magic eye of the wireless shine. Give it a rub.

– Careful, it's collectible.

– Find an ARP helmet. Today please!

The helmet has a dent but no rust. Authentic props and good effects tune actors to a period. Brings out their best, it's all you can ask for. Airborne petrol engines bell the bay.

– I hope they're British kites.

The classic Spitfire has a V-12 liquid-cooled engine. The vee construction produces an irregularity in the exhaust note. The cooling damps the higher frequencies to produce an unmistakeable growl which has become a legend. The planes passing overhead have a broader spectrum of sound, the timbre of a flat four. They toll over the hill incognito.

– Intermittent, sullen, didactic.

Rapid beating of oil drums in an anechoic bunker, maffets muffled.

– Speed the audio fifteen points. Keep the pitch steady.

– Voice after three.

Sabbatha pango I determine the Sabbath funereal plango I lament funerals fulgura frango I break lightning excito lentos I rouse the lazy domo cruentos I tame the cruel dissipo ventas I disperse the winds.

Exhaust notes of clashing periodicity dissonate the berceuse estuary.

– I prefer the toucans.

– It's ten cans, big uns!

England is celebrated abroad as the ringing island crackles the pocket set. Today our church bells have been silenced until the threat of invasion is over. We must hope the wait is not long.

The ganging altos of a cathedral choir mute the oil pans to the daily times that big ben chimes are radio times which we are interrupting this evening for an official announcement on behalf of Her Majesty's Government.

> Spitfires and Blenheims,
> Say the bells of St Clements,
> Aren't built for five farthings
> Say the bells of St Martins.
> Donations, I pray ye,
> Said the bells of Old Bailey.
> On account of the Blitz,
> Said the bells of Shoreditch.

A peal of Hurricanes, dogfight trebells, tenor Junkers jangled out of time and harsh. Before this I took much delight in ringing. My eyes, Joan's eye, follow changes across the ceiling, bobs and dodges, hunts and firing. Neither of us speak. I began to think how if one of the bells should fall? I stand under a main beam where I might stand sure. Tumult in the clouds. Melodic propellors. I balance all. What if one fall? This thought shook my mind.

I was forced to fly.

I scale the sea wall.

I pitch into midnight bruise, the bay's dark lap. I jog black shingle, leap unlit, hurdling groynes. Pebbles cushion my knees. I roll. Spotlights reverse from the harbour, a barge tugged by a groan. The lamps revolve, doubling in the wet, snouting the swell, grunting up, grunting down, darkling. At Reeves Beach cables clack on alloy masts, a slack harp. I climb the wall again, stepping down to rubble.

A military jeep makes a slow pass on Meerstrasse, enforcing the curfew. A mouser scouts ahead of me, hightail, its eyes sparking. The atmo is zithery. I demortice my gate. At the base of the street lamp, gleaming, I see the perforated toes of a pair of brown brogues. White pelt buffs one kicker, catlick damps the double. Company murks the alley. I confront it.

– Do you want anything?

The Watcher's mute.

— Have you been following me? Who's your boss?

I'm irascible, due to drink perhaps.

— Step out here shortarse whoever you are.

An upper window squeals open.

— Seien Sie ruhig. Gehen Sie weiter. Want sleep.

Alley illuming, hat forming, brim lifting, I clock the scar.

— William Joyce!

— I'm taking shelter from the wind, that's all.

He grins. A truck rattles past, spanners in a tureen. The alley's empty. A man's shadow sheers across the tilted facade of the Yacht Club, an outdoor projection. Running feet reverberate on Harbour Street. The strings of the zither twang. Stand clear!

The strings break, scoring the road. The cat nyans.

Nape still at the window.

The pocket radio fuzzes. I tap the side. The grille shreds a thin voice.

> *although my mind recoiled in anger when you asked and I shudder to remember I shall begin it's a long and winding story but I shall trace its outlines for you*

— What do you remember of the war Joan?

No response. She lowers her right ear to the window sill, eye closed. There's a cervical crack as her scapula stretches, cleak of a head jamb in heatbloat, dew simmering on the apron, a beetle gristling bark, feathery bluenotes, leaves birching ninetail, malacca beaks golloping bees, ribthump, ridges of coins milling in a Watcher's pocket scarring queens, shoals of shoes spanking sidewalks, the bay basin bassing, waspy jetski, steady skyline hum. And cloudrolls, clouclap, drizzle of electrons, prefix sig.

— Joan?

> *the war it just was*

The nape rises and revolves, antenna tacking to a source. Artillery, distant crumps and yells, drift from the set at the foot of the bed. Wet sand on drums, spectral guns.

> *on the slopes at Tankerton you could hear artillery pounding the Somme heavy doors slamming on the sea a beast growling in the air bombardment drub everything shaking and trembling so fragile just a blue shawl brushing the water*

– I meant world war two Joan the next one.

> *men young men sad unsmiling smiling was bad form up there by the Military Hospital some were lewd filthy mother took me to the slopes for my tenth we sat on a blanket we had biscuit sandwiches biscuits from the baker with butter icing for a treat father's over there she said he's thinking about you today listen carefully listen in the lulls the empty moments you will hear him whistling happy birthday to you father tootling happy birthday dear Joannie close your eyes and listen dearie send your smile to father over there*

– The menace at the frontier.

– It's overused. A trope of last resort. Lost parent too.

– But real.

> *for years I kept going back I sat and closed my eyes I strained to hear him all I ever heard was gulls trucks dogs barking no signal at all let's pray for father mother said forkful of good that did pardon my frog twenty thousand men dead on my birthday we were listening to my father the man I called father emordet by the engewehr o-eights as we nibbled on bickies it's a week before we hear*

– A telegram?

> *a deeply regret to inform you yes I didn't understand not really not till the lucky ones came home what luck they laughed without bad we've none to speak on they were different creatures altogether bakelite brittle men flint for eyes back from the trenches to nothing five in a room no work strangers living with strangers who used to be their mothers wives sisters*

– The second world war Joan let's get on to that.

I knew a little about Germany not much I didn't go there till thirty-three everyone knew they were inventors and efficient and that the ruckus wasn't over I saw the Graf Zeppelin come over that was up on the slopes too it circled the world went to the arctic you could go to sleep on it and wake up in America it was a round Britain tour forty pounds a trip a lot of money then a flying marrow a bomb shaped balloon that's how I remember it but I wouldn't have seen a bomb by then ha groaning over the sails of the regatta the last sails of the day were coming back in but the zeppelin steals the show

– She nods to the right, sighing.

a sky whale a motel in its gut a fat boche finger pointing to a future where clods like us wouldn't be needed it could go eighty miles an hour it was a wonder August 1931 a wet summer evening Hugo Eckener was the captain in charge the radio club was fishing they caught German voices some lads cheered shiner the silver sausage they shouted but mostly it was a silent crowd upturned faces private thoughts someone yelled take cover one man said they're making maps for next time the older ones remembered that throb bombs grenades smashing through the rooftiles red glare in the small hours it was barbaric killing civilians in Kent as if we were Tommies at the front babykillers that's what we called zeps till we caught on how to burst them our pilots flew higher they fired incendiary bullets the flare lit up the sky for a hundred English miles we took gin in the Marine Hotel after the military hospital as was and such a crush a man went round the bar mickeying a paperboy flapping a copy of the Whitstable Times guard against zeppelin raids he says use brown paper from Cox's to darken your windows he had us all laughing that was on the front page every week of the war extra large sheets for a penny he shouts sticking wet pages wet with beer on the windows a real comedian that night brought back so many memories church bells attracted zeps that's what people said the skating rink's electric organ too even the Sally band got flak ha as we leave the hotel there's a girl singing for coins a rhyme we all sang as kids

Children they sing along with her, cheerily then querying, softer then sad. Uniformed nurses and wounded men appear at the windows of the former military hospital.

> Do you think a Zeppelin, a-sailing in the sky
> Would see the lights of Whitstable and pass them kindly by?
> No, it would drop a cruel bomb, and blow it in the air
> So darken up your windows, little Whitstable beware

The verse thins along the Parade as the voices disperse, a phantom broadcast fading.

That's lovely Joan I say. Half an hour wasted I was thinking.

– The next war Joan, what about that one?

I didn't see much of the next war dear I was kept away from the worst of it ha under lock and key I was raids confused noise garments rolled in blood burning fuel fire and after it was the same again hope yes there's hope peace planning hospitals schools but the same numbness again afterwards the ache for the gone and the selfish and brutish ways of strangers you once loved who once loved you

– The people's war they called it.

it was not Lord Snooty didn't share the shortages or have the same war as the rest of us factory lives the farmer's long hours greed of the spivs having no appetite for what's on your plate and being hungry aren't the same thing waking not knowing if you'd last the day bedding down would you last the night it was no news bad news more bad news then we knew we'd win it wasn't a war it was wars imperial colonial antifascist democratic theirs ours I can tell you living in Archway wasn't a patch on a country barracks with three meals a day or somewhere leafy far from the Luftwaffe I can't talk about it bad for my blood pressure I know I've agreed to but let's use today for something else

– Of course, take a moment.

Willy I heard Willy in the raids I was waiting

The looping welt in the bedside photo rises to a wire mesh lollipop,

Neumann NrM7/123, a Rundfunk station mic, Jairmany calling, wave on wave rolling to the raised chin, breaking at the toothtash, spuming airborne over occupied France.

Ack-ack raps the broadcast. Our window rattles in its frame. Bowled by Willy's pitching jaw, taunts tossed from Axis Europe vault the Channel, clearing cliffs of chalk. Caught high by Joan, swept down, owzat, they splay the walnut staves of the bedroom wireless.

– Mr Churchill's able leadership during the last war will be remembered by all those who lost their relations and friends in the holocaust of the Dardanelles.

Willy, dog with a bone.

– Can the ordinary British soldier understand why he should have been expected to die in 1939 or 1940 or 1941 to restore Poland whilst today he must die in order that the Soviets may rule Europe? Surely it must occur to him that he is the victim of false pretences.

Tenders blunder through the blackout. She presses a postcard to her cheek. I'll be seeing you soon it says. In Latin via Dublin from Berlin. London can take it Joan of Archway lays her head on Willy pillow wireless. Her blinders drop.

– Going deaf ma?

– What I must have nodded off.

She scurries to the backyard shelter with a pail of water, a sleeping bag, a skin of wine, the *Evening Chronicle*, leavened bread, a child, a smart phone.

– War's a constant.

– War is.

Fire crackers, slowed to a quarter of their speed. Rolling thunder with a long tail. We puff at our mics, old mics with vast rumbling diaphragms.

> when they sound the last all-clear
> how happy, my daaaarling, we'll beee
> when they turn up the lights
> and the dark loneleeee nights
> are only a memoreee

Joan's tea-slaked lips spittle the wistful air on to the bedroom window.

> *when they sound*
> *the last*
> *all-clear*
> *how happy*
> *my Willy*
> *we'll be*

– Is it possible to love a fascist?

– She did. It was. Today, I don't know.

– You're sure you want to do this?

– I have to try.

I'd made a bargain with that hair and all the windings there.

Play, key with a triangle boss.

I pad the plastic peg. As the lever yields my finger senses metal sliding, mech engaging, motor vibe. Check the aperture. Rings of plastic teeth are meshing, slow circular saws, a reeling unreeling side by side, revolving rustle of hiss. Spoooooooooool. Discs of digits riding rotors track duration. Reset to zero. Thumb the crenellations, slip the slider, winch the volume.

> *I have resolved to spend the remainder of my years in sincere*
> *penitence for the wicked life I have lived*

Joan's disembodied voice, seamless as a Greek manuscript.

> *these are my last times there are grey hairs on my soul hag*
> *bristles I've the pulse of a corpse sicknesses cleave my bones*
> *consuming agues dwell in every vein I tune my breath in*
> *grones*

Schlip schlip. Riffles from a softback butterfly she's browsing.

> *my story's ending time so it's time I told it truthful ever since*
> *I was a child I've loved to make up tales pretend I've done*
> *things that I didn't as a bit of fun yes but mostly to get by*
> *at school I wrote on cards I'd killed my mother I hid them*

about the place in other children's desks teachers' pockets
the library hoping they'd be found hoping they would hang
me yet I was very fond of my mother

Traffic grumbles below my window. Tyres rattle a drainlid, jazzing the street. Voices fountain. Where's the letterbox mate harbour oyster restaurant can I park here where's the sea? A Watcher's waiting by the gate, no mouth no ears no bladder. Lidless eyes, a lens not a woman. Gulls are scroking, are they on the tape or here, they're here I think but how to tell. Joan resumes.

I knew her Dot O'Grady knew her in stir Holloway she died
ten years ago I'm going to make the millennium I've got the
years left in me I do want that so go easy with your cuttings
and your clippings if you're going to make me walk coals
show a little consideration prod at my yesters if you must
just let me last a few more candles though lord knows stuck
up here Rapunzel in bed I could do with a prod ha a nice
fellah a man to make me laugh and feel wanted then hold
me after while I sleep oh chance'd be a fine thing nothing
down there works anymore drips when you don't want it
dry when you do like washing on the line at twindicorn any
pleasure would be yours alone skin's rind is life's last lesson
if I let my hair down now who'd climb it nobody it would just
pull out it's mould in a jampot look

Chinkle. That would be her glass. A real glass, not spot. She always had a jug and tumbler by the bed, crystal cut, a beaker scored with curls of red.

I remember a filigree handle on the the bedside cupboard, the drawer at the top, a plastic pearl with a deep scratch. By her ring, she said but she didn't wear a ring.

– Buy herring?

Fingers flick water.

– Silver darlings.

– Won't rollmops do?

What I can't remember I'll create. She'd want that. A sliced loaf of books, staling. Who delivers those? A library service? Please tell. A carton of tissues, sprouting.

A clump downstairs, a cupboard door.

How long has she been back? Will she stay this time?

Twindicorn? Where's Twindicorn?

Schweeeeeet-a-clunk.

Arrowheads descending. Blur of teeth. Stop I tap, then poke the spear.

> *drips when you don't want dry when you do like washing on the line at Windy Corner any pleasure would be yours alone*

Her voice a bell in my stairwell.

– Who's that you're listening to? An old flame?

– Hi come on up no. It's an interview. From back in the day early nineties.

Tapdance of her feet. Windy Corner, note it down. Was it called that then? Dead Man's, when did that slop find its name? Scent of absence, ex not over, tell me all and tell me true, current to my nape. I didn't turn. I daren't look.

– An old lady in Whitstable. She knew Sir Oswald Mosley. Our one time would-be Adolf. To her, he was Tom. She had an affair with William Joyce. Willy, ditto.

– She shagged Haw Haw? Are you serious? You have to tell Hairyall. There's a programme in this.

– I hope so. Don't call him that.

– Airy all over Hairyall Ariel.

– He's a mate.

– How can you work with the radio on? And music playing?

– It's lively, how I like it. How long are you staying?

– I love the tech.

– The cassette player? Twenty-three quid. I found it online.

– Copy the lot to digital.

– I will, I will. But for now I'm rolling old school.

– Luddite.

– Futurist.

Static whistling in my ears. No sound on the stairs.

– Don't go.

She's gone.

> ***yes I knew them well my glory was I had such friends I
> worked in the Black House the headquarters we travelled
> together did the rallies wined and dined I went on marches
> beat a drum in the ladies band I've got some stories I'll tell
> you what I can***

I'm not little lady make believe. She said that too. Which bloody tape though?
I need development funding. A budget to finish the transcript. I need it now.

Canterbury, the Stour draining east.

– It's slow progress I know

– How much have you got? Enough for forty minutes?

– Hours and hours. Yes Mark, I think so.

A gate open to sundry folk.

– A series then. I'll chase development. Is there a book in it?

– That too. I've drafted a few sections. I've notes from the time, I'm
  gathering my thoughts. A book will take a while, a year and more. But
  there's a series here, that's for sure. The original tapes are good, she's
  articulate and she's a story.

– But?

Bells scour the streets.

– It's hard to hear my questions, that's one problem. I usually sat behind
  her, sometimes the other side of the room.

– On the edge of the dead.

Bells like trumpets, the last.

– Amateur.

– It was part of the agreement.

– We'll need to establish exactly what was agreed.

– Sit there or no go she said. I sat facing her back.

– A bit odd?

– Whatever worked for her was fine for me.

– Work the rough cut. We'll see.

– Great.

The wall firm despite the breach.

– Bloody sensitive stuff though. Ultra awks. Local Nazis, living relatives, antisemitism. We'll be scrutinised to death. You'll be accused of promoting fascism. Nostalgia for our homegrown Hitlers. Normalising the far right, that at the very least.

– It'll be worth it. They're all wrong.

– Her views are bound to be controversial. She'll need placing and balancing. Do you have the stamina for this? Are you sure she's worth the effort?

– Joan's not what you think. Yes, yes of course.

– Persuade me.

A seat of learning, disputation.

– She knew Mosley and Joyce personally. It's the inside track on British fascism. She recalls details and incidents that aren't widely known, I've details confirmed. It's national history, there's a high level of interest. Her account raises questions about the role of the security services that need answering. What more do you need?

Twice a week I catch the bus to Canterbury where I hotdesk at the regional radio station. I copyedit scripts. I advise on unsolicited material and programme pitches. Bin or borrow, I'm called. I tell Mark Ayr, my boss, the task requires the patience of Job.

– A better paid Job.

– Noted. Go over this again will you? I need final by five.

I don't have wheels, not wheels of my own.

A car has too many downsides–insurance debits, speed limits, parking permits, roadside bizzies with breathalysers and zits. Friends cop rides, strangers wheedle lifts. A cab to fetch your car from the bar the morning after. Ferals key the paint job after dark, crack the mirrors. Where's the pleasure in driving? That's what I tell people.

Magnets for bugs, that's what cars are. An open goal for Trackers. Cars shout over here! to every camera in the facial recognition network. Wheels are shackles. Can you cut through a wood in a Kia? Can you merge with a crowd in a Mini?

I sit upstairs, at the front of the bus. It's a bit of reading time. The local paper, lately deceased, is a jigsaw of ads and news.

LORD JOHN SANGER'S CIRCUS. The Salts, Tuesday August 31st. Performances 3.0 and 8.0 pm. See JUMBO THE ELEPHANT GOAL GETTER. Jumbo will challenge the goalkeeper of the Whitstable Football Club to keep goal against him. MONKEYS, educated HORSES, comedy BEARS, a host of CLOWNS, Clemens Merk and his troupe of forest bred LIONS.

I look out of the window, coaxing lines from what I see. It's a daily ritual on which my freedom depends.

 — Tall bores at a boar stall, watching ice pies.

As we chute from Pean to Blean I leave a tangled trail. Orc bats in pork orchards pending. Flying trapped peas. Iron lion incisors, shredding sheds. I do this to deter pursuers, to delay them at least. Three are on my frequency today, half-seen figures tracking me through the streets, logging each encounter, noting every word. I must push ahead, stay out of their reach, or they will take me down. I detach suppressors, unleashing ticks and crackles. I drop dead letters in the breeze. They scurry after scraps, distracted. I let it be known that I write with invisible ink. They draw candles from their pockets. My code slows them. I billow smokescreen from the exhaust of the bus. Coughing, they double up.

Go, go, go.

As you went on buses, Auerbach recalls, you saw the sites of bombed buildings with the pictures still on the walls, the fireplaces and so on. I spy Joan's house in Gladstone Street. The front wall is a road rug, frayed, facedown.

— Crimes swept beneath it?

— The home exposed like a diagram.

You'll have to excuse me. I grew up speaking to buildings.

In the cramped sitting room, a crack cheek mannekin, slur-drunk, shouts at a miniature wireless set.

— Jewsury! Thugmorton Street. Thieves!

— Willy darling. It's late.

He drips himself a thimble. Reflected in a sequin, Joan pets her hair.

— In the City today new loans were announced for trade with India.

— Jewsury!

— Hush now Willy, come to my bed.

Joan extends a hand. Willy downs the thumbler. He tips the last drop twice, three times, his scar hooking, runner of a rocking chair. He clamps her palm. He stands, unsteady. Joan unlatches a cupboard door. She leads him up a set of steep and narrow stairs. Willy stumbles. His toecaps rattle risers, treads baton his knees. The ceiling muffles their voices. Creaks, wooden. Drips below, blop, a tap in the blop scullery. Have they gone to sleep? Blop. A sudden groan, springey in the stillness. Again, clanking and quickening. Blop. Creaks. Boots descend the cupboard. The door slaps open. The nub of the latch chips plaster. The dwarfling blop shrugs into a leather coat.

— Where's my hat, Joan? My muffler where'd you put it?

Hmmomaghyow! The street's unlit, silent but for a cat. There's a bus approaching, a stop nearby. The passenger upstairs, that's me. With my forehead I melt the windowpane. Yawning, I sentence the high street.

Willy is a colossus.

He towers eighty feet above the terraced streets. Willy, swirling a dark pennant across the face of the moon. The victory streamer snakes in search-light. Feldmarschall Joyce snipes lightning at resisters retreating to the harbour arm. He thorbolts. He thunderzags.

– Which way's the bus stop?

Whitstable cowers. A grenade detonates outside a council office, shattering shop windows. To those ychained in sleep the wakeful trump of doom thunders. The Jewish tailor shop smoulders. Old scores are settled in woodyards with boots and clubs. A union card soaks in the blood of a railwayman on platform one. Books blaze behind the library. Willy stamps approval. Clapboard homes shake, windows flop and break, horses bolt from grocers' gates. Willy looks down at the vanquished town. His scar threads the stars, a new constellation. A blackshirt retinue throngs at his feet. Peaked caps peck at his calves.

Rothschild and Gandhi are snared in the painter's mark, a scrawl of barb wire.

Passing the tower of St Alphege, Willy nips the blades of the clockface shut. His boots sink deep into the diosoil. He flicks each of the bells twice, imposing midnight.

– Hour of crimes.

– Stimulate some action gonna get some satisfaction.

– Midnight. Midnight in the century.

With a back kick, the heel of his boot, Joyce splinters the gilt frame. The church carillons a warning, a nippy klang that quickens tocsin over the town. Church-bels beyond the starres heard. A black squad hatchets the oak door.

Joyce doesn't look back. A ferocious hem storm, his leather coat slaps roofslate, toppling terra cotta pots. Alarmed by falling debris, attendants bellow warnings.

– BRITAIN FIRST chim at ten BRITAIN FIRST! watch it! HAIL MOSLEY halt I said halt KING AND PEOPLE keep tut middle ut road KING AND PEOPLE steer straight BRITAIN FIRST man down!

High street hutches rupture open. He sees a woman washing herself: and the woman is very beautiful to look upon. He will inquire after the woman. He resolves to return and find her when the battle is over. How can she live till in her blood she live! Through a scullery rift she pleads:

– Don't go.

Seeing Red! baying for the blood of Red! bellringers Red! trade unionists, Red! aliens, Red! plutocrats, Red! Indian nationalists, the black pack flushes out Reds! – no passaran they pipe, workers of the world unite – flushing them toward the makeshift checkpoints that local patriots, lids festooned with apple blossom, have set up at all the major junctions.

– Apple blossom?

– Nationalist voodoo, wooing the Orchard of England.

– They used to throw it at Hitler.

Identity papers are checked at major intersections: the Cross in the town centre; the junction of Nelson Road and the High Street; where Joy Lane joins the Canterbury Road; by the castle and harbour gates; in rural roads to block any backdoor flits. Translations are added to street signs: Fahrbahn Frohlich; Oxford Strasse; Hafen Allee. Armed volunteers patrol the back streets.

– Ensuring community safety.

– Protective custody for Jews.

– Rounding up disorderly Natives.

– Taking pets as hostages!

A day of trouble, and of treading down, and of perplexity. Move along. Geh jetzt weiter. It is like a babble of hissing, screaming, humming and grunting.

Gulliver Willy wades into the estuary. Galway's Gargantua fords the moat. General Leviathan strides over occupied France. Goliath Joyce orates into a microphone mounted on the Eiffel Tower.

– He was only five foot six!

Eyes as lamps of fire, the voice of his words was like the voice of a multitude.

– How is a country transformed into a single economic and cultural whole?

Europe waits on his answer.

– By means of communications.

Nods rapid nods knowing nods willing nods growing.

– It is imperative in the political interest of the state not only that the whole nation participates in broadcasting, but that the entire nation is ready to receive radio programmes at any moment.

Invisible waves ship tablets of stone.

– He scorns the pebbles of our feeble slings.

New radio nations merge in a Radia Reich, a structure of hearing an eardom of orderly listening in.

– The man who can hold the people's ear – or most of their ears most of the time – will acquire the most astonishing influence.

By hearths, gathering at bars, in the cool shade of colonial verandahs, huddled toe to toe in storm tents, twenty million ears Britannic tap Willy's nasal whine. As if on stalks, the ears of the world revolve towards him.

Joan talks at the grey window. Her words glide like gulls. Inform.

> *radio is invasive rootless cosmopolitan nigh on uncontrol-lable the hertzian wave doesn't respect maps wireless dissolves borders with tides of new voices songs welcoming everyone radio draws on us all to make things new in the early days that wasn't so obvious radio was a technology that could construct nations win unity from disorder engineer souls mobilise the bioelectric mass Tom and Willy loved it but didn't get it they longed for their own station for a wireless nation of imperial Britons the new scientific radio race*

– I transmit therefore I am.

– We receive we are.

Citizenship is conferred by wireless, citizenship is listening in, politics is radio is politics.

– The most modern most important instrument to influence the masses, a true servant of the volk.

The first People's Receiver, the Volksempfanger 301, takes its name from the date of Hitler's accession to power.

– In fascism radio becomes the universal mouthpiece of the Fuhrer.

– His voice merges with the howl of sirens proclaiming panic.

– It beats in the heart like a divine understanding.

The VE301 is half the price of previous sets, the cheapest wireless in the world.

– National Socialists understand that broadcasting gives our cause stature, as the printing press did the Reformation.

With half the power of previous sets, the VE301 only receives German stations.

– The whole of Germany hears the Fuhrer with his Volksempfanger.

Adverts offer a Bakelite set the size of a house, aryan masses listening in a ring.

Soon the DKE1938, Goebbels' Schnauze, sells at half the price of a VE301.

– The Fuhrer's metaphysical charisma is the omnipresence of his radio addresses.

– Cue the scar two one red.

Gin Willy Joyce, Giant Thighboots, declares the final victory of National Socialism in Europe.

– This is our new order a corporation of corporate states planning the movement of peoples and the scientific health of the race.

A state of listening, state of the ear, Earope. But the order is unstable. National Socialist leaders are troubled by a new obstacle, the advent of the shadow ear. For each lug that listens to a wireless, one is turned away.

William Joyce informs the radio nation that every shadow ear withheld from the wireless – the broadcast voice of the People, the People speaking as the Reich – every averted auricle insults the dignity of the Fuhrer, every redirected eardrum weakens Earope's defences, every misaligned auditory canal drains strength from the broadcast race.

– The Fuhrer has decreed that all National Socialists, each and every citizen mobilised by the State, will from this hour forward listen in to official broadcasts with the right auricle only, sealing the left to eliminate distraction. Deputy Gauleiter Mosley in London has welcomed the directive, recognising the more effective public messaging, and shared sense of citizenship that will result from a consistent drill for listening-in.

– Heil Hitler! Hail Mosley!

- Don't be forgetting O'Duffy.

- Plugging the left ear when listening to the wireless is the duty of every citizen.

- Adopt the drill today!

- Block interference by the ear sinister!

- Irreconcilable enemies of the state will have their left auricles humanely removed by expert hearing technicians before World Radio Day.

Entertain. We traffic in mockery.

As the Berlin Reicharmonic plays the overture to Wagner's Rienzi, a hundred million people turn to their sets. Cupping their right pinnae, they finger or cover the left. Citizens jostle for listening spots, foreheads clash, hearing cones compact to fists and cone again. Families fight over ear plugs. Large numbers of listeners swivel their heads from side to side, putting shadow ears to equal use, ending the distinction between left and right. The new movement wins support. Tens of millions of wireless sets blur in a frenzy of patriotic headshaking. The continent tremors with manic naysaying.

- Quiver down my backbone.

- Shaking all over!

Goebbels rages in the Funkhaus. He paces up and down.

- This is mock-obedience! Am I surrounded by fools?

- Radio has made life even more fantastic and ridiculous than it was before.

During a live broadcast from Bayreuth, opera-goers are ordered to adopt the decree.

- Deviant ears will be removed from the hall.

- We had to turn our faces from the stage!

- There was no refund and it was very uncomfortable.

One listener, best seat in the house, defies the order.

- I recognise, each time I see that opera, what mistakes I might be in danger of making, so as to avoid them.

The directive is withdrawn.

– Anyone can change their mind. It's good policymaking.

Twelve men sit at a table. In bursts a larger number, armed. A diner hacks off an intruder's ear. The host replaces it.

The people will not tolerate any act of clemency, says Joyce.

– Was Lambeth a bid to lop off your right ear?

It's when it all began, he says.

– Next job I do I shall clip the ladys ear off and send to the police officers just for jolly.

Two men in a warehouse. One dances, holding an open razor. Tied to a chair, the other begs through a gag. An ear is tossed to the floor.

Never shall misdeeds be forgiven, says Joyce. The English are unhappily given to compromise.

– Crop the shell-like.

– Shades of Prynne.

– Slice the ear that listens to Satan.

Round three, two boxers in a ring. Teeth bared, lips to lobes a clinch, one bites one rips. I don't know how much, he says, I spat it out. Later, in an ad, he returns the rind. It's pickled in formaldehyde.

Educate.

An insolent farmer's ears, clipped with garden shears, served in a little covered dish.

That should see off the Watchers, flummox followers, slow down the Trackers.

– I've won some time.

– For what?

– Joan and I to talk alone.

– Make doubly sure.

I open the rear window of the bus. I fling handfuls of caltrops into the road.

I'll invest in a stinger one day. A chase car hits the spike shingle. It pops and sighs and stops. The blue bonnet contracts. Job done.

I return to my seat.

The coach burrs along the dark High Street. I cool my forehead on the window. Willy steps into the road, waving his arms.

– Stop. Stop please.

The anchors yowl. We bow to the supplicant. F/X returns the bugle to the table, softly, so it isn't picked up. The bus judders and halts. Steel blocks, scrubbed slow, Jew's harp.

– BOING!

Slung to,we spring back erect.

– Yer left that late mate coulder runyer down.

– Thank you. I'm sorry everyone. Canterbury please, a single.

The coach is snug with pipe fug. Framed by headscarves, female fares frown.

– Shameless. Drink you can smell it.

– Spetacle of isel'.

– Stepping out like that who's he think he is.

Women of Canterbury. Their men nap in felt. Willy takes a seat towards the rear of the coach. Joan, gin, Jewsury I hear him mutter. Joan, gin why do I? He's two or three seats behind. I don't turn. Swindling swine he says.

– Seven bloody miles if I'd missed it!

He burps audibly.

– Bellamy better be up when I get there.

The last bus climbs the hill, rocking its freight gently.

In the sound library there is a disc of heritage bus engine recordings. It has twenty-two tracks. Tilling Stevens, Lances, Leylands, they're all on it. Grind seven, muffled with a blanket, confirms we're on board.

I rub a tennis ball on greased glass.

Lurching Willy pads for balance on a large globe in a sawdust ring.

He holds a hollow rubber hammer in one hand, a balsa sickle in the other. Both are red. They jerk and plunge as he footles. Sanger's big top bloats with stripes of boo. From upper seats men hurl upholstered lightning. The front row flings asparagus in bundles. It's a Willy-shy. Ambushwhack the amballator! Willy's had enough. He dumps his props, leaping from the squashalloon. He draws a Mauser, fires it in the air. The powder wakes a lion.

Willy levels his chin, Willy raises his heels, he rises on his toes, he stiffs his spine, locks shoulder, locks right elbow, arm thrust palm down bayonet fingers fixed he spears roman. The limb doubles in length, his hand inflates. The audience rises, a forest of raised forearms. Hail Joyce! The woken lion rolls to its feet and roars. The forest flops. The audience gasps the audience holds its breath the audience yells run run get out get away and Willy scarpers.

The bus drives into its own illumination, a projector screening documentary hedges.

Silver bat swooping, a hand shakes a hankie in the headlights. It's the stop at Blean. A scarf and felt get off. A sniffler boards, collars up – shields of twill – his peak pushed down. The bus lurches on. The new passenger sits directly behind Willy. A hand grips the holdrail at his shoulder.

Hatched furrows of freckle scale a lee of peel rising to the fist's cortical ridge. Scab knuckles camp in hide, wispy gold phalanges top the cliff. The distals are locked by his thumb, the nail harbours a black moon.

Willy rubs his prickling nape. I do the same to mine.

Gates, hedges, the docureel resumes. Pistons rattle pipes snort Willy nods. Run get out the lion's behind nobbut a claw away. He doesn't look back. He zigs and zags to a set of goalposts standing by the entrance to the ring. An elephant clad in a Union Jack fells him with a trunkswipe, GO JUMBO! hoofs him into the back of the net GOAL JUMBO! and rolls him in the knotting. JUMBO JUMBO the audience chants, JUMBO BOJUM laughing clapping, UMBO JUMBO stamping in time. Jumbo tosses Willy's lightning cap high. An aerialist yoked with elliptic wings swoops across the canvas sky. He scoops the cap. HOORAH! Jumbo rises on rear legs. She sprouts moustache. She prods a blunt salute.

Teeth raked the lion roaring leaps at Willy, massed muscle arching through the air, harmless, a costume thrown aside by an elegant man in a Kippah. The laughing Jew waves at the cheering crowd. The applause mounts as the fake pelt engulfs wriggling Willy last stop St Peter's Place last stop sir calls the bus driver off you get it's the end of the line all change.

I'm first out. Using the tradecraft Joan has taught me, I reverse my coat and switch my hat.

make your shadow as the night in the middle of the noonday

– I'll try Joan

unobserved unseen invisible to mortal sight

– I'll do my best

Covered in sawdust, drowsy Willy steps onto the pavement into daylight OW! A tourist rucksack knocks him into a pedestal bin. He bottoms into the eggcup I SAY, a stuckbutt, knees folded to his chin, arms and legs dangling from the brim.

– Help me out of here!

Parents carers buggies nippers bustle by the wriggler on their way to school. High collar of Blean watches from a distance. Has he clocked me? Did Willy? I'm late for work already.

– Help me out of here dammit.

Children giggle at the bawling humpty numpty.

– Someone please a hand.

I snatch a photo. Work can wait. As I negotiate a coffee at the grab and go – six origins of bean, five stylings, three milks two non-dairy, lid or no, size stay or go and cash or tap – a car swings hooting through the medieval gate. It's the hunting pack. They've cleared the caltrops from the road, they've cracked the code and caught up. Doors break open as the blue avenger mounts the pavement. Two guys rush to Willy.

– Bloody get me out of this!

– We've got you sir.

They raise his arms and feet high over his head. Groin to thigh, chin between knees, an agent lifts him free. Feet shuffle, their foreheads crock.

– Put me down!

The back of Joyce's trenchcoat is smeared with ketchup and kebab. He pulls a copy of *Action* from a pocket, wiping off the worst. The rescuers – move along now, on your way now – encourage the crowd to disperse. Arms perpendicular, they revolve slowly, rotor blades in a law enforcement folkdance. I step back reluctantly. With a theatrical flourish Joyce jettisons the soiled newspaper, the blackshirt rag that bears his name. I wish I'd caught him on the phone cam. Director of propaganda bins the party's paper! Front page for sure, and William Joyce a standing joke.

– Fascism isn't a laughing matter.

– I know. But they hate ridicule.

– No sense of humour?

– They're funny like that.

– Upstairs they say you're making evil into entertainment.

– We'll show them they're wrong. You'll see.

As the coach pulls away, Joyce makes for Bellamy's. The unpurged images of day recede. The rooms are five minutes away, above the Union shop, just west of the cathedral. Bellamy's up but he isn't in. Chap might be anywhere, the woken neighbour says.

– You're avoiding my point. You can't treat fascism as a joke.

Diana said fascism is too serious to be dealt with in a funny book. That's a little unreasonable, Nancy replied.

– It is now a notable feature of modern life all over the world. It must be possible to consider it in any context.

Will Joyce go back to Joan's? He's light on cash. I trail him for an hour as he wanders between the cab rank and cathedral. I count monks and drunks and engines clanking the crossing. It's a draw. Six of each.

I return to Whitstable in a minicab.

I get out in Century Close but the care staff won't let me in. They say Joan's asleep. I don't believe them. Light lines her curtains. I hear a dance tune, faintly, and a phone-in too.

- Can no platform and free speech coexist, the gentleman at the back please.

- Zing went the strings of my heart.

- Arguments are more effective than bans, even the most heated arguments.

Walking away I notice a blue car with tinted windows, engine idling, in the slip road to the cul de sac. As I pass it, Rienzi is playing on the radio.

- Put the ladder to the window.

I step behind a parked van, as if crossing the road. I wait then drop to my knees and lay flat. I elbow forward, palming oil, under a dark ceiling of struts and props. My jacket's biker, it can take it. I'll need new jeans. Wagner's exhaust cannons crud, streaming my eyes. I heek on the tar and bite on a cough. I suck cool air from the kerb.

Footsteps. Shins and shoes approach. They point right at me. Driveside they pivot to the opera, eyelets aligning, shins inclining, heels lifting.

- Everything okay?

And you, Rienzi asks the people, have you forgotten what you swore to me?

- She'll sleep soon enough. He did show up, we sent him away.

- We saw.

It's hard to make out what I hear, her head on his chest, ancient Rome the queen of the world. Thick ankles seal the mouths of both shoes.

- G'nite then.

The shoes dob close, so near I smell the leather. They bat the road behind me fading faint. It's just me and the tailpipe now.

- You besiege the road like bandits!

When the interference is outside the premises a suppressor is often effective.

- It should be mounted on the apparatus itself.

I snake beneath the front valance and roll on my side. I wedge a tab of soap into the hot exhaust. I burn my fingers pushing it home. The booming mutes and stumbles. The blue car bloats. As it lifts into the night sky, swelling, the floating chassis thins to foil. I hear soldiers marching with the bells of morris dancers at their ankles.

– For Colonna!

– For Orsini!

The surveillance car is a carny inflatable, a barrage balloon saloon, a pork bladder bubble bobbling blue moon.

The Watcher and the Wheelman panic. They stand on their overblown seats, calling for help from widening window voids. They disappear from view.

Falling co-ax cable fountains in the cul de sac, rapidly mounding, fast unwinding, one end tied to the underside of the soaring surveillance car.

I lash the lead securely to a gate. Kites are unreliable antenna lifters as changing winds change their height. I open the gate by degrees, tuning the vehicle in. Maid the hinge wings. The latch clats hay. May the hinge, the latch day.

– Mussolini banned May Day.

– Hitler declared a holiday.

– Dissolved trade unions the following morning.

– Shut offices. Seized funds. Sent leaders to the camps.

The soap melts.

Dead moving ever to a dreamless goal.

William Joyce's spectacles are retrieved from a glass display case in the top floor corridor. His gold ring is withdrawn from the National Archive. He signs for them in an interview room in Wandsworth and is returned to his cell. After declaring himself not guilty at a hearing, Willy is taken to an airport. He's flown to Brussels, then driven to Flensburg in north west Germany, where he's handed two passports. One bears a false name, the other his own. Joyce is released at gunpoint in a wood above the harbour.

Am I free, Willy asks, am I really free? A guard shoots him in the leg and leaves. The wound doesn't scar. He makes his way, painlessly, to a cottage where his wife Margaret waits. She scolds him. Willy, wroth to see his kingdom fail, swings the scaly horror of his folded tail.

A few days later, after meeting with local officials, they board a train to Luxemburg then to Hamburg and on to Berlin. Joyce makes propaganda broadcasts to Britain from the Rundfunkhaus. He predicts German victory. He criticises the British government, its armed forces, the impact of wealthy Jews, of left-wing Jews, on public life. British planes bomb the station during broadcasts. After three years his name is removed from the credits. Out of work and friendless, the Joyces catch a train to Ostend, then a ferry to Dover where they are met by Joan Cade.

Shortly after returning Joyce receives a phone call, a heads-up from the Secret Intelligence Service. He's no longer on the wanted list. He joins Oswald Mosley's British Union of Fascists. On his first day at headquarters he is welcomed with a parade. He's handed an envelope stuffed with cash, he becomes a director. He deputises for Mosley at speaking engagements. His accent downshifts, from landed elite to London Irish. His followers march in black uniforms. Willy is rapidly demoted. He marries and divorces. His public meetings grow in size, the opposition dwindles. In Germany, Hitler falls from power. Joyce joins the Conservative Party. His breach with Mosley is final, they never meet again.

Mosley launches the New Party. Soon after he is elected as a Labour MP. A popular campaigner for full employment, he's tipped to become the party's leader. Joyce studies linguistics and publishes *The Mid Back Slack Unbound Vowel A in the English of Today*. He remarries and moves to Galway where he helps British mercenaries to target republicans. Little is known of his last years in the United States. The documentation is patchy.

There's no one else I talk to.

Walls of mist encase the hill. The estuary is abstract, two horizontal bands, grey over white, her nape a pale peak.

– A view to gloom whatever window we look from.

Astra my daughter won't hear a word there's no one in here

who really remembers only Mr Samuels down the corridor
he was red he's rude a vile vile man it was him scratched
MOSLEY'S WHORE on my door it's not the first time I've been
called that not by a long chalk we used to call each other
Tom's whore Willy's whore a giggle it was cutting words can
always be turned though there'd be trouble if I cut PERISH
JUDAH on his door I've been tempted I can tell you plain old
PJ no one would know what it means it wouldn't be right
granazi abuses elderly Jew care home hate crime that's
what the local rag would say I'd be out on my ear I won't
make that mistake again never the smoke of their torment
will rise for ever a grave in the sky Willy felt no remorse he
was obsessed fixated to the very end antisemitism was his
cross an illness it made men mad he didn't see we are all
chosen England is Israel and Israel's struggle is England's
battle that was the penny that didn't drop

From 4569-4610 on tape 17 there is silence in the room. The grey at the
window mists the mist greys and clears. Salt fresh Thames gape, Whitstable
blister on the lip, tidal cut to Teddington lobe, churning rut to Chelternear.

– Try to make a silence.

– We cannot.

Radio always radio passing radio distant radios play.

we didn't know what was happening in the camps or if it
happened the way the Russians said it happened we know
that now but what was that to do with us we aren't German
at the end of the day we're different people

Clotting cloud, white sprigs. Container ships cruise the water windfarm,
passing behind loft conversions and solar reapers, vista clutter. Trampo-
lines, she says, I've never been on a trampo, they're lucky the kids today.

Childe Joan scampers to the paunch of the hill. Open fields, oak trees, a
market garden edged with paths. Still you may find there, lovely together,
flowers crushed and grass down-pressed. The landscape of my childhood,
she says, it's where I grew up look it's there now it's gone.

Laurence and I, she says, reaching for a book, we sat like this in the black
mill, she says, looking out the same as this, she says, naming the horses

counting sails listening in as Laurie had a crystal.

– Laurence?

– Irving, the designer. Older than me, gone.

– Tell me about him.

My most daring delight, reads the nape, was to climb up into the cap, to straddle the fat windshaft and, clambering through the spreading spokes of the great driving wheel, to work my way to the square trap door that opened onto the huge iron axle into which the intersecting sweeps were wedged.

he's describing the mill listen to this bit

Unbolting it and lifting it to one side with difficulty for, like everything in the windmill, it was solidly constructed, I could gaze from my Olympian perch over the vast panorama framed in the massive butts of the sweeps.

> *massive butts of the sweeps that used to crack me up chubby butt of the local chimney sweep more like it was his joke everyone missed it straddling the fat shafts of intersecting sweeps ha Laurie was a clever one but you wouldn't want to get caught back then dear shame shame and hard labour were the price you paid for being gay when we were young*

– What was she reading from?

– Not sure. I'll find it online.

> *Harry Irving his father the actor lived in the house all the celebrities of the time were visitors actors writers journalists I'd come up here to spy through the hedge so grand it was tennis flannels bright dresses silver trays a gramophone playing Laurence noticed me he was nice I see you Joannie he'd shout from the cap of the mill he'd sketch up there I'd shave the pencils and watch oh I was happy up here with Laurence away from everyone*

To a curious boy each floor had its own enchantment. The second floor was rammed with rough hewn machinery – wheels geared with apple wood cogs, grading drums driven by leather belting, and stone governors hanging from the ceiling like giant bats. Though these mechanisms were, as it were, petrified and would rattle and rotate no more. In their suspended animation they made a cave of stalactite wonders.

Laurence had a crystal set the first kind of wireless no lecky needed nor batteries very eco just a cat's whisker don't go animal rightsy on me not a real one we catch an orchestra it's very faint but it's music through a headset a performance in a hall in London you can't imagine how exciting that was to me sitting on the stile and there was drama too

– We chose the balcony scene from Cyrano. We sat round a kitchen table in the middle of the wooden hut, with its shelves and its benches packed with prosaic apparatus, and said our passionate lines into the lip of our separate microphones.

high in the cap squeezed up close twiddling with Laurence whenever I can my brother says plying the knob ha crude but not altogether wrong Laurie was a pilot in the first war like Tom hush hush in the second something secret

Wireless readies for war, boosting valve production, raising masts.

Two grey biplanes, propeller-driven, fly towards a radio tower, both at exactly the same height. A collision seems inevitable but they are static, two dimensional, pareidoliac, eyes to a steel nose. The aircraft and the mast are enclosed in a white circle, the face of the moon. Smaller planes orbit the circumference. As they pass a red planet, Soviet earth, they change course, drawn by wireless signals. The Flying Proletarian asserts the revolutionary futurism of the world radio party.

– Attention! Moscow is speaking!

An object of constant fear for neighbouring nations.

Three years later, Joan and I visit the Funkturm in Berlin. From the observation platform, we look down into a cantilevered web of climbing steel. The restaurant, half way up, conceals the concrete heels, each supporting a ceramic sphere. Shadows ribbon the diner's rectangular roof. The garden is studded with parasols, tables and seats. So high here, dizzy high, a steep sway of giddy struts. I go back down. The sonneshade are furlen. It's closing time. Moholy nods as he passes. He's on his way up.

A radio mast is the nape of a city. Moscow Shukov, an aviary of voices. Echelles de Jacob, Eiffel. Deutsche Welle Deutschlandsender. Daventry dauntless. Diamond Blaw Knox. Steely ambassadors.

Joan's summit bed hosts crisis talks, wireless head to head with plastic, grim-faced valve to diplomatic pocket tran.

   – I mass one will from the will of millions.

   – Dinosaur! We co-create with active listeners.

   – Commercial broadcasting weakens nations!

   – We let peoples speak!

   – So open up the airwaves!

   – Television will destroy us all.

   – Sound is more suggestive than the image.

   – Then we agree, a broadcast should not be envisaged.

I try to reconstruct the setting, nonetheless. The window's expanse, mast Cade. The bed, the poppy curtains, cupboard, chair. Two radios, no, three. A jug, the glass, her books. Clutch and dressie, coats, at the door. The portrait of Joyce. More, she says, there must be more, of course there was.

what about my medication

Plastic pots, screwtops with labels. Pills in bubble strips. And tissues. The windowsill, she says, what's always in my reach?

   – Your glasses. Your specs are always there.

and next to those what do I have next to my glasses

   – What are you driving at Joan?

what do I keep beside my glasses

I look to her right. An enamel clasp for matches.

I've not seen that before. She passes it over. Blind as a bat you are, she says.

a memento what else have you missed or failed to mention listening to me not using your eyes

   – But it wasn't there. I'm sure it wasn't.

Coated metal, commemorative, it's folded like a taco. Inside it's rusty. On one panel there are three portraits framed in gold. Roosevelt smiling, Churchill grinning, Stalin stern, turning his back. On the back a show of allied flags.

Willy one side of me the big three on the other you think about

***that for a moment a little more envisaging will balance your
report our listeners will appreciate it***

There's a tribute on the spine of the clasp.

*Our Deepest Gratitude and Admiration to the Allies who stood
United in Defeating the Greatest Tyrant in History.*

I bought it for Laurence on Victory Day, she says. I went to see him again
she says, we'd both come through.

***he was a squadron leader and in the movies famous by then
but it stayed in my bag dear oh dear I should have realised
otchy cotchy did I hurt his words were bayonets***

– Mosley's whore if I'd known what you'd turn into into I'd have pushed
you from the top of the mill. Haw Haw's mattress I'd have set the dogs
on you.

It wasn't unusual for the concierge to see women hurrying from Mr Irving's
rooms in tears.

– Get out you Nazi Jezebel go!

Leaving the care home that evening, I take a closer look at the black mill.
It's undergoing restoration. The smock is holed. New weatherboards are
stacked at the base by a heap of rotten shards.

– A post mill, wings spread.

– It can turn but it doesn't.

– Wreckage at its foot.

The cap throbs bloodshot in a yellow sky crusting with blue. Blades hew
blurring whorls of spattering sunflower. A high door yanks shut. Who's up
there? Props and ladders gutter red to dazzling lemon puddles.

The mill post emits a deep hum. I hear beating in the air, eurodisco you're my
dance girl. The iron windshafts declaim drama harry it's not safe up there do
stop fussing I'm alright aaaa. Harry what's happening? The fantail delivers a
political speech: the bag makes the tea stronger the longer it remains. The tea
keeps its strength if you exit, the metal fence replies. The clipped sails gale
with laughter, all eight sides of the smock shake, black planks clapping.

As I walk on a car reverses away from me, fast, very fast, towards the hill.

Rubber shrieks, urgent. Rad and bonnet veering left swing right, bobbing and rising, hip-dipping rearend into startled traffic.

Nothing that has happened is lost. It flashes, is seed.

A care home, what's that like to live in.

– I try not to think about it.

– What F/X do we need?

– I asked her to write down what she could hear.

– And did she?

– She gave me a list.

1. Nothing at all below 20 hertz. 2. Nothing over 8000. 2a. So a lot less than you! 3. Wheheezery tungslop swallop sluck. 4. They thud, my teeth do, they give me headaches. 5. Shapeless voices. 5. Skelecrack my knee my neck my back. 6. Windbust, coffings. 4. Snatches of song. 5. I sometimes laugh to myself. 6. I do talk to myself. 7. I read aloud as well. 8. Coughapercussion and antic gutsiphone. I could form a band. 9. Bangle jangle beadclink ringting tink. Our first album. 10. Scripts of the carers. How are we today? Soon outer your hair gran. Laters. Carboof, doorblam, doomp cloomp all day.

> ### plup of these pills from the pods plup plup

– Cuppaclop of a spoon clup clup.

> ### chirrups coowoos birds return when the Watchers go

– Phone fret ting. Fret ting gring. Fret ting gring in a house on the hill.

> ### Vera's vacuum's a banshee it kicks the furniture

– Pat pot pit spit spat rain sodden paper sodding buckets.

> ### ha you your fool questions pipes that chime warming up and sing when they sluice snoring always my own boys and balls bawling church bells faintly wind permitting fireworks on the beach faintly wind permitting bursts with a slight delay

– The dustbinmen.

Willy Tom Mosley ma their counsel and correction my
wireless my pocket and zista

– She wrote that list? Did she write it?

– Trust me. A nudge was all it took.

drooze honey in the rock garden murgling fount of milk
wine sloaking over the ridge the swump of Century Close
plashing yaps and playful growls a fox and badger frolic
beasts of the forest without their wildness apples pattle
from aching branches fruit without labour each cherry each
nut on its stave a tremolo bud

– These are her own words?

clotter locks falling from doors squeams chaste windows
unsealing floorp a fence falls a thundulate flush as the sea
voids smuck and dreg and oyster racks

– She's on a roll.

– Could be the meds.

heart of a man I truss maddling mine

– The signal's going.

nomo deth nomo sorro nor crine o pain.

– We're losing her. Nurse! Nurse!

No chips.

– Beg pardon?

my son's no chips I'm sorry to say

– You've got me there Joan.

chips the prince gave Hetepheres the queen his mother a
fold and go bed it's what I need a flying bed wings to get me
out of this room I can't smell the sea taste salt on my lips
through a window all I can see from here is the lid of my life
I want a hoverbed rooves with hinges like the dolls house I

had as a girl I'll lift the slates and look back in

She grasps the view with a roll of her wrist.

the Bear and Key hotel we held the first British Union dance there kindling tied with ribbons decorating the tables fasces on the banners in the dining room mister Tester with a swastika on his lapel the boys in their uniforms saluting as the cars came and went a glorious night

I squat outside the hotel, now a pasta joint. Reaching into the passage on the right I unhook the façade of the building and swing it open, closing the junction with Harbour Street. The panel bats against the pub opposite, sealing the front entrance and blocking its windows. A tiny landlord storms into the road, shaking his fist. A model bus halts and hoots. Won't be long I boom, minute or two at the most. They plasticise.

Each room of the exposed Bear and Key is a compact stage. I squat for a closer look. On the ground floor, blackshirt mannequins greet and seat ticket-holding dolls. The guests smile red ink as they are shown to matchbox dining tables decked with writing paper. The men wear felt suits and foil medals, their wives and daughters colourful evening dresses made from ribbons. Seeds pearl on cotton thread. The dining room is lined with gift wrap. The carpet is flannel. Scissored white lighting zigs across a scrap of red velvet. A waiter in an origami jacket steps from a side room.

– They're out of butter in the snug.

Peering into the small compartment I see a family tucking in already, gran, ma, pa, an adult son. In woollens and workwear, they haven't dressed to dine. Is that why they're banished to a side room? It may be due to the diecast dog, or the waxy infant in the wicker pram. Granma chomps the blade of a shovel. Her daughter gnaws a handlebar. The carcass of a bicycle is on the table, waiting to be carved. No veg no gravy no trimmings. Pa wolfs a chain, the son gorges an iron weight. Charcoal hazenkreuz and a postage stamp fuhrer adorn the walls. Below the table a mutt licks thread from a bolt. The tot sucks the edge of an axe.

I hear shouting, a wet mirror rubbed by a finger, behind the dining hall. I poke some swing doors open. It's the kitchen. A dove is impaled on a bayonet, ready for the grill. It hasn't been plucked. The chef in the chop frill is angry. Spit of Joyce, he roasts two galley hands.

Standing up, I lift the roof. I rest it on a stable to the rear. In a third floor bedroom, a couple carved in candlewax roll on a hankie as a pastry radio plays. In the next room a lead figure stands at a window, studying the street. The room after that is empty. In the last a rubber maid scatters minute rose petals over a silk bedspread. I rub them between my fingers. Shredded rose, real.

I've seen enough. Lines of model cars fill the streets in every direction and I am ringed by an angry horde of figurinees, peg metal and painted. Knocking them over, sweeping the casualties into Harbour Street, I swing the façade of the hotel shut, hooking it to an eye high on the side wall. I lower the roof back onto the gables and walk back to the care home.

– That was great Joan I'm starting to get a sense of

> *the Horsebridge nearby the building where the Union's café and headquarters were they're long gone we held the drills the parades the open air meetings there we sold Action in the street every week over to the right up by the church is Morland Hatch we launched the women's branch there in Bessie Pullen's sitting room standing room only that day it was kitchen chairs bath chairs all sorts and that's the church I went to with Willy look at the sunset tonight the bay's glass shot with fire it's why people come here sunsets I know it's all changing down there all states rot it's what they do but up here by the mill the tragedy slows the sails stop turning here we may make some sense of it all*

A movement starts in Joan's bed, a ripple of quilt mounding, falling, mounding again, continuous cotton waves radiating from her spine, wide arcs broadening rolling tugging at the undersheets. The bedpost taps the bedside drawers, the transistor shakes and rocks and creeps towards a fall, the cotton keeps on surging tapping shoving cupboard batting the seat of my chair, ripples repeat on ridges on rolls of bedding rising and bulging and breaking.

– Channel one, top end and lively.

The engineer ups the current. I bump up the volume, way up.

> *me back on my feet wouldn't that be nice go out without a carer or the chair never again not for me never everyone's so young these days the staff are children often when I meet*

a newbie I recognise someone I knew the passed resurrected as stupid ha I'm at a window in a Stanley Spencer watching them clamber from pits and tombs I bet that seems like zombies to you I don't care if it does I love that painting it's hope on a wall gladness redemption love returning it only lasts a moment the gone here as kids then its outta yez hair quicks ma making the bed with one hand messing it more like phone on the go reeling in lads when they should be tending to me

Bulging and rolling cotton breakers crest on crest shaking the footboard jolting the wireless waves rebounding nodes of anodes storming bedframe twister buckaroo Joan.

– Cue two, ready, push the bass.

Down at the footboard I dial down the tone.

I don't grudge them their luck cash in their purses credit on plastic and contraception but do their men respect them dow they don't that hasn't changed one bit birth control we did it of course we never felt safe I fell ha it was a difficult issue the Union said it was a private matter to keep the Catholics onside the pill came way too late for me some of the girls work hard some don't fit in not expecting to stay girls from the town have careers much than tending to coots like me good luck I grrrrnnnnn

Self oscillation sets in when the tuning control is rotated to the low frequency end of the wavelength.

– Back to one speed it up a nudge.

Cotton waves crack and fluct. Joan tosses in a crosswave sheetstorm.

– What's with the music bed?

where's the country going doesn't anyone care people today are shopping mad unwholesome in their selfish thoughts they get the politicians they deserve Tom and Willy were a fresh start we'd sweep old skirts out of the house close the private members clubs put banks on a leash purge the Mayfair parasites Britain first war on want a corporate state the first step to socialism rights for workers rights for

women a shift in the balance a better place to push from the
rising class stepping up culture shift a new Britain where
there's discord harmony where there's error truth we were
going to squeeze the rich till the pips popped the press turned
against us Germany went off the rails our house of cards
collapsed they jailed Tom Willy was gone then murdered by
the state I miss my man I've missed him so long fifty years
I've been kissing my pillow no one else came close no one

Bedlegs stamping bed pitching quilterupting nape tossing schedule-busting wall slamming at my back.

– We're overrunning.

– Joan!

what is it dear

Bed at rest, end of transmission, Joan composed.

Willy and Joan are invited to a ball in Mayfair

– By a wealthy Italian supporter of the Union.

– He's about to make a big donation.

I love a party dancing a chance to dress up the donor wanted
me there me more than he did Willy I had the upper hand
for a change so I say as long as futurism is the theme Willy
wasn't pleased he had to go along with it ha

Here we destroy passeist clothes!

– No to revolution in a suit and tie!

the tailor's was called Modavanti it was in Old Burlington
Street

We will need to meet three times says Spurinna, the aruspex fitter, when Joan rings to make the appointment. At the first session, the Dynamic Declaration, he says we will inject your gait with a warlike spirit, multiply agility, and proclaim the opportunity. Next will be the Progress he explains – the Non Abbatanza! – where we will supply elastic prototypes to serve your genius. We adapt these to your will for the Glorification and that will be in roughly four weeks time.

it all sounded very exciting I couldn't wait

The receiving room is a chaos of bricks and debris. Strips of wallpaper trail from a half demolished wall below a holed ceiling. There are slots in the floor where boards are missing, slots containing propellors, speedometers and poems on sticks. Joan and Willy seat themselves on an opulent black leather sofa. It is sprinkled with ball bearings and bullet cases. Sandbags serve for cushions .

– Joan what is this madhouse?

– It will be worth it Willy you'll see what larks!

By the door there's a poster in motley typography.

Pattern changes ARE AVAILABLE by pneumatic despatch
CHANGE YOUR CLOTHES **according to policy or need**

– Good morning mister Joyce e buongiorno Joan mwah mwah.

Spirinna is wearing a pleated brown sac, forked below the waist and gathered at the ankle, wrist and throat. A flamingo ribbon spirals round his torso, a vortex. Springlike, it comps and thrusts as the fitter – bending and squatting and rising – logs Willy's vitals.

– What's that you're wearing?

– For too long Italy has been dealing in the second hand style. We have abolished static lines in cut and design.

– Absurd, a bloody Bloomsbury ballet.

– Signore Joyce prefers the more austere outfit?

– That's right. Clothing free of emotional slither.

  Britain is dying in its contemptible wardrobe. Part a little, please.

– Outrageous I'm not putting up with this.

– Think of the donation we're going to receive Willy.

– What happened to dress anonymously? The smoking jacket?

– We invent go-ahead menswear for modern times. Garments with brilliant colours, a mechanic beauty, and electric contours.

– It's going to be fun!

Dynamic Declaration frees the physique from mediocrity, Spurinna explains. It's a simple procedure, he tells us, no time at all. Look forward ten years. Scorn the obstacles which stand in your way. Dream the desire. We will dress you for your part. Accelerate the genius of your race!

We've come prepared, says Joyce, we'll see it through.

That's the spirit Willy, Joan exclaims hurrah!

– Marvellous, the floor is for you.

Willy hammers his feet bapbapapapapppp, a machine gun. Joan holds up a sign saying ENEMY AT 700. Willy flurries pokes and punches oosh oosh oosh, furious gunfire. Joan nips her teeth on the tip of a sipstraw, stem of an orchid. She drops to her hands and knees. Fanning his arms, Willy signals the sector on which shells must fall. Joan is a tank. She throws back her head. Blast orchid recoil. Joyce ululates victory, pirouetting on his toes. Joan orbits contra, convulsing to each of his whoops. Haw Haw springs into the air spreading his arms and legs wide, a mast signalling, a leaping transmitter.

– Bravo bravo. And now you will view the samples?

Modular zinc gossamers. Chromium chestguards. Aromatic shoulder pads. Steel wools, silk lined asbestos, copper thread tweed. Lining inflaters, under-lighters, crownless brims. Chin release collars, button batteries, dynamo zips. Necktie antennae. A decanter of cream.

WHY DRINK MILK WHEN YOU CAN WEAR IT?

What on earth says Willy, wear it milk? We do Spirinna says spun milk. He strokes his bag. Milk and veg says Joan, his brown cocoon is dairy.

– The fabric is woven from lanital, an Italian invention. Artificial wool made from cows' milk. The pink vortex is viscose rayon, silk from cellulose. They extract it from wood pulp it's big in Milan.

Forgetta the steel, the fitter says.

– Build a new Europe with the lanital.

– Cream of all suits!

– Cholestorol threads!

MILK MADE OF REINFORCED STEEL
MILK OF WAR

– What about the cotton mills of Lancashire?

Willy was never comfortable with the Italians, says Joan.

> *futurism was a song of the left anarchist and socialist till*
> *Filippo flips and joins the fascists abolish the monarchy*
> *they said expel the Pope public ownership of land water*
> *property a free press an eight hour day equal pay for women*
> *the seeds of futurism were sound they grew into a travesty*
> *war's beautiful what an arse Marinetti could be metalisa-*
> *tion of the body cold manthink so cold meadows flowering*
> *with the fiery orchids of machine guns yes I know but balls*
> *balls balls they were against war with Germany sure but*
> *not against war itself Marinetti and Willy had boners for*
> *the battle ahead oh don't be embarrassed I can feel that you*
> *are I thought a battle lay ahead battle always lays ahead*
> *somewhere but preferably a way off so we never get to it*

Two weeks later Willy stands in front of a full length mirror. He's dressed in a loose fitting grey rayon suit overprinted with white isometric girders and yellow transmission towers. It's paired with a black milk shirt and a red bow tie whose upper curve replicates his scar. The soles of his running shoes – uppers cut from a Union Jack – are rubberised copies of the *Communist Manifesto*. His trousers are secured with a belt and brace antenna and a grey ceramic buckle. Crouching behind Willy, Modavanti himself – sweaty, obese, spilling from a morning suit – slashes both trouser legs behind the knee. Fresh air, he says, hygiene, he says, be free in the movement. Modavanti clips flexible tubes to vents in the shirt, running them through the arms of the jacket. They connect to bulbs in the cuff, he explains, the vaporiseurs.

> *line the seat of his pants with emery cloth I say make the*
> *grit coarse number forty do the back of the shirt too we must*
> *keep this man of action moving*

I can't go out like this Joyce says, I'll be a laughing stock.

– He was intensely vain.

– Who's there? Show your face!

– If you want me Willy you will. We need the lira.

101

I went for a full length coil dress made from copper wire it was slinky and springy with a low impedance neckline I had a kinetic hat with a fascinator interleaving metal plates a condenser it opened and closed as I moved and my shoes oh a pair of dreamy ankle boots steely audio jacks with tight black nubbins instead of laces I looked the mutt's nuts

No foot silent in the room, no mouth from kissing nor from wine unwet.

Tom had no design sense whatever black sportswear buttons on the shoulder that was the uniform he came up with for the movement so insectlike and morbid

– The black shirt is the outward sign of an inward and spiritual grace. In a black shirt all men are the same, whether millionaire or on the dole. The barriers of class distinction are broken down.

– Had he put his followers into blue pullovers instead of black shirts much would have been forgiven him.

– Show your face you Red!

fencing's for fops and frogs sportswear's not a way to change how people live and see the world it's tat

– The uniform made us much too military in appearance. The old soldier in me got the better of the politician.

that night in Mayfair I felt like a futurist princess and we got the donation too one hundred thousand smackers all down to me and Willy

Joan puts on her specs.

Over her shoulder, I see what she sees framed by the left lens. Flotillas in the bay. Poky prewar kitchens, smoky offices. Postcards, coffins, a pink-sunset. Montage, things falling, maybe into place.

– Tell me about Tom.

A man in grey pops into focus. I wait. Joan jiggles her head. The lens smogs green.

– What did you make of him?

The figure reforms at the window, rising lifesize. He must be on stilts.

It's Mosley in his mid-thirties, sky thrusting, legs many times the length of his trunk. A well-tailored pylon, an invert victory vee.

Trouser pockets sheathe his hands. Wrists pin back his jacket, flaunting an hourglass waist. Swollen pedestal neck, head smaller than his kneecap. Sharp moustache, the smile a blade.

One of Beerbohm's assets – as a caricaturist – is that he cannot draw.

Tom avoids Joan's eyes. He looks to his right, warily, watching the entrance to the close.

– Such a tall poppy.

– Sir Oswald to you.

– From thirty-one, the year he walked out.

Mosley resigns from the government. Mosley leaves the Labour Party. His New Party flops.

– He could have been someone.

– Leader. Prime minister?

Joan's mesmerised. I stand on the bed, face to fascist. I will him to back off. He ignores me. Loser! I shout. I'm not sure he can see me. Placing my hands above the window I lean forward, looking down for his feet. His hop pole legs are severed at the ankles.

– Caricature should be exaggerative.

– It should be personal and particular.

I step down from the bed and return to my seat.

Mosley turns to Joan. He says the four words. She comes back to life.

> ***that was a turning point they changed everything nothing
> was the same again I'll never forget what he said never***

– No Joan nor will I.

Tom and Joan were dining in the Grand Hotel in Llandudno. His proposals to end unemployment had just been rejected by the Labour Party.

I sent a telegram to the dog walker I say to the girl taking it down just put OM reaction stop then four words

And they are?

– This means a dictatorship.

Now's now not then.

– What do you think about today's fascists Joan?

hideous hateful people not forward-looking like Tom at his best they've no idea what a more efficient state would look like they hate black people rag heads Muslims that's all like Tom at his worst with Jews the Union stood against war unless it was war against communism or financial democracy to him they were one a snake with two heads a huge Jewish snake that's how they saw it Willy especially Jewish international finance and Jewish international communism how he made them one's beyond me the heads weren't joined at all they weren't Jewish either not completely anyway now's not then today communism and total war the way we used to fight it aren't a danger anymore the future of Europe's what matters Tom saw that didn't he Europe A Nation after the war these people they're small minded they march and shout about the wrong things they're second time as farce third rate mugs for leaders mugs directing thugs they're the snake now

No mosque here hissss crush jihad ban the terrorists slither respect the poppy muzzie scum fascist islam shall not pass hissss no to islamification halal equals animal cruelty one nation one enemy slith-hiss everyone's had enough this is what a patriot looks like never fucking surrender ever.

– Was the Union really any different?

Willy was out to win elections he pressed and propogandised persuaded he is a powerhouse he reaches ordinaries on the street civvies like me in the markets and the factories pubs and shops on farms he was raising a mass party not a fantasy army but he was sweeping water uphill with a broom from fifty thousand in thirty-four we drop to half that size inside two years Promethean it was with vultures pecking especially after the farrago at Olympia

– Mosley spoke effectively and at great length. Delivery excellent, matter reckless. Interruptions began, but no dissenting voice got beyond half a dozen sentences before three or four bullies jumped on him, bashed him and lugged him out.

– An honest looking blue-eyed student type rose and shouted indignantly Hitler means war! Whereupon he was given the complete treatment.

– There was a wild scrummage, women screamed, black-shirted arms rose and fell, blows were dealt. The arena was soon full of hooting and whistling and chairs and boots and shoes were flying in the air.

A week later, returning from a rally in Leeds, Joan and Willy share a compartment with an affable Yorkshire businessman. I was sat in your hall last night, he says.

– I came to hear how fascism would save the wool trade.

– And did you find out?

– Did I heck. All there was to listen to was a lot of silly claptrap about the Jews. I don't approve of the growing antisemitic tendency of the movement.

– They're wandering itinerants with no loyalty to Britain. Their hold must be broken

– The price of South African wool, now what do you say, is it fair?

– For wool to prosper we must rid ourselves of Jewish plutocrats, aliens imported from Palestine, hairy troglodytes who creep out of ghettoes and take sanctuary in the British Museum, the political crimps of Judah, of the loathsome fetid purulent tumid mass of hypocrisy which is the Tory party, politicians who have yielded to noisy fakirs and chattering babus.

– How the new agreement's going to work, that's the crux of it.

– Churchill and his lousy gang of crooks must go, the spoilt darlings of Mayfair, verminous Bloomsburgians, wop viscose vendors too.

– You've made your point Willy.

- Australia, the clip from down under, it's getting bigger and bigger.

- Neurotic crusaders for pacifism, myopic printers' hacks, fuzzy wuzzies Mr Bleeding Bevin and the scum of Transport House, Yiddish Bolshevik scum that's where we need to start.

- But what about wool?

I was just a secretary but I could see what was going on the HQ penpushers were flattering Tom the numbers leaving the main reason for funds drying up was kept from him Willy was the master of detail you couldn't deflect him he knows Jew-baiting will keep the men keen no blowing Willy off course he's always shoulder to the boulder even the day he marries Mag we're at the registry one minute down in Shoreditch for local elections the next up the aisle for vows straight down Hoxton Market for the vote I've got a photo of that somewhere

She hoists a box on to her lap. She rummages. I hear the contents are mostly paper. Small metallic items too. Lifting and riffling, her knuckles strum the wicker. Timpani footsteps sound in the corridor. Joan lids the box and lets it drop, backheeling it under the bed. A slow tuba booms lento. The passing nurse wipes her nose. The flutes refill with phlegm. Twoooor twoooor the booming. As the footsteps fade, Joan sings softly. It's hard to make out her words from the tape. Some one, a voice I don't recognise, says I'll get it. Who went out, I wonder? It sounds as if no one came in, but someone goes out. When we're alone she hoists the box back to her lap.

A photo at her shoulder flaps.

Mag's overdressed for the market look at that hat Willy's in a trenchcoat you'd never guess he's come straight from the registry marriage didn't distract him from the movement for a moment Tom and Willy both wore their wedding rings loosely Germany was their bride by then Willy tells Mag pretend you're my first it goes down better with the voters Tom keeps his marriage to Lady Diana secret for two years well he had to didn't he make it common knowledge half the girls would break with the Union not that Tom took advantage not often sleep Tory he used to say he was a Tom Jones the Tom Cruise of his times a poster boy really not an

organiser a star it's what being a pilot with land and a limp
did for you then

It is always impossible to completely eliminate stray couplings, particularly in a superheterodyne.

one of his legs was short by an inch and a half not that
you'd really notice not with so many in far worse fettle
I'm not short where it matters he said ha it's hard to
understand these days the glamour of the Union how you
felt when Tom came into a hall the rush Willy had it too
the erotically provocative effect of rhythmic goose-steps
they say the libidinal thump of powerful uniformed men
lean muscular warrior lovers salesgirls and secretaries
understand it

– Does Adolf wear pajamas?

The footboard wireless has a faulty circuit. Draughts from the door silence it. A cathode won't emit electrons unless it is hot. If a valve cools in a waft from the corridor, reception cuts out. Warming, it resumes. A Scouser sings with a dance band.

Does Adolf wear pajamas or a night-shirt?
Does he take his teeth out when he goes to bed?
Is that unruly lock of hair a detachable affair
Which he hangs up on the bedpost overhead?
I wonder what he thinks of in the night time
Does Goering just to make him feel at home
In a merry widow dress do a waltz with Rudolf Hess
Accompanied by Goebbels on a comb

Joan laughs at that. My how she laughs. She doesn't how to stop.

I loved Tommy Handley hahaha that was hu it was huhu it
was humour for the troops dear oh what a scream ha it must
have made Tom and Willy so angry to hear that I hope Willy
didn't I wouldn't like to be near Willy when he heard that
haaaaa can you get it me on a tape do you think Goebbels
on a comb hahohaha

The window frames a banana idling over molasses. It's late. I unplug the recorder, bundling the leads in a bag. The bedroom door is slightly ajar. But

I closed it when the nurse left. It was shut when the tuba passed by. I closed it again after that. Someone looked in on us. There's no other explanation.

The Watchers were always nearby.

I became aware of the shadowy regiment of Watchers and Trackers and Hunters, of Frustrators and Deflectors, soon after the interviews started. They are there beyond the window. They are there outside the door.

> *they're always with us dear they provide a structure of sorts*
> *a semblance of order you'll soon get used to them I have*

I switch protocols immediately. From that day on, each time I visit Joan I use two taxis. First, I ring for a cab to an address in Tankerton, east of the town. As soon as I'm on the back seat I direct the driver west to the Sportsman, a remote inn from whose windows I can check for Trackers. I have to pay a hefty supplement for radio silence. After a decent interval, I call a different firm for the ride back to Century Close. The mounting expense is a burden.

I call Mark. When's the development funding coming, I ask.

Where'd you get it?

I ask Joan if she bought the valve wireless from the radio shop that William Joyce ran in Whitstable.

– Did Willy sell it to you? Is that why you've held on to it?

> *he never owned a radio shop here not Willy he didn't work*
> *in one either it's a myth I know people say he did but they're*
> *remembering someone else a shop run by two other chaps*
> *who join the Union they mix Willy up with them can you see*
> *him fumbling in a greasy till*

– I didn't think it likely no.

> *Willy never worked in a radio shop in Whitstable I'd know*
> *wouldn't I Astra's mother would know he couldn't have*
> *stepped in a wireless shop in this town without me knowing*
> *ha the traders on the hight street are so hungry for celebrity*

***branding they're talking up a fascist oh the irony the shame
it's all a put-up job***

She was right.

There's no evidence that William Joyce owned or worked in a radio shop in Whitstable in the 1930s. Claims that he did draw on false folk memory and an error published on the website of a lax museum.

Some say Joyce was a resident in 1936. But he was living in Chelsea then, travelling to rallies all over the country three or four times a week. By 1938 he had relocated to South Kensington, where he tried to launch a language school. In 1939 he moved to Earls Court, then he left for Berlin. There's no Whitstable address in the Special Branch or intelligence files. The records show Joyce was living and working somewhere else throughout those years.

In the 1960s some people remembered William Joyce selling wireless parts from the Assembly Hall. A self-help centre for the unemployed did open there before the war. But Joyce wasn't on the team. The fairy tale about the radio shop has been repeated for eight decades. In 2015 the local paper reported William Joyce cycled through the streets delivering radio parts. That didn't happen either. In fact there's no record of Joyce visiting the town except on one occasion, in 1936, when he gave a speech in the Forresters' Hall.

– So why does the story persist?

– The war, we're British.

– Racism, I'd say, stubborn racism. White flight from London driven by hostility to minorities. A nod and a wink that Joyce was one of us, whatever he did, and they're not.

– Traders eager for footfall. A bigger catch of the day. Beer and oysters, Krays, British fascism, anything to bait the hook.

– He made some good points old Haw Haw, everyone listened didn't they. He had a radio shop here.

The station gives the spat five minutes of airtime. The interviewer clips a microphone to my tee shirt. The neck sags, obscuring the message on my chest:

Destroy All Dogmatic Verbal Systems.

She taps a tablet.

- Say anything.

- Law Haw Haw Lord Horror Lord Ha Ha.

- Ok it's good. Ready?

- Sure.

I sip water as she burbles the intro. Soulless places studios, and airless.

- who has looked into whether Lord Haw Haw owned a radio shop in the Bubble, as the town is fondly known, speaking at open air meetings and unwinding afterwards in its many lively bars. It's been folklore for years Kevin but you're not convinced are you?

- It's a complete myth Samantha and I think it's very sad that parts of the community talk about this genocidal antisemite as if he's a local celeb. Why is William Joyce, a man that historian Colin Holmes calls an exterminatory Jew-hater, part of the town's story at all? He didn't live here. He may have come down from London just the once.

- So there's absolutely nothing to it?

- Almost nothing. Joyce did speak here, in 1936, at the Forresters Hall, now the museum. His speech that night was a ninety-minute hate crime. He said Hitler was freeing Germany from the control of Jewish financiers and Mosley would do the same in Britain.

- So why do people cling on to the radio shop?

- I think I can tell you where the myth comes from. There was a wireless business here in the early 1930s called Radio Services. Two men ran it, E D Hamilton and E L B James. They had a shop by the harbour gate. It was a golden time for wireless, sales were booming. Hamilton and James, two men on the make, wanted a piece of the pie. They played broadcasts over loudspeakers at football matches. That's nothing special now but it was sensational back then. They held radio dances at the Bear and Key Hotel. But despite their flair, the firm collapses. Three years later James is Officer in Command for the Whitstable branch of the British Union of Fascists. Hamilton is his adjutant. They've found something new to sell, National Socialism. Well known local blackshirts, they have installed radios in homes across the town. I think after the war people confuse James and Hamilton with Joyce. The excitement of radio, the novelty of the blackshirts, the passage of time merged these men in a story with no foundation.

- So William Joyce, Lord Haw Haw, didn't drink in the Prince Albert after all?

- He did not. At the high point for the local BUF, a few brief months from 1933 to early 1934, there were large meetings outside the fascist HQ at the Horsebridge, close to the Albert. Parades and drills took place outside a British Union canteen overseen by fascist police in blackshirt uniforms. Speakers from London came down to help recruitment drives but there's no mention of Joyce. It was someone else at the bar of the Albert, two someone elses in fact, denouncing the Old Gang and cheering Hitler on. It was James and Hamilton, not William Joyce.

- How did you find this out?

- I was told the legend of Joyce's radio shop a dozen times. I didn't like the bizarre sense of pride that came with the story. I'd read the Branch and MI5 files on Joyce, so I knew it didn't stack up. I did a bit more homework and read the diary of the town, the local paper in the library. Anyone could have done it. No one had. Why not?

One take, it's done. But now there's another puzzle.

I'd know wouldn't I Astra's mother would know

Joan introduces sleeps.

If I lay down, the nape says, if I lay down and nap, keep the questions going.

- Even when you've closed your eye?

yes sleeps will help me retrieve forgotten material that will be useful to you surely try it and see

The curtains are drawn. She's resting by a field of poppies. The bed is cased in copper. Soon she has a neck of brass, a lens for a head. The lens scans the brass pillow roll.

- I was expelled from school by the Jesuits after pulling a gun.

Things discovered in the deep when only body's laid asleep. He left school early, familiar with handguns and logic.

Post-mortem wireless is a metallic medium. The pillow rotates slowly.

– Do you need to sleep Joan?

She lifts her head.

> *don't you ever listen just carry on like I told you listen just*
> *listen can't you now what would you like to ask*

– But

> *do as you're told just once*

– I'd like to know more about your visits to Berlin.

The nape realigns to the mattress, shoulder to roller.

> *I'm sitting next to Willy he's snarling at the front page of the*
> *Times we're flying we're over Germany it's chequered with*
> *orchards acre after acre of rosebush and medieval market*
> *towns it's Kent with mountains the posters in the airport*
> *say SUN AIR AND HOMES FOR EVERYONE it really is a*
> *vitalising sun a purer cleansing air*

And when you land, I say, what then?

> *a kadet takes me to visit working Germans they have good*
> *teeth better teeth than I do the housing is superb light and*
> *roomy well built secure we don't have apartments that*
> *good now not today the rivers are banked with vineyards*
> *spotless hotels food is wholesome prices fair there's a lot of*
> *undressing by the lakes I'm no longer young not firm but I'd*
> *like to the towns are overdressed too many uniforms ridicu-*
> *lous so many flags and banners*

– Did you say that to anyone?

> *of course not you didn't did you not me anyway*

As we are walking through the park, she says, we pass some tiny tots in
uniform. They greet us with a smart salute, she says, brisk pipings of Heil
Hitler! You certainly believe in catching them young I say yes indeed my
escort replies.

– We're designing a special uniform for embryos.

Joan is shocked. The guide chuckles with delight.

– Joan what about Germany awake, the Jews are coming?

well what about it what do you mean

– You must have had a sense of that?

yes Judenhetze yes of course we hear it all over everywhere no one conceals it but I don't see any Jews mistreated we don't see that many Jews the numbers I'm told are wildly overestimated I see nothing amiss I can't speak for Willy but it's kept from our eyes did you know there were thirty-six women MPs in the Reichstag just imagine thirty-six

The brass roller halts, brass lens retracting into neck.

– She doesn't talk much about the Jews.

– Ashamed, I'd say. You couldn't go and not know.

– She always swerves.

– We'll tell it for her.

Humiliation. Abuse. Robberies and beatings. Murders, forced labour, more murders, starvation. Genocide.

– What was your view of Germany at the time?

Her shoulder rolls, lens engaging the drum

the Germans had been treated badly war reparations at impossible levels squeezed more than any country could afford by the French mostly they post black troops to fuel the flames the National Socialists stand up for the nation part of it not all I know they say they are the only way to halt the Bolsheviks which mattered at the time I remember a cartoon an arm with a swastika on it another arm a red arm holding a flaming torch to a roof the swastika stops the burning of a German home people have forgotten that red is pretty pink to you now

– Where did you go?

a break in Bavaria some meetings in Berlin and Munich oh it was exciting Tempelhof the largest airport in the world people sat all day admiring the planes fifty up fifty down a few marks to watch I lose interest after half a dozen but the wine and service at Tempelhof are wonderful

– What memories do you have of Berlin?

The lens skips to the outer edge of the roller.

no one in rags no beggars little in the way of cosmetics most women don't wear much the shops are full of prams endless rows of black hoods and chrome arms prams are spooky in large numbers long rows empty wireless everywhere radios on sills and balconies speeches long ones public announcements music playing classics marches not a lot to dance to I saw aeroplanes tattoo a swastika on rainclouds that was striking a little frightening I think of God by this symbol you will conquer Willy says as they go over most of the meetings were dull nobody says anything I hadn't read in the papers we go to parades too

– Tell me about them.

I remember one in Bamberg climbing a hill like a carpet up the stairs rich patterns colours and brass the orderly weaving of arms and men gleaming boots rifles shining like table legs spades spoons on shoulders braziers burning regiments threading the avenues families cheering from windows an open air opera national pride back in the saddle

No house without flags, no door without greenery. Grandstands, incalculable masses, one cheer. A marching column, marching ram. Flaming torches loudspeaker towers waterproof against the rain.

I may remember it from films more than the day itself when you're actually there it's long waits waiting and nowhere to pee them looking at you you looking at them everyone speaks too fast to follow I wish I'm at a window wonder if I'll get a view when he comes the fuhrer standing in an open vehicle no one knows what to do till then singing to pass the time once I nearly fainted you have no conception how painful it is to stand with your knees locked for such a long time cold too people in thin coats bored salutes slice into my view did I see him did I think I did a sleeve a cap for sure I think then it's back to the hotel bar you went so you could say you had

If I knew then what I know now, she said, I'd have seen it differently.

Paris with Willy on the way back, sparkle and arches the bank of the Seine.

– Up there Joannie look.

Another couple, high on a roof. A field lass and a factory hand, skystriding, side by side, her hook arcing his hammer thrust.

– And there.

Bronzing on a loftier perch, wings spread ready to strike, the eagle.

Will it fly at them when?

– Art, upholder of our race.

– It's wonderful Willy.

> *oh do we have a lovely time in gay paree we do*

The nape lifts, the brass pillow spins, the lens descends.

– Joyce does not model himself on the lines of the ascetic Hitler. He drinks, plays about with women, and plans.

Max the spook is good at thumbnail.

– He is pleasant to those who do not oppose him but never friendly.

> *that's right he was a cold fish with men standoffish*

– He is irritated sometimes to the point of insanity by older men above him.

> *oh yes that's Willy yes he had issues with authority hahhahha*

Tell me about the two of you, I ask.

– Your story, as a couple, from the start.

> *I fell for him I spread myself on a slice of toast before I met Willy I had no life none to speak of not really first home I remember was a hutch in Albert Street schooling and churching a step away no funeral for father work in a shop work in a hotel a few boys having a grab hormonal that's all just names to me now Wilfred and Samuel off the barges no faces they're gone we walk out at sunset go to the pictures soon as I can it's off to the smoke for me*

London, a large and gay City took with me mighty well, who, from my being a child, lov'd a Crowd, and to see a great many fine Folks.

Willy's a revelation he talks about rights for women I catch his eye we click we rode forth conquering tours the halls and squares of Britain with the Union's message he's welcomed he's admired everywhere he's hated too of course it goes without saying Frolich he used to sign himself Frolich a pun it's German for joyous frolich Willy joyous the professor that's what people call him a nickname professor Frolich such a voice he had in Newcastle he strikes down one thousand protesters with the jawbone of a donkey he uproots the gate at Whipsnade tears a lion in pieces tell me the secret of your great strength I ask

She sleeps.

The nape plunges a headless torso.

A *Radio Times* drops to the pillow, browning and brittle, plucked from under the bed. The coronation issue. On the front cover, a lozenge microphone mounted on a wooden block, its wire trailing from Joan's sill. A brushwork crowd fills the pavement penned by khaki lines of Tommies. Where's the king I ask. He's coming. Curling slabs of red and blue, scarlet veins on yellow, bunting breezing overhead. Horseguards hoof, dragoons despise the dancing plumes of lancers.

– Nevinson for tuppence.

– Collectors item.

A day of shame, she says, a crowning of the wrong king.

for king and for people I chalk that in Holborn for the Union to a patriot king and people are the same thing that's why the abdication's such a cause for Tom save the king a people's King being forced out something must be done he said so he was well liked the coup gave us a focus

Room service at the Adelphi. Trolley linen wine a toast the King cigars.

– He's in direct contact with the court.

– There's a plan to govern without Parliament.

Joan leans to the lozenge.

the abdication is a blow to Tom with Edward gone there's not a hope the palace will give him office it was a political pipedream but hey ho you never know do you

– Mosley's in a state of great excitement.

As prime minister, he says, I will be able to broadcast as often as I wish.

Turn away or lose the thread.

The nape at the window is reflected in the glaze of a framed print hanging on the rear wall. The image beneath the reflection seems abstract, green and blue horizontal streaks, a bright bisecting vertical. It may not be, I can't tell because of the glare. An outdoor scene? It may be a print of a woman sitting at a window. It's hard to say. I cross the room for a closer look. It's a sketch of the coast. Chalk smudges, light in a downpour bouncing.

The print defies the window. When the sun sets, it hints dawn. Before us the bay, back there steep cliff. All merging, back to back. Week on week, as sunsets drift east, acting contrary.

– Hold to the Joan thread.

I broke my resolutions once let everyone down I heard the boys agree to torch a synagogue in Dalston I alert the dog walker straight away carrying the Listener was our signal for an urgent meeting he doesn't show then right out of the blue Willy asks me to go on a jaunt to the coast not for a meeting just us I couldn't say no

– Dog walker?

a concerned friend I didn't want to say no I wear a red dress red Joan he calls me at Victoria well I'm shaking I wondered if I'd given myself away slipped up but no

What do you mean slipped up, I ask. It's a form of words she answers.

Joan an English rose he says as we walk through the dunes near Sandwich we talk a little he spreads a blanket in a quiet spot he's attentive kind he tells me how alone he feels how

*bleak o bliss inspired by guile boldness is a mask for my fear
he says I reach for his hand we embrace I hold him in the
sand by the tide he's in a hurry he's rough great wings beating
I make him stop I make him wait we talk some more Willy
tells me he will serve Britain when the crisis comes no one will
understand it will look like the reverse of his intentions I pass
that on of course but I don't get it then he paws at me again
love's not choice but fate he says something like that I have no
bloody choice at all he shouts he was getting angry I push him
away my teeth clack a sudden blow not hard but I was scared
I scramble the sand I nearly get away*

Close behind his sounding steps she hears, and now his shadow reach'd her
as she run (his shadow lengthened by the setting sun) and now his shorter
breath with sultry air pants on her neck.

*he catches a sleeve he grips my arm he whirls me round please
Joan he begs had he kisses a thousand I can't get free he
pushes me over leg behind my knee over I go flat on my back
he's close as a mask ignoring me arms a tight strap his knee
where it shouldn't be heavy so heavy Joan no Joan I could
not escape his sucking five men were watching from a boat I
was soon engulfed my shoulder throat my ear I grab past him
nothing to hand only water I'm slipping he swallows oh Joan
ah Joanah his strange heart bruting no foothold no way back
I sink the disc of sun slots black*

– Though foul be my face, my hands hold thee fast!

I heard a sea-mew cry. I saw a flake of yellow foam that dropped upon my
thigh. He sports me on a dune.

– Joan, I

*it doesn't matter now dear it was a long time ago you get
over everything but after that it was just push pull the single
double throw if you knew how wireless works you'd know*

I hold my tongue.

*when the lovebug bites anything can happen vileness too
we come back separately he buys me a dress after a green
one I find out the boys took paint not petrol to Dalston they*

trashed a Rabbi's room no one badly hurt a tooth clean bowled a shiner minor really a relief Dalston's lucky I am too no reprimand

I failed to ask from whom.

Could her spoken word have checked that whereby a house lay wrecked?

On Friday evening last, seventy-two-year-old Rabbi Aaron Hertz was brutally attacked by three men with metal bars. Rabbi Hertz has lost an eye. He is being cared for in St Leonard's Hospital Shoreditch.

– Bastard fascist scum.

I report the raid what I remember anyway it might have been a test I wasn't the only one alerting them did I pass I think so I must have done but I knew I'd lost my footing fallen it was a strange time a brutal not a caring start and I'd failed in my duty I feel ashamed now I atone for it still

– Poor woman.

– Yes.

After which I wet a finger, pluck my lip.

PLUP

– She was an informer.

I play the sound back slowly. PLOOOUUUP.

– Sounds like it, yes.

I cue the bay. Evening. A pearl, pink, settles in the filth and sinks.

Ha tart an voice an Godod saaaaave thek ing.

Chairs scraping, twenty rows of babble.

– Remarkable speech a remarkable man.

– Man of action and vision.

– Will he fight I couldn't tell if Hitler comes our way you think?

Mosley descends the platform. After a moment with well-wishers, he is guided to a perimeter corridor. Boots tramp tiles, the escort arriving.

Willy issues a final instruction to the guard.

– No scum to get near the Bleeder today!

Joyce, boss on the shield.

A few minutes later, as the squad halts in the foyer, Mosley winks at dreamy drummist Joan. She blushes. Her companions giggle. He departs through the high arched door, mock gothic. In disarray the escort follows, the wedge of ladies drums ungainly in their wake.

Chanting detonates in the street.

– Mosley means hunger and war! Mosley means hunger and war!

Fifty yards away Tom's stately black Humber eases forward. It stops, caught in a knot of men waving their arms.

– Hitlerite!

– Do the tyres.

They bang on the windows of the chauffeured car.

– Bugger off back to Berlin!

The road in front of the hall narrows. Fisting roars punchuate Hunger and War. Tom steps to the holler, chin high, disdaining the mob.

– You cheered me here once.

– Did these cheer him here?

– Who's turned on whom?

He bares his teeth top step. Mouths roar Hunger War on they come. The Honour Guard pulls the Leader back. It forms a wall. Cobs erupt from bunnets banners rise on staves MOSLEY DEAD OR ALIVE and THROW HIM IN THE RIVER. A cricket bat wafts in a barbed wire vest, umbrellas jab. Still chanting – osleyeansungeranwor meansungeranwor – the surge brims. A communist in a leather cap – red star sparkling – climbs on the bonnet of Tom's car.

– Comrades a most important stage in the consolidation of the united front must be the establishment of a national and international

A rush on both flanks seals the pavement each side of the steps. Joan is carried backwards in a slow reverse of blackshirts to the hall. Behind her, yells and commotion. The door slams shut.

Chain clanks through brass handles.

– Damn!

Record an anchor dropping. A lavatory chain detaching.

– Stand your ground.

They know what's coming. Fingers slip to steel rings, teeth arm knucks. Hammers slip from sleeves to hands. A spanner flashes, head grinning.

A helicopter thuds low. Joan's the other side of the road, sitting on the steps of a war memorial, walking stick across her lap. The hall opposite has been booked for a rally by the National Front. There are posters on the arch. IMMIGRATION ENOUGH IS ENOUGH. Dreadlock bloat lips balaclava blackface soil our flag YOUR LAST CHANCE. She can see the spot where forty years before she drops her drum.

– Move along madam or I'll have to take your cane.

Thousands all ages tote yellow placard lollipops yellers yelling darts red on buttercups jostling between Joan and the hall, a catcalling flyer-pushing badge-selling paper-vending shrill-whistling river of carnival protest stretching thin banks of prussian blue. On the far shore there are more constables, tiering the steps to the venue. Cars buses cabs are caught in the antifash flow.

We'll start the push from here says the steward with the red armband.

– Out we go.

– Right oh.

Two sidekicks breach the seam of uniforms. Pointing to the memorial, they direct marchers to leave the road. They've a megaphone but they're not using it. Put granny top step, the steward says.

– Keep her in the middle look after her.

A snapper pops half a dozen Joan shots. She is handed a placard saying NO RETURN TO THE THIRTIES. She watches the slowing tide from a copse of raised fists and lollipops. As the yellow swell breaks its banks, surging up both sets of steps, she holds to the shaft of the granite memorial. On tiptoe, braced by her stick, she looks across the buttercup flood, searching the steps of the facing hall. Willy's there.

Stay close, Joyce tells the guard.

– Our men inside are on their way.

Tom calls to Joan through a railing of legs.

– Stand firm Joannie. Someone see to them! Hold your ground ladies.

Stone and steel and sticks in hand, sizing up the guard, young Reds and democrats – troublesome socialists yahoos Jews antifascist thugs trade unionists – take the lower steps. They're readying, rush imminent.

A drizzle of spit arches through the night. Black uniforms glitter with mucus gems.

When I shout go, says Joyce, break right.

The cricket bat rises, thorny baton bating.

– Go!

Some are blocked some fall, a chaotic descent. Joan drops the drum, she leaps three flights and runs. Snagged by the hair she's held and shoved to a wall. Whore! Spit spats her face. She crouches, forearms raised above her head. Hail of spit, a kick.

– Fascist bitch.

– I'm going to ram these sticks right up

How bad will it be?

– Let the whore go, leave her be.

Joan rises, eyes down she hurries away. Bye bye blackshirt sneer the men.

Clawing women knock her to the ground.

Shrieks, pounding, slaps to a table, slaps to the back of a sofa. Clothing clubbed in a dry tub. Gasps, grunts, female. It doesn't last long, a few seconds of hate and run. Joan watches from the memorial as Joan picks herself back up.

I remember the road empty between us just myself and me

***looking on but there must have been hundreds of people
there all running in different directions and shouting***

The steward with the red armband swings his megaphone from hip to chin.

– This is not a march past. Stop the Nazi meeting. No Platform. This is not
a march past. Stop the Nazi meeting!

The demonstration halts. Lollipops and darts congest, not a march past stop
we're stopping. Cracked margins of blue look forward look back searching for
an officer. Do they stop too? The march deltas. More protesters lap towards
the war memorial, its steps now full, the backwash swamping the steps to the
hall. The blue corridor dissolves. Police helmets are drop-kicked like rugby
balls, curving overhead, every shot a goal cheered to the skies. Bareheaded
constables link arms, forming chains which break and slip to side streets.

Wild crowing. Stamping on the terrace steps. The demonstrators celebrate
with hugs with leaps and roars, pummelling the air.

– The National Front is a Nazi front smash the National Front

– No platform. Close the hall! No platform. Close the hall!

– Comrades we have stopped the Nazis today but we must dismantle the
system that creates fascism to

Willy's squad shields Mosley. Knuckledusters showboat, handtools swing,
a path opens. Huddled men at arms, a black tank shuffling through the
fire zone, fists for barrels. They crab and lunge at Dirty Jew! and Stinking
Red! the way widening. A rescue party scrums towards them. Bizzy whistles
scree. The assault thins. The tank unpacks and jogs to safety. A face well
known to the boys, a staffer, drummer in the band, steps from a doorway.

– Out she pops, right in the thick of it.

– She took some but she didn't run.

– She's a tough 'un that Joannie.

She bags the weapons, steals away.

Tomorrow morning Tom will speak to the press.

– Red members of the Boiler Workers Union drew copper pipes from their
sleeves. Market traders threw weights.

Willy calls a radio journalist.

- The Jews of the Building Workers Union were wielding trowels sharpened like bayonets.

We threw soiled nappies at the Nazis, the Nursing Union boasts.

The foreign methods of a German dictator have no place here, says the mayor. We gave them a lesson they won't forget.

- Why'd you hire the hall out in the first place?

I got the bastard's flying lady, says Tommy.

- I bust it from the bonnet of his car.

Hitlerites will never be equals here, vows the Labour candidate.

And now the National Front can't get into the hall.

- Black and white unite and fight!

Only one thing could have stopped our Movement: if our adversaries had understood its principle, and had smashed, with the utmost brutality, the nucleus.

Ordered to clear the road, police officers with transparent shields array on each pavement. Swing gates, they push their lines to. With wooden batons they drum the screens. Half bricks and broken bottles chip their view. Protesters kick and thump and throw themselves at the shuffling shields.

Backing away, the glittering heel of a pink platform shoe ruptures the skin of a hand-painted drum.

Willy gives Joan the thumbs-up from a high window. She waves back from the memorial.

> *he hadn't changed a bit not by a day not a jot I was glad*
> *I didn't miss him I wouldn't have missed him for all the*
> *world*

A young fascist is lifted into an ambulance, a stabbing is the word.

- A rush down the gangway.

- Scuffle with the stewards.

- Flash of a razor.

The siren complains as the river refuses to part. The red armband wades in from the bank.

– Make way for the ambulance please move for the ambulance make way!

Herded towards the hall by bobbies, National Front skins gob sput at buttercups. A bottle rotors in the air. Glass shatters on the memorial.

Tom places his hand on Joannie's shoulder. Show respect for those who made the sacrifice, he barks at the skinheads. They flick vees at him.

– Fuck offan die loser.

– Kosher fascist! European!

He's gone. Joan leaves the memorial to buy a badge. Southall Youth Movement. Come what may, we're here to stay. She pins it to her mac.

Horses hoofle marbles. One rears, legs flailing like truncheons. The mounted officer falls.

– You want some rozzer?

– Want some you Jew bastard?

They repeat history.

On the town hall steps two men are swinging a bicycle. That's my living, a courier bleats. They heave the frame high over ducking helmets. It lands in a howl. They jubilate, arms high, cupwinners.

– They with them or us?

A strap of cops bulges. Bulldog fists swing at posh buttercups beyond their reach. Boots kick short no bovver dem. The strap holds.

– Self de fence is no off fence! Self de fence is no of fence!

Placards part. Kitchen staff from an Indian restaurant mount the memorial. They carry dustbin lids like shields. They shake forks in the air.

– No to knife

– Don't use knife

– Not knife.

Joan sips from a styrene cup. She's sitting on a low wall. Wooden staves, denim falls, leather hangings give her cover. Two Asian punks have been detailed to look after her. Joan signals to a passing superintendent. She flicks a little finger twice at the boy on her left. To say blade, she rubs her left knee. The super nods and doesn't stop. He speaks to his lapel.

Officer Beechcroft removes the number from his uniform. He takes a rubber cosh filled with lead from a holdall. A snatch team assembles.

Joan sits at her typewriter, smoothing carbon between white sheets.

Joan, blouse ripped, sees Tom by his car.

Joan, eye blacked, sees Willy closing in on the steward.

They wave to her.

Rising, Joan enters a narrow alley. The two minders follow, Beechcroft behind them.

Joan in the briefing room, looking at mugshots before the march.

Joan after, sparkling in the station pub.

Joan, her back to me, mic at her hip.

– Is this how it was?

It's me looking back, she says, it's how I see it now.

> **a memory at a moment of danger**

I switch the walnut on.

It takes a few seconds to warm up. Look in the back, you'll see the valves glowing. Tubes toasting dust. They kindle Joyce. His voice scorches the air.

– The inheritance of mental and physical characteristics, the existence of insuperable differences of environment, the laws of biology and psychology make it impossible that there should exist a real equality between men. But make no mistake – we are opposed to many of the inequalities and snobberies of our present system.

> **Britain wasn't democratic isn't now it's a degenerate financial democracy to this very day Willy and Tom were right to call out the banks no argument about that but**

saying money power was all Jewish that was driven by something else not reason

– Hore-Belisha, his melon-like physiognomy expanded in a horrible Moroccan Jewish grin, an Oriental pedlar of furniture.

Lansbury leads Labour he makes headlines no headway he was going nowhere the left pulls its punches boxes for Moscow the blackshirts are the real socialists boof boof a modern state the right a cross equal pay the uppercut a knock-kneed establishment sprawling on the ropes

Her paws are up, she's jabbing gracefully at the window, swinging weight from hip to hip. The shoulders roll and return, the nape dips and feints. Willy was my coach, she says, I put on gloves we danced around a ring.

– The corporate state will put Britain first, punish the moneylenders, and insist on equal pay for women. Don't drop your right hand. Friendship with Germany will prevent another slaughter.

A bell sounds from the walnut. The puckered hands tumble to her lap.

just for fun in the black house gym a lovely afternoon

– National socialism and socialism are different things.

– Opposites.

– Opposed, but you didn't challenge her.

– It wasn't that kind of interview.

John Beckett had been a Labour MP Bob Forgan too John Scanlon he and me came from the ILP together George Sutton Bill Risdon Labour organisers Mary Richardson the suffragette Tom Moran Rex Tremlett McNab Raven Thompson came from the communists there was no border no gulf between left and right really just people who wouldn't give up or kneel to Moscow

Look at the hill, says the nape, the road up the road down are one.

– I found in the British Union of Fascists far more sincere and earnest socialist convictions than I had seen in the Labour Party for the last ten years. The great majority were either converted socialists or young people who years before would have found their way into the socialist movement.

- Many of Mosley's followers and a surprising number of headquarters staff were former members of the Labour Party or ILP.

- OM who may some day do the things of which we dream!

Vox pop voicings from the tran.

- How many blackshirts came from the left?

- Wish I knew I don't have a number.

- Fallen angels.

- There's no study.

- Damn well should be. What else are historians for?

> *the left lost its way I soaked a copy of Rise of the Soviets*
> *in beetroot before a meeting of the book club I slop paint*
> *between the pages too as the talk begins I take the dripping*
> *pamphlet from my bag I spoilt that bag I hold it up I flap it*
> *splattering the useful idiots well did they jump I tell them*
> *the truth about Stalin's terror the famine and the purges we*
> *weren't afraid to name the beast or stand up to it historians*
> *make me laugh they make me angry they've no idea how it*
> *was they don't ask us on principle what principle is that*
> *evicting us from history*

- The important thing is the anticapitalist sentiment that is permeating our people.

Applause from the pillow pocket-set, stamping feet below the bed. Industry must serve the people! Dustcast on the wireless. National ownership now!

- The protest of a people against a state that denies the right to work. If the present economic system is incapable of properly distributing the productive wealth of nations, then that system is false and must be altered.

Footsore hunger marchers straggle the road. Struggle or starve, one shouts, struggle or starve! Struggle or starve let's eat let's eat, a shaming parade on an empty street, struggle or starve let's eat let's eat, boots and slogan finding the beat.

The signal dissolves in a seething shower of rain. The ganging's not right. There are powerful stations on similar wavelengths. The marchers duck for cover under awnings, ledges and trees.

I hope you caught that, she says, reaching to the dial, the case for socialism.

– Who was speaking, was it Stafford Cripps?

Not him says the nape.

– Young Bevan?

No says the nape but it could have been.

> *it was Gregor Strasser killed on the night of the long knives*
> *we must take from the right nationalism without capitalism*
> *he said from the left socialism without internationalism it*
> *seemed to make sense but Berlin betrays the socialism ha*
> *when's that not the case internationalism meant Marxism*
> *and bankers with no loyalty to a nation a hole in the head*
> *that was Strasser's fate Tom would have done the same to*
> *Willy in the end it was a dangerous time an urgent time*
> *affairs of the heart made it harder*

Correct second channel interference with a wavetrap. Adjust for minimum response.

> *the whole economy led by one body a third of it the trade unions*
> *a third consumers one third employers would that have been*
> *worse than nationalisation it'd be a damn sight better than*
> *the grabbing hands of the free market we have now*

Nape Joan taps the side of the wireless. It's playing up today, she says, turn the pocket set up till faithless recovers.

A thin voice fizzes at the bedhead.

– Never before had I met a personality so terrifying in its dynamic force, so vituperative, so vitriolic. The words poured from him in a corrosive spate. He ridiculed our political system, he scarified our leading politicians.

> *listen closely he's talking about Willy a careful choice of*
> *words scarified not scared you have to hear it said or you*
> *could easily miss it*

– He has a titanic hatred for Jews and for capitalists. These two hatreds have been the mainsprings of his adult life. He thinks the Nazi movement is a proletarian one which will free the world from the bonds of plutocratic capitalists. He sees himself primarily as a liberator of the working class.

Who are you, I ask the pocket radio.

well done dear you're getting the hang of it now at long last

Shirer William Shirer it sizzles back.

– I was a journalist in Berlin until America entered the war.

– You knew Joyce there?

– Sure did sonny he was the war's outstanding radio traitor.

A donkey brays at a microphone, one eye winking, the other enlarged by a monocle. The cartoon mule is dressed in a day suit. Its lower jaw shovels, its upper jaw hatchets. The script rests on a nameplate: LORD HEE-HAW CHIEF WINDBAG.

An amusing and intelligent fellow, Shirer says.

– If you could get over the initial revulsion.

Willy had powerful obsessions the Jews were behind it all you couldn't shift him from that not Willy it was widely believed there was plenty to it bankers industrialists press barons socialists communists sweatshop owners cut-rate shopkeepers they argued the toss all week but in the synagogue on Saturday they spoke with one voice calling for war on Germany oh dint they get one too

I couldn't shift him, she says, no one could we tried everything.

– He didn't have a softer side?

he was vulnerable like any man he confided in me told me there were bowstrings seven of them they could make him as pliable as any other man well I misunderstood I thought it was a hint you know pervy so one night when he's sleeping I tie him up with knitting wool

Footsteps sound round the bed erratic motifs on a violin settle to calm cello bass hush a pause. The walnut wireless revives.

– Raaarrrrghnahhreeeu.

I get that wrong don't I how he roars as he breaks free you'll need a strong rope and better bloody knots if that's your plan he's furious

The hush bass flickers. A voice sings remorsefully from the transistor.

– Ever toiling for him alone.

Willy darling I'm sorry I say combing his thinning thatch with my fingers he didn't like that how about shaving your head I suggest it's a manly look it might be the making of you

I trust your dishonesty whispers the tran, as the bass hands back to the cello.

– The breath of gentle breezes.

it would look very virile I whisper to him he doesn't go for that either Willy wasn't very adventurous or trusting he'd say sometimes Joan you annoy me to death to the very death of me then he'd fall asleep and in the morning he was gone

– Love has been forsworn by me.

A declaration, broadcast violins strident.

– Beware of my army of night!

he had to be strong we all did the venom of international finance had weakened England's heart the poison of Bolshevism too he was right about that just wrong so terribly wrong to blame it on the Jews alone Jews at all Tom said tackle Jewish criminals just them not the race but there were voices to the right of Tom you know they called us British Jewnion kosher fascists what does that tell you

– I am everywhere hidden from sight.

Heavy drumming waps the violins, a fierce onslaught of bass thunders the room, the joints of the bed crack, I can hardly hear her. The wireless rasps hoarsely do you believe me now?

the Union wasn't what the falsifiers say not at all no not at first anyway force decides everything history's written by the

dog on top

– How small should I be?

A cataclysmic chord a closing smash of cymbal nape a dot in the bedchamber auditorium.

the past rewritten as monstrous as something else erased replaced and silenced

Light out but no applause.

– That's bollocks. Antisemitism was there from the start.

– As far back as twenty-two Mosley blamed Jerusalem.

– It was always present Joan.

yes yes it was everywhere so it isn't the reason people join they join to get rid of the Old Gang unemployment war that's what fires them up some say things are run for the Jews others say by the Jews but that wasn't the spark antisemitism the socialism of fools that came later when members were quitting it was a way to call them back

I challenge and expose tonight, says Tom, the corrupt power in England of international Jewish finance. Perish Judah, he snarls. Stronger than the stink of oil, the wireless says, rises the stink of the Jew. The parties who oppose us are Jew-ridden jackals and flunkeys of Judah. Old sets have an appreciable hum which, though it was tolerable at the time, is not so today.

– She won't admit it.

– She is admitting it. So terribly wrong she says.

– Mosley was inconsistent at best. He made concessions, lost control.

– An antisemite biding his time.

– Joan, that note by Mosley, the illegible one. What did it say?

you're asking me what an illegible note says do listen to yourself

It may be shown from now the Jew is the aggressor and ter ession may be launched of .

– I see what she means.

- We'll have to find a way to challenge Joan Cade about her beliefs.

- But she's dead gov.

- Introduce some balance. Board of Deputies. A respected historian.

- A misleading last word, she'd have snorted.

> *there's no end to my story or ways to tell it dear you're in for*
> *a long haul it unwinds winds down just when you think it's*
> *wound up there's more not the same I feel like Winnie you*
> *know in Happy Days wondering what her Willy is up to I*
> *cried when I saw that onstage may one still speak of time*
> *it is a long time now Willy since I heard you it sent a chill*
> *down my spine when she said that I laughed out loud*

Hang Mosley high!

- It went pear-shaped after Olympia, didn't it?

HEAR MOSLEY antifascists mobilise ALL ROADS LEAD TO OLYMPIA resist with all means. Ten thousand attend, drummers and a band. Flags and arc lamps, ovations booing a few salutes. Highly organised groups of REDS Tom complains. Loudspeakers fail, Sir Oswald mimes, chairs volley. Beatings enforce free speech. An aerial protest, a chase along a girder DOWN WITH FASCISM glass breaking, the fall unseen, ejections, the ousted arrested.

- I was appalled by the brutal conduct of the fascists last night.

- Two dozen in cells for halting free speech.

- Thanks to their stand the present universal outcry against fascism has developed. Before there was silence or indifference or amused toleration.

RED TERROR SMASHED a FASCIST VICTORY a MIGHTY COUNTER DEMONSTRATION a COMPLETE FIASCO. Lord Rothermere backs away, the *Daily Mail* withdraws support.

- Mosley has suffered a check which is likely to prove decisive.

- A spectacular own goal.

> *pressure was brought to bear on Rothermere Jewish*

advertising managers turn off the taps Lyons Carrera Willy calls it a Hebrew siege more exodus I'd say cash dries up the bragging and the bullying grow

– Fewer members?

– Ten thousand down. And short of funds.

– Much falling out?

– Headless chickens. People leaving.

after Olympia the tide turns it gets choppy the Jews and the reds are relentless it gets harder the Union is smaller down to Shoreditch Stepney Bethnal Green and Hackney not much else that's when they lose the plot pettiness and nastiness and hatred obsession with Jews and cut price shops Sunday traders overcrowding clatter from the house next door sewing machines shaking the table steam presses jolting beds at night soon English people turn on us good people angry and struggling themselves it was all over but we couldn't see it not for certain not yet

They take me late that evening.

It's a well-timed raid, professional. Joan and I are in the vitrine. It was a little later than usual. Joan was reminiscing about the man she claimed was her real father, an American. She tugs a string of beads to close the curtains.

it's a mirror at night this window

– Sorry?

I can't talk to my face

– As you wish.

Lew Misz was his name my real father mum met him in London before she married he went to Italy after the war and didn't come back a rolling stone Willy reminds me of him yes Willy was very like my real father was that was the attraction

I can't find a person of that name or its most obvious variants anywhere. Lew or Lou? Misz, Mistz, Mies? She may have mispronounced him. Or made him up. Lew Misz I wrote down at the time. Twice in fact. ~~LOU MISZ~~ then LEW MISZ. Did she spell it out? I was a fool to let a half heard name pass. What was I thinking?

> *I tracked him down I did go to see him on two occasions after the war twice in the fifties he was distant yes a little distant he wasn't well but it was important to me I found him in New York sitting in a deck chair in a garden he knew about Willy he said he wrote to Willy*

– He knew Joyce? When was this Joan?

– Impossible!

– Joyce was dead by then.

> *dead no not when he wrote to Willy he wasn't no he couldn't have been hahaha*

– Lew who contacts Joyce when is this?

> *he sent Willy letters during the war they never meet two of a kind brown-nosing radiomanics talking past each other they didn't hear each other men like that don't*

– I should be glad to profit from your experienced criticism.

– Your methods are unique, nobody could imitate them successfully.

– Poets are not to blame for how things are.

> *pass me my juice will you*

I raise the carton to her shoulder. A squeezebox on which apples blush, a sucker hooking from a puncture. She takes it. Her crown is the spider of a speaker cone, her ear disfigured microphone. I retreat to my seat. Slurp bubble, slurbubble, death rattling.

> *put this somewhere dear will you please*

The box wheezes in my grip. It sprays sweet mist.

The crimped straw crooks up at me, blind, hissing.

– You mussst find thisss man sshe callsss father.

I stand the carton on the cupboard, next to the tran. It won't let up.

– You need to know. Yous knows yous needs to knows. Whyss don't yous ask?

Syrup drips on the back of my hand.

– Asssssssssssssssk her.

The twister swivels, pointing at Joan.

– Asssssssssssssk her. Asssk

– Joan, who was Lew?

Lew who's Lew who do you mean?

I don't hear them enter. Watchers, two of them, grab me from behind.

When I come to my hands are bound. My arms have been roped to the back of a chair, my ankles to the legs. My mouth is stuffed and sealed with tape, I gasp through my nose. Brilliant light sears my eyes. I can't focus. I can't see anything. I strain I squeal the chair. Something moves by the wall. A raised rock, the silhouette of a stave, shadow of a truncheon. The shape swells and sharpens. It's a taser. Barbs crackle spining trunching jab and rock it's gone.

The Frustrator snaps questions.

– What has she told you?

– Grthhhhhhwhoog?

– Who has read your research?

– Grthhhhhhwowt!

– Any more questions keep them to yourself!

– Grthhhhhh! Grthhhhhh.

If signal is considerably down in strength, choke is in order. Connect the choke across the condenser. A good high frequency choke will not cause much loss in strength.

– Who put you onto her?

Moisten a finger tip. Touch the grid terminal. The speaker will make some noise.

– Grthhhhhhowwrg!

The Frustrator leaves the room.

I study my bonds. Joan's words stream round my ankles, my knees, climbing to my elbows. My real father Lew who don't go did make me laugh. Dog walker an urgent meeting. Word fetters, incoherent meaning chains, I would know Astra's mother would know. I wrig I twist I bump the chair across the room. My knees bang the bed. Ghhown! Ghhown! Joan's oblivious, a burbling nape, mic at her thigh. Her anecdotes allusions testimonies run through diaphragms, magnets, testers, multimeters. More cable coils beside her on the pillow, metallic word straps, a roll of gaff tape. There's a man leaning in at the open window, a man in a raincoat, a man in a hat with a brim with a dent. A Communicator giving Joan instructions. I catch a snatch.

– Let your words be few

– He won't hear it from me.

I wake with my head on my desk. Red inflammations ring my wrists. Ink stains my arms. My ankles are badly bruised. No one heard me return.

– We had an early night.

– Thought you went up ahead of us.

– Big Bro watches not me man.

At the time of the interviews I'm living in a shared house. Twelve adults and four children, more at weekends. Footsteps drub and stub the stairs all day, all night. Nobody pays any mind.

>   ***tell me about the children dear I'm interested in the way you
>   live together what it's like***

– What happened last night Joan?

Some things, says she, you have to work out for yourself.

One evening, my turn in the childcare rota, the kids loot my books. They build a wall of paperbacks, topped with battlements, across the front room floor. At one end – blocked by an upended tray – the legs of a chair serve as a gate.

– Walnuts is the password what's the password what is it say it.

– Walnuts.

– Yes you can come in.

One Way Street Vegetarian Cookery George Fox Whole Earth Catalogue Naked Lunch Andy Capp bond defiantly on the face of the fort, a regiment of rainbow spines. I step over the ramparts. Piling them is OK, I say.

– But no knocking over do you understand no knocking over it will damage the books they cost money they are my work.

Safe in the fortress, the kids lay flat on cushions poking weapons at the door. They open fire on an ankle length patchwork skirt, shooting plastic swords and guns and rulers.

The four-year-old hurls a satsuma grenade. It skittles a figurine Che. Sorry, she says.

– I didn't mean to I didn't mean it.

The fusillade continues bam bam perkoosh bam rah! The skirt shields her breasts with crossed arms – oh, oh – she drops to her knees she bows her head.

– Mummy's dead!

– Give me some more bullets nahnah I'm the ambulance nahnah.

– Don't cry mummy.

– Danny it's your turn to come in come on.

Dannee Dannee! they chant. He fills the door. Yeay bang boosh pyshoo Danny's dead Tina where are you they call Tina Tina come in.

Pap pap I go pap pap pap.

– Now you're all dead!

– You're on our side you can't shoot us!

– Don't you mustn't.

– I'm on mummy's side and Tina's.

– That's not fair!

That's it for tonight I say, as the book wall topples. My daughter crawls through a rubble of Penguin Specials.

Pick up the book bricks, I say, everyone ready for bed.

– Not yet not yet please no but we don't wannooo.

I think I would have liked to live like that yes I do think I would

The church door is being repaired.

Two monstrous footprints indent the lawn, like open graves. To disguise the spoor of Haw Haw, a Thorkell the Tall walk has been created for the arts biennale.

A Viking defector, Thorkell the Tall captured Alphege. His men killed the archbishop when no ransom was paid.

I'm late. It's going to rain. I hurry up the hill.

I spin my umbrella in the foyer of the care home, speckling the tiles. I girdle the cone, dripping the stairs two at a time. I tap at the door and enter.

Joan's framed by storm streak.

not a word not yet just look

The sky above the bay is sheet steel, scored diagonal, drilling steeps of downpour. Upwells of ink flood every vector. The plunging steamer is a pair of pitching funnels. Two blackened rectangles tilt. Ripped shards of paper expose the lurching hull. Above the ship, behind the ship, reflected all about the ship, a pall of boiling sootstain.

The weather's turning, she says. Watch, she says.

Slowly the cloud thins. The bay mustards under sallow sky, the shafts reset upright. A beetle on its back, feet smouldering, a blue field. Tide as constraint, wind and waiting for the turn.

Then oh a sailship dazzling in the noon, swelling to the sheer, dipping gliding spotless.

That was time well spent, says Joan.

now let's get on

Hitler had a foothold in England.

– There really was a fifth column?

> *resident Germans were forced to join the Ortsgruppe no work permits if they didn't a journalist ran it they were told not to work for Jews not to mix with British fascists Bene was top dog he says Tom is a person of little importance a political adventurer Bene was a jumped up snob I meet them at a Viennese restaurant in Soho the German Hospital in Dalston they have rooms in Paddington hotels in Bayswater boats from Hamburg moor in the Thames the ships are German territory closely watched so I board in Tom's place a man called Thost tells me he'll be ambassador one day the swastika will fly over the embassy he was long gone when it happened*

Workmen demolish walls in Carlton House Terrace. They are extending the first floor drawing-room. It is one hundred feet long. Vast mirrors enlarge the chamber at each end, doubling each other, cubing each other endlessly. The embassy is unbound Lebensraum, reflected photons rebounding blasting a corridor unconfined. Guests replicate, hosts multiply, one race infiniting.

– Enoptromancy!

> *it made me dizzy standing there*

Speer, Hitler's personal architect, oversees the work. Galleries are plundered to dress specular walls. Lucretia, by Cranach, has pride of place. She multiplies, serial blades rising in concert. The women stab their breasts a million times. Blink, they stab again. Columns of Ribbentrop view the revue, pouting cigar. Europe and the Atlantic cloud, the earth retches and spits.

> *vertigo it threw my balance off I didn't like it at all*

– Cover the mirrors.

– Cover them for seven days.

> *Lucretia was blackmailed she's blackmailed and raped she tells everyone she takes her own life her suicide triggers a rebellion she's virtue the rising leads to a republic*

– Wow. So why that painting?

a German masterpiece a woman of principle they don't identify with her do they no way ha self harm as politics that's crazy revolutionary suicide they called it in Guyana nine hundred dead in the rainforest not to mention hunger strikers in the Maze

– Those I know.

by this blood I will drive the tyrants hence you have to be brave very brave to turn a blade on yourself brave or despairing Cranach paints Lucretia more than thirty times why do you think he does that was there a cult was it a compulsion that poor woman was out of place in the embassy

I've got a postcard of the painting, she says, it's in the drawer.

The recording is thunderstorm. The microphone booms like a drum.

– It's impossible to tell who's talking or what is being said.

– What's going on?

– We were searching for the postcard.

It's four and a half minutes before coherent voices return.

pearlescent that's a nice word pearlescent I wish I was pass me some tissue dear do you think I'm pearlescent I'd like you to say so but one thing I'm sure of ha I was never well known for chastity

Plug, press, probe.

– Joyce had the gab a talent for speaking didn't he?

compared to Tom yes Willy was deffo the better speaker he was a real persuader the first time we met he was inspecting a course I was on a course in public speaking for women he listened to us all he's encouraging to everyone he says I've got potential so he coaches me I'm an eager learner he makes this mouth a sharp sword I know he's with Margaret I don't consider that will last so with our lessons as a pretext

we abandon ourselves entirely to love our studies allowed
us to withdraw in private as love desired with our books
open before us more words of love than reading passed more
kissing than teaching his hands stray oftener to my bosom
than to the pages

A cassette dated one week later tells a different tale.

I fell in love with Willy in thirty-four at Chelsea town hall
I was working for the Union as a typist I'm lonely I wasn't
seeing any of my old friends I was at a low ebb ready ripe I
suppose he spoke out against the exploitation of women how
it has to end well had I no eyes but ears my ears would love
that man that's how he made feel

My heart was like wax, melting within my chest.

Stew simmering on a gas ring, female laughter.

He drinks, plays about with women, and plans, agent Charlie notes in
S.F.96 British 2 v19 906a.

the Union is the first British party serious about equal pay
for women the wireless today says we still don't have it and
might not for years equality was one of the reasons I stayed
put in the Union women were more equal respected it was
hands off unless we said so and no smutty jokes some of the
men waver of course they want higher wages for themselves
so they can keep a girl at home the arguments we have
about that I can tell you some of them only support equal
pay because they think firms will stop taking on women not
Willy he speaks up for us

– Didn't Mosley say we want men who are men, women who are women?

It wasn't kinder kuche kirche here she says, no not at all the German way
it didn't wash with Tom.

Peals of wedding bells, chopping of root vegetables. A wireless plays, a child
calls Mutti.

– Take a pot, dustpan and broom and marry a man.

– Preserve family preserve the blood preserve the race.

- The granting of so-called equal rights to women as demanded by Marxism does not confer equal rights at all. They draw women into a zone where they can only be inferior.

Splice two seconds each in here of lathe and hammer drill and gun.

- Can we get back to Chelsea Joan?

> *that night outside the town hall he comes over he asks if I'd like to join him in the car well you couldn't say no to that we talk about art and books I'm tongue-tied we go to a club Willy quotes Byron love is a woman's whole existence he buys me a cocktail he cracks jokes about poof poets*

- Destroy the old language, powerless to keep up with life's leaps and bounds!

I'll drink to that, says Joan, you've changed your tune from talking up tradition.

- Throw the old masters overboard!

> *paintings or politicians I ask both he laughs ha*

- War Joan war is the hygiene of the world.

What's hygienic about wounds and infection and sepsis, she replies. Such nonsense, she says, it's cracked.

- I like you Joan.

- You're alright yourself professor.

- What year was this?

> *nineteen rosy four he rolls me up like a poster and takes me home happy days one afternoon we're in the meadow near the station I lay my hand on his I lose all sensation in my other arm my legs it's gone all I feel is nestling palms a bird swoops by Willy snatches it from the air I lighten with joy I rise like a kite in the cubic clouds Willy holds on to me Willy with a piping finch in his fist we exchange I soar weightless as signal the bird's compelled below Willy is the pivot of our revolution his collars curl and fill like wings the fields are green the houses green lawn green a horse is grazing a hill the picnic cloth is red and rumpled there are no flowers in*

143

the meadow not a single bloom Willy brought a decanter but only one glass why I think is he going to let go he doesn't I fall in love with him dear head over heels and vice versa too

I thought, the nape says, one day by his light the nations will walk.

I knew I'd have to own him in rags as well as silver slippers that I'd have to stand by him bound in irons

It sings, shakily, from the cassette.

I shall never relinquish love
They'll never take love from me,
Though Valhalla's glittering pomp
Should moulder into dust!

don't turn your face away dear you asked me about our relationship and this is what it was

Six times she slaps the duvet, beating the metre of her reproach.

I'm trying my best to explain the least you can do is listen

The eye fixes on me, a bombsight.

I look away. I frown. I look up, suck a breath. There's a small crack in the ceiling above the bed. I sketch it. Three toes forward one back. It's the footprint of a bird.

– A bird with one foot.

– One foot upside down.

It chirils and flits. Joyce was violent to both his wives I say.

I'd been warned he beat Hazel but it was a shock when he hit me he really hurt me but I loved him it sounds ridiculous I know it was something you accepted no one would help you the anger didn't last for long the first time I thought he won't come back but he did I threw my arms round him my bones leaped for joy that night I dreamed angels were whispering in our ears as it turns out that's what happenned

Ariel hits stop.

– She's saying Joyce fathered her child.

- Seems to be, yes.

- Why doesn't anyone know about this?

- Would you broadcast it?

- How old's the daughter? What do we know about her?

- Astra's seventy-plus, in good health. Public interest?

- We should speak to her.

- I've tried, believe me.

- And?

- Nothing doing.

> *in the middle of all this felicity one blow unhinged me Willy
> told me he and Mag were to marry oh I'm old furniture an
> armchair with a lump Mag's a firm new sofa no more letters
> hotels no tea for two nor smiles not real ones not a friendly
> word for weeks Mag phones its me who takes her call me
> who books the tables books the room I felt pointless hollow
> the evenings were lonely chasms weekends were marathons
> I don't know what I'd have done without the wireless I get on
> with the work my work is valued that is something at least*

- Which campaign was that?

> *campaigning oh campaigning yes we were against another
> war the boiled shirts the brass hats they're getting us ready
> to fight another Willy says the Jews are too because of what
> is happening in Germany it was unjust but not a cause for
> war it wasn't why we went to war either at Earl's Court we
> held a peace rally what an event a white podium Tom in
> black twenty feet above us in the air the voice of truth people
> were ready to hear him again*

- Enough we have had of alien quarrels, enough threats of foreign war,
enough diversion from what matters. A million Britons shall never die
in your Jews' quarrel. Peace with honour, the Empire intact, the British
people safe.

> *I was a drummer in the escort one rolling thrilling tempo
> as we beat Tom in he was back in the saddle it felt good we*

were righteous chosen the men lining the pavements and the corridor salute us we parade below raised arms a roof of muscle and respect protection for women

The Earl's Court meeting has created enormous interest among circles which had been led to believe that British Union was dead. Now is the time to take advantage of that interest. To organise such a meeting during mid-summer demanded great courage. To take advantage of the interest aroused calls for hard work. We are asking all our friends to assist us in our endeavour to push the sales of ACTION during the month of August. In the Autumn will probably come the General Election. Yours in Union.

Joan pats the duvet flat. Her nape shutters as she looks to the ceiling.

That crack's been there a couple of days she says.

it was all Tomtopia really he'd have been a useless prime minister he always wasted half the year in France the south with petticoat he'd have been a minister of twerps dangerous twerps he wasn't being honest about fighting German invaders but Earls Court that night is the old Tom a climacteric the best of days oooh what a lovely word climacteric what a night we had just like our first time will be hahaha

– She never gave up.

– But you didn't, you know, anything, did you?

– What do you think I am?

– No. Quite.

Voices come they go.

– Radio is the most modern, most important instrument of mass influence that exists anywhere.

Faltering frequency fuzzsh, off signal swoosh, waves racing by forty-foot deep and forty-foot high, caught, tapped, undiminished rolling on.

– This is the great miracle of wireless. The omnipresence of what people are singing or saying anywhere, the overlapping of frontiers, the conquest of spatial isolation, the importation of culture on waves of ether, same fare for all.

– The truly modern house must be, for a man of action, a home linked by an antenna to the prolific waves of his time.

A young lady in a gown, two gents in evening dress, standing in a bright room. Reading from scripts, they simulate the horror of entrapment in a coal mine.

– Who'll feed the parrot?

Outside, a young man cross-legged on the floor has telephones on his ears.

– As he heard through the receivers the progress of the piece he signalled to two assistants on a lower landing to make noises to represent the action of the play.

> *no bodies sounds with no source a spook speaking a voice in your head very odd some said even evil speaking no sign of a speaker like listening to neighbours through the wall but nobody's in*

You heard the sound of words but saw no form; there was only a voice.

> *voices in a box one voice then another you had to work out who was who they put in patterns quirks to help us out they were speaking at that very moment miles away they called it in the ether the science was hard to understand*

– Just think! It takes five hours to get there on the train.

– The ether was chock full of voices striving to gain one's ear.

– Like ghosts.

– Spirit presences, frightening.

– The reception and amplification of voices from the past with thermoionic valves will destroy time.

– It made me feel queerly.

> *we got used to it eventually learnt the way of listening who was who who was where near what the announcers never had names voices like the vicar with your eyes closed one man a comic his catch phrase was a song a smile and a piano they change it to a joke and a piano cos you can't hear a smile*

A shower head gusts over a string trio.

> *music through an earcap you can't imagine how exciting*
> *that was a silver shower of sound the sky speaking voices*
> *from the past what next the other side wireless walls to read*
> *taste rays smell rays one listening world one people all in*
> *the same time*

Such power, through the wireless you can enter every home.

– The public pays for our warrant!

> *you wouldn't find out what was going on from the papers*
> *anymore events would be announced in your own home*
> *anything that matters we'd hear it and live it together*

– It was a new world it was nowness I listen in for hours.

– Angels, angels singing in the air.

Once triggered, an electromagnetic wave continues ever forward unless matter absorbs it. A form of light, it travels at the speed of light.

Sound converted into impalpable light is turned back into sound. It is caught by a detector or coherer, a coil or receiving antenna. It is matched in a tuning circuit, amplified by a valve, sent to a speaker. Diaphragms bat matching molecules to eardrums.

An apparatus of relationships pulsing power popping pleasurably playing on ears interminably.

Here in the air, I key voice to a screen.

Why should anyone want to buy a radio?

– Nine tenths of what one hears is second rate jazz.

– Degenerate sax players, sickening crooners.

– Blatant sales talk, so many interruptions.

> *digital internet world wide web computerising paging*
> *they're all very well but I don't see people getting better at*
> *listening*

It's late. The window starts to mirror Joan. She screens it with poppies. A sad clown in ruffs and poms warbles from the wireless. One hand palms his heart, the other reaches to Joan.

> Little Betty Bouncer loved an announcer down at the BBC
> she doesn't know his name but how she rejoices
> when she hears that voice of voices!

The pierrot, singing at night on the crowded pier, knows the value of a tranquil moonlit backdrop. A sea of silence for your background, the Lissen Super Transformer. That is the sort of silence you get in your set when you have a Lissen. You get no rustle. All else is still. More pure volume, clearer reproduction, sharper definition. No motor boating.

A chub negro, white lips and collar, checker trousers and no hat. He climbs the facing page, a banjo saucepan on his back. Bald, shiny with sweat, he's headed for the pierrot. As he treks he sings I'm going back to Old Nebraska.

– It's one of the Darkie songs that sets the feet of Europe's broadcasters moving. It is one of those tunes for which you must have volume. Putting a Lissen New Process Battery in your set is the surest way of always getting both volume and purity of tone from your loud speaker.

> *the waves never stop you know if nothing gets in their way and soaks them up they keep on rolling Marconi said sound never dies it keeps moving he was building a receiver that would pick the voice of Jesus up imagine tuning into that Boudicca cursing the Romans Lilburne fighting the gallows Willy's broadcasts are still moving his words are pips and seeds on their way to new planets*

The man who spoke was a man named Colson.

– He spoke from a distance of 186 million miles!

> *I suggest a policy for the Union manifesto let's convert radio from distribution to exchange I say from a broadcasting machine to an apparatus for communication but no they don't like the idea at all Willy puts his foot down it would jeopardise the function of leadership he says it can't be done we shouldn't even try*

– Organise the listeners as suppliers.

– A vast network of pipes, that's all it would be.

– Every receiver a transmitter.

- Pointless. We'd hear everyone. The Babbling British Chaos.

- The people!

- Do I have a radio so my enemies can talk to me?

With coils it is necessary to establish continuity through the winding. Any looseness of the terminals should be corrected. Oxidisation and corrosion are always a possibility.

- I'm afraid Mrs Cade isn't well today.

- What's wrong?

- Sudden fault of a component.

- What's wrong?

- Grid leak, the doctor says.

- When can I see her?

- We're waiting for parts.

As I leave, Joan knocks loudly at the bedroom window.

I spread my arms horizontally. I raise them both forty-five degrees. I level my right arm, swinging my left across to replace it, left elbow to my nose. I drop my right arm. Seven-thirty. With the left I point above my head.

A paper aeroplane sashays to the flowerbed.

B CAREFUL

Watchers emerge from the treeline.

I hop it.

Transistor sunlit on the sill.

- Neofascist groups in Italy opposed to immigration Forza Nuova, Flamma Tricolore and the National Social Front will be protesting

A shrieker bites hedge, a motorised blade below. That's heavy duty gardening I say, nodding at the window. Ignore it she says, I'll shout if I have to.

something about the radio doesn't sound right today I've

moved it but it's no better I don't know why

– That hedgetrimmer I expect let me look.

She turns away. Old faithless is on too. What are the wild waves saying?

– In France the Front National of Le Pen has secured fifteen per cent of the vote

Breakers from the bed foot. The tip of the zista's aerial tinks the view. I level it and take my seat.

– Shopkeepers in Rome were boarding up windows at sunrise today

that's a bit better a pity the news isn't

Mast, mane, chalk, glaze. Nape, never the face, always the scruff. The half bell on the wall her shadow.

Sickert tells her to sit on the bed. I know her immediately. He paints Joan from behind. She studies herself in the mirror on the sill. Mired and brown and only twenty-five. Renoir catches her young, red under roses, reading indoors, nape a wan clay. I see Joan in Richter's daughter, the snap of the back of her head as she turns away. Whistler is close, his mother in grey.

don't be offended if I sit this way it's my hearing just the one good ear or is it slow oh slow my beating heart because you're a handsome one haha

Thy neck is an iron sinew.

Thy neck is a tower of ivory.

Thy neck is comely with gold.

history's one way to describe what we're up to I should be in a museum these days a glass box are there taxidermists for old trouts like me fill out these folds give me a stuffing I can set the record straight with you what can they do to me now

– At a hearing in the high court today the director of public prosecco

Joan picks up the transistor. She gives it a shake and puts it down.

– New exhibitions opening in London galleries this spring in club.

why's it not working what's wrong with it

Outside in the cul de sac, the howling hedge sheds leaves.

people don't want to hear our story they shout over us iron wrinkles into it treat us like a stain they want history simple self-justifying dumbed down truth gets in the way of their tall tales us socialists who wouldn't stomach the soviets they dress us for panto as fifth-column Nazi stabs in the back

She shakes the transistor, slapping its side.

– Violence has broken out during a street protest against the European Union organised by the British National Party in London today we go live to

we're in the same moment now it's always the same moment the same emergency the same mistakes

She bangs the mute plastic on the sill. It dints the paint.

– Don't bang it Joan you'll break it.

Tom and Willy aren't memories she says.

the living seem more shadowy they're here they're now they're on your tape Tom and Willy in this room my poor Willy snared and stretched run my darling rabbit run

A silence follows. I imagine a rabbit bolting across the close. Brown tuned ears vee antenna, kickback legging butt tupping tail flash airborne, burst burst off.

was ever grief like mine

Footsteps in the corridor. She puts the tran down.

and you dear do you have someone

The shaky flute my voice.

– What do you remember of the trial?

you little wriggler full of sap denying an old lady pphah why don't you get your hair cut it would be like bedding a girl

– There's no one Mrs Cade. At the moment.

yo yippity doo I'm in with a chance

I laugh. The tape confirms it. Did I blush? Yes, hot prickling. I feel it now.

– How did you put up with it?

– Oh easy it was fun.

– There's something here but a lot of work.

– She's worth it you'll see.

– I need to hear it. Work up a rough cut.

– Yo, you won't regret it thanks.

I think we're nearly done Joan.

– I've got enough for a programme. You've been great. I've really enjoyed it. I'll still come see you though.

The nape stiffens. She doesn't respond.

– If you'd like?

Oiieeengeeoioooooooooo... A high pitched piercer sounds from all the radios simultaneously.

– Joan? Anyone at home today?

Woman at window. A cloistered life, bright light surrounding. A Dutch canvas. My ears, zinging with alarm.

– Are you alright? Joan?

I haven't been entirely honest with you

– How do you mean?

you don't know the half of it

– What are you saying?

The nape stares me down. Severe attenuation of speaker sound.

– Vintage sets should be considered inherently unsafe until they are tested and prove otherwise.

there's something you can help me with

– Of course what is it?

Her neck swans right, to the top corner of the room. A drip? Cornice repair for conservationists? Stay cosy with cobwebs. Keep the top storey free from inflammable junk. What does her gesture mean?

– The crack in the ceiling?

> **there's rot up there rot I've seen two starlings come back to the eave they're nesting in the roof there's flutter and flap and wriggling all night I turn on the radios its still there the nurses say I'm imagining things they live such noisy lives they don't hear the blust of the pillow crut of a nest the starlings stop me sleeping sod all's the help I get**

– You sure it's birds?

> **two starlings.**

– I can't hear anything.

If all other tests fail to reveal the source of background noise it is well to remember the possibility of a faulty cap inside the detector valve.

Out in the close, a new recruit drops from a covered truck. Hoisting his kit bag and rifle, he heads for the guardroom. Pigeons mill on the care home's lawn. The soldier pauses.

– Any messages?

– You had to ask!

Plosive whines winging, lips blasting multi-mic.

A boy in a bed by a sealed hearth. The transistor, banned after light out, is fading. Tim's bro is the deejay, two villages out. Insect voices, moog morsing through a downpour. The signal's weak, the batteries low.

– As soon as he speaks, it's light again.

The curtains are flimsy. When cars pass a sail of spangles sweeps the ceiling, panes dashing from headlights, cross on the wing. He listens from the blankets, waiting for burr at the bend. Night prowling Victors, barking Escorts, Hunters hugging ditches all break cover to snarl through the village. Drowsiness whelms the light show.

The boy jerks to. Sturbs and flot, inches from his face. Scrab and squea in the null. The pirate reviving? Scrape scratch squeep? Sound no source, a ghosting. Scrab and scurry, acousmatic.

Frantic Foley flappling.

The penny drop. Spoon around a metal bowl slowing, tap. It's pigeon thrash. Fluefall. A pigeon behind the panel on the fireplace. He knucks the board. It flails. We beat a table with towels. We cease. In soot they sleep.

Wingscuff. He shouts.

– Mum there's a pigeon in the chimney!

– Go back to sleep.

– There really is. Moving in the chimney.

– Iss wind. Stop that shouting now you'll wake the others up.

– But mum.

– Go to sleep.

Pidge flip pidge flares squeep sleep.

Dream fingers binocular, scanning for curl brace.

– Trap's empty sir. No message, not yet.

– 161 will make it sergeant. Keep watch.

A second night straining. Burb bat abat board back.

– Mum. The bird's still there!

This time stamping angry stop this nonsense up the stairs it's late. Dark her gloom the bedthick. She looks at the fireplace.

– Well I can't hear anything.

– When it's quiet it comes again.

– There's nothing, go to sleep.

– There is there's a pigeon.

– Stop this now or I'll tell your father.

– But mum.

– Sleep or there'll be trouble.

The Dickin medal for conspicuous gallantry and devotion to duty was awarded to thirty-two homing pigeons during the war. White Vision, Winkie, Tyke, Beach Comber, Gustav, Paddy, Kenley Lass, Navy Blue, Flying Dutchman, NPS 42 NS 2780.

– Was it pinned to their breasts?

Sixteen thousand birds are parachuted into occupied Europe. Two hundred thousand serve in all. They report landings lost aircrews, bring messages from agents, microphotos, warnings, wants and whereabouts.

– Magneto-receptors. In the beak. That's how.

– Racing Pigeon News, is that a good read?

– If you can't sleep.

On the third night, faint fluting.

– Mum!

– I'll give you shouting this time of night.

– But mum there's a pigeon.

– Where?

– There. Listen.

The bird scrapes and calls.

– Damn me if the boy ain't right. Ossy!

– I told you. I told you.

– Get up here you'll have to come up.

Plodder slipper farder up the stair.

– Swun a your damn pigjen.

– What?

– Open the hearth.

– This time a night?

– Will it die?

NPS 43 TW 161. A twig foot, a green canister, a curl of fine paper.

NVNCIE VERA TEGO

– She came through!

> *first you hear them then you don't you know you will again but not while you wait you wonder is it there you know it is a scuff a rustle says it is but silence stillness leaves you unsure did I hear it did I its hard to tell to fall asleep the uncertainty goes to the quick of things*

– What happened to the pigeon?

– Dead in a bucket next morning. Foot upside down.

She reaches for the portable.

– I'll take a look. I know where the trapdoor is. I'll have a look now.

> *would you dear that's wonderful I'm tired so grateful how do birds avoid the rats there are probably rats there's mice critters take care up there look to see where the microphone is don't touch it get the location close as you can*

– Of course Joan, that too.

She raises her left hand, fingering the loft. The transistor whispers lullabye. Making for sleep, she lows to the pillow. I soft sof fff close the door.

The recorder registers tosses, turning, sniffs a snore.

The reader will no doubt have heard whistles and groans produced by an oscillating detector valve when tuned to a carrier wave.

The pitch of the heterodyne note varies from a high pitched squeak to a deep bass note vanishing at silent point and then rising again finally to disappear as a high pitched squeak. The interference is very often found to be caused by equipment on the premises of the receiver.

She was right. In the void above her room I find an array of delicate apparatus, microphone buttons, ceiling probes, antennae. It's all active, green spot and red.

Next morning I'm called to the desk.

Reception directs me to a room on the second floor. I'm to go no explanation to E2. My heart races as I scale the stairs. Bad news how bad is she? I know she isn't sleeping but. A block on the interviews? Doctor's ruling, family complaint?

I knuck the door. It's Joan who calls me in.

– You had me worried.

so you should be

We're in a meeting room, just the two of us. Joan in a wheelchair placed with her back to me. She's the far side of a nest of grey tables with a lesser view of the bay, vantage point lower, foreground leafier, cluttered sky. Whitstable looks different from here, I say. Joan doesn't reply. The rubber grips of the wheelchair bookend a tape recorder. Panasonic RQ-2102. Sit she says. A microphone signposts an empty chair.

I thought we'd do something else today something my way

– What are you up to Joan?

it's my turn now I've questions too you know

She twists a hand behind, she hits record. The view resets. The bay tiles with floating folders. Facsimiles, cuttings, photos, film clips. Faces from the past, my past. It won't take long she says. It takes an hour.

Spits skim treetops chasing Schmitts. The bomber's American, fitted with cameras, a psychedelic monstrosity. Cheering, a child, I wave at the dogfight. An airbase back under plough, the Battle of Britain restaged. A control tower, grain hangars, a flooded munition store. Runway crumbling fieldside, gun mound, cockpit vets Carlino. My war.

british boys own I bet it's left your head a right mess

– I don't think so Joan.

All white all white awlright? Tea break in a midlands factory. Screwdrivers by saucers. Skinhead moonstomp on the radio. Paki-basher last fellah in the job, a knitter says. Ya din look like ee wi yer longhair. No black on the books.

I hope you stood up to them

– I tried and yes I did but

158

Head mechanic Mick, former bomber pilot, Daedalus in grey nylon. If I'd known what the Germans really stood for, he says, I'd have refused to fly. We knew sod all we were youngsters they didn't tell us owt. Look at city now, we've lost it it's gone.

some truth in that I suppose

– I learnt a lot, pushing back. I enjoyed it there.

My face yelling between two police helmets. Fingers flicking vees, my badge a fist. The community hall fills standing room only with NAZI SCUM! people I work with NAZI SCUM! strangers neighbours NAZI SCUM! They win a quarter of a million votes.

you made a stand that's something

– Well I thought so but

Me a day later, face down in a pile of yarn boxes, nose bleeding.

small price compared to some you got off lightly

– Yes I did.

Leaflets, handmade posters. No Nazis on the campus! Eggs fly, shells crump the lectern.

a university is no place for violence what were you thinking

– It was eggs Joan just eggs.

Tyndall at the station in Brighton. Their leader alone, combover suit and tie. It's late, it's quiet. I circle him twice. Facing me, he turns with me. Stares locking I spin him again. And once more. Turd. All I really do is make him dizzy.

you could have snatched his case you let him off the hook

– I should have.

Razorscalp, combat jackets, eighteen eyes of boot. We are many, tens of thousands, they are few and feuding. Queues and dancing on the grass, stage left is right and right is wrong better decide which side you're on.

that's more like it I was there too that day in the park

– You were?

Two battlements of helmet, one holds them back, one us. Me in no man's land. The National Front is a Nazi front smash the National Front the National Front is a shut it or I will hands behind your back.

no record of the arrest what happened

– They let me go.

A funeral in Tower Hamlets. A young man from a clothing factory. Stabbed in the park on election day. Silent banners. Black unity! Here to stay here to fight! It's raining. Joan's quiet. She doesn't speak.

– A turning point.

Every Saturday they try to sell their paper in the shopping precinct. We outnumber them five to one. Keep the Nazis on the run! They're stubborn then they take off fast, the chase is on. Some of ours fall behind. At the clocktower three race warriors make a stand. Come on then, bleeding come on. We slow we stop. The odds have changed. One goes through a window. We circle the other two, they're harder, up for it. Howlers bill from two directions Babylon cops go go go.

playing at soldiers but you tried someone had to

– Yes we did but

The charred window frames of the burned out community centre.

Willy wouldn't have done that

– Yes he would it's what they always do.

Racial awareness training, a residential weekend. Typed schedule, handouts, minutes. A role play, monitoring protocols, impact targets, draft strategies, reviews. Hate crime, report it, we've systems in place.

managers won't save us top down tick box twerps

– It makes a difference. Maybe not a lot but.

Tapes and notes of three interviews, frail women in their eighties and nineties, former blackshirts. Memories, excuses, alibis, photos. The hands of one shake, the second she has a twinkle in her eye. And Joan who always faced away.

it had to be done to get to the roots of it

– It's why I'm here.

I understand you better now dear I see where you're coming from I'm glad we did this aren't you I'll see you tomorrow come in the evening eightoclock I've something to tell you

I haven't been entirely honest with you.

– In what way Joan?

She doesn't answer.

– It may have been a ploy.

– I know. I didn't want it to end either.

– Before your beak let her drop.

– I wasn't indifferent.

another bombers moon look a gold bowl glowing a glorious incarnation the push the pull do come a bit nearer

Headlamps sweep the tresses of a birch tree. An engine dies. I can't see the vehicle from where I'm sitting.

my protectors

I stand to see the roof of the car. Blue I think, it's dark so hard to tell. Lit below the windscreen, hands dance the knobs of a console mixer, rows of sparks of green and red. The driver is explaining something, clasping and parting his hands, compressing the range, gripping a wrist, working the filters, the palms turn upwards, a query. They withdraw. The near rear window drops. A sleeve revolves a hand. Headlights snuff the trees depart. Stocky nurse Vera crosses the cul de sac. Her shoulders shield the face of the hand she shakes.

where were we dear oh yes well here's the thing in thirty-two I joined the blackshirts to keep tabs on them

– Tabs Joan? For who?

I wasn't a believer you know quite the opposite I put on a black blouse to save the left from fascists kept it on to save

*democracy I put a spanner in Tom's works I was pushed to
join by Jimmy Maxton's set I was asked to stay on by Max I
was only with Tom and Willy half the way if that not even
half I couldn't get out I was stuck*

Sing out the song sing to the end.

– So the last few weeks Joan?

I know I'm sorry I was doing it by the book

Her left hand kneads her nape.

*I thought you might stop visiting I rarely see anyone no one
really*

– The reveal?

– One circuit resonating with another.

– Cynic.

*when I was a girl I joined with the independents not the
Labour you put up with no no the real thing the Independent
Labour Party how I ached with longing for a better life for
all but they asked me to leave to snoop to live a lie I agreed
I was an impostor eavesdropping hiding in the Union at my
wit's end until I met my Willy*

Cough, car ignition. Birch trunks, strip lights. Reverse, a whining.

*do you think people see us sitting up here turn the light off
dear I'd rather see than be seen I would say that wouldn't I
the job I had ha I'll tell you all about it I signed I shouldn't
have no one knows no one I'm not meant to talk about it I
can't go without telling someone this is my chance chances
are for taking safer taken as two it's cosier when it's darker
isn't it much more intimate*

All the while her needles pulled the gold and silver thread.

– Spying's immoral.

– Not when you're dealing with fascists.

– Gentlemen don't read each other's mail!

- Send agents, God told Moses, spy out the land of Canaan.

- The greater good, that's the nub.

   a friend of Jimmy Maxton's sent me to join the New Party
   and report back so I did after that to stay near Tom join the
   British Union of Fascists that went against the grain I must
   say speaking out honestly is my way it's what got me into
   politics straight talking standing shoulder to shoulder then
   they told me to do something underhand

A drink in Battersea. Singalong piano, chinking glasses.

- It's jolly in here!

With a nine track fader you make space in the centre for dialogue.

- Anyone can hand out leaflets. We've halls full of women for that Joannie.
  You'll be our amazon knight, a samurai in Mosley's typing pool.

   a Mata Hari I said and we know what happened to her

- You have the looks girl.

   enough I said but I was flattered

- You might help Tom find his way back.

   really I said that would be so do you really think he might

He contrived so subtly, as if he had known as well how to catch a woman in
his net as a partridge when he went a-setting.

Six boot broomstick Maxton, one pair on, two idle. Lappet lashed slabheel
coal cupola toecapped Maxton. Glasgae Jimmy folded sideways on a wooden
chair, hand stash in a pocket. Specs, furl hair, lampshade brows. He leans in.

- Willya help us Joan?

   Jimmy and the boys made snitching feel saintly my socialist
   duty Jimmy was a smart one Tom's headstrong he says
   ambitious he was furious he'd been blocked by MacDonald
   by Thomas lame men in lead socks he could persuade people
   against their interests turn them round I didn't want Tom
   turning on us I had good ears was good at flaps and seals
   yes I said yes and after a bit I was sold on

- In the thirties we thought it was fascism or socialism, Mosley or Cripps, a two-horse race.

- Deception's an honest thing in a good cause.

- They were over in two years, done for.

On Sloane Street Joan covers her eyes with both hands. The contact puts a hat on her head. The brim drops to her shoulders.

- A basic precaution. It won't be for long.

Underwater effects. Muted traffic, high-pitched voices, directionless.

She's walked to a nearby apartment block. Someone takes her elbow and leads her up some stairs. A door opens.

- Let me take that from you. Have a seat Miss Cade.

- It's so bright. I can't see.

- Shade your eyes for a moment, they will soon recover. I believe it's a blackberry gin?

- Yes. Thank you. Yes please.

- I'm sorry we're unable to meet face to face.

The voice has a towel wrapped about its head. A small oval parting in the folds enables it to smoke. She sees an eye. It reclines on a sofa in pajamas, head propped on an embroidered cushion. Joan watches the seesaw ciggy. She sips sweet fizz. Her eyes are drawn by the fingers drumming his paunch. A signet ring leaping. An irregular dance with no discernible pattern.

- Get effects to drape the mic.

- Will do.

- Track upholstery rub.

- Done.

- Run it again from the top.

And they came up unto her and said entice him and see wherein his great strength lieth and by what means we may prevail against him that we may bind him to afflict him and we will give thee every one of us eleven hundred pieces of silver.

– It's your patriotic duty Joan.

he said Tom was a born leader Tom could lead Britain into
trouble away from democracy but you Joan may I call you
Joan he says you can help us bring Mosley to his senses
save him from himself Major Attlee and the Labour Party
need to know what Tom's up to we'll keep them conversant
the authorities need to know the future of the country is at
stake Joan England your people we need to win him back to
commonsense Tom could contribute a great deal to Britain
help us turn him round they need a window on Tom's plans
his thinking they need someone he would trust someone he
might talk to would I help to save him from Tomself would I
help to save him from the enemies of Britain

He spoke this in so much more moving terms than it is possible for me to express, and with so much greater force of argument than I can repeat, that I only recommend it to those who read the story, to suppose, that as he held me above an hour and a half in that discourse, so he answered all my objections, and fortified his discourse with all the arguments that human wit and art could devise. He said says she I'd need to be as wise as a serpent.

– One spy in the right place is worth twenty thousand men in the field.

it was all unnecessary really I was young it sounded
thrilling he offered me four quid a month and I said yes
sealing my fate for cash like that I'd have caught kippers
with me kisser I didn't need asking twice

Joan identifies the officer to me. She describes his mannerisms, his pets and the approximate location of the apartment.

The towel is enigmatic, debonair. The towel's accomplishments are extraordinary. It plays drums in a jazz band, it is proficient on the clarinet. It has published thrillers. The towel's a crack shot, a collector of antique guns. The towel knows more about the occult world than W B Yeats.

I withhold his name and his quirks from publication as this book will certainly be read by fifth-columnists and foreign agents to whom myself and the publisher wish to give no succour.

– A plump man with grey hair and a grey moon face, in rather shabby grey clothes.

– A motor salesman maybe, a retired tea planter.

I'm sorry I misled you dear but now you know the truth of it I went into the blackshirts like a corkscrew to get at their plans their sources of funding to spill the beans on Tom ha spill a bottle of beans words take you where they will Joan the Giantkiller Max calls me I find that out later it's not what he asked me to do was it bring Tom down but I didn't have many scruples dear not really

I felt tremendously bucked when I saw that they thought me clever enough to be a spy. I had never been anything before.

– See if you can lure him into showing the secret of his great strength and how we can overpower him so we may tie him up and subdue him.

It made me feel somebody says the nape. I was carried away it says.

at first it was just getting dates from the diaries who was meeting Tom and where who'd refused to meet him share the gossip steal some headed paper learn his signature that was easy then they say it's time we had the membership list soon I'm getting paid double bubble the shekels twice over then they ask me to find out about the bank accounts and German contacts

That's when I target Joyce, she says. Willy, she corrects herself. He was close to Tom he was privy she says, he was Tom's stand-in.

– We knew that he knew the script.

– And all of the cast.

– We calculated he'd show off. Brag to a dolly.

– He did.

Germany oh Mr Joyce I wish I was coming will you bring me something back something nice what was Germany like Mr Joyce no it wasn't hard soon he started seeking me out

– We're setting up a club to woo the Tories, Joan, the January Club.

– Lovely Lire of Charing Cross, she'll pick up the tab.

– Let's go to Blackpool, we're giving the ballot a miss.

Her hair mounds, falling in curves to her lips, framing her face in a heart. A swelling blouse, the Union Jack, silk bloom at its collar. Cartoon fins for hands, her knees are closed like eyes. The lead of a powder puff puppy trails from a fin. Looped on the other, a hockey stick dangling, a trademark on the blade: MI5 B5(b).

> *from that time on I was neither fish nor fowl not left nor right nor centre I live one way I think something else a right little Joan Bull I'm fake a dissembler I end up lying to everyone*

A choice constantly renewed in solitude.

– You saved the future King from embarrassment.

– Timely calls, they tipped the balance.

> *I wasn't a mercenary I was patriotic it was a civil war oh yes very polite at times ha I'm a fascist for five Eva Braun for the crown blackshirt labour dissimulation's a terrible thing I was snared penned in on all sides a socialist in a fascist party a fascist in the eyes of the world a reporter for the service that blocks our way but somehow I make a go of it undercover is a fanciful word there's no cover at all you're on stage twenty-four hours a day with a suspicious audience back seat critics a script you don't understand pages missing but the show must go on I was always rehearsing scenes in my head calculating every gesture a wrong note at any point the song would stop and I'd be in for it*

– The country comes first Miss Cade.

– Until Hitler is halted.

Sacrifice, and the heart made stonier.

> *old friends who see you call you traitor say you're sleeping with the enemy not that I did not with Tom I wasn't a honey trap they think you've turned you make them think you've turned then you start to see their faults five year fantasies fake stats fingers in their ears so I'm on my own no going back I do not do the good I want to do I'm friendless but I have my wireless I read novels they're my company*

– We'll keep you supplied miss Cade. Mark any books that you'd like in the Listener. I'll see they're placed on your shelf. It's the least we can do.

Too long a sacrifice.

– Spying is lonely and often depressing work.

> *tell me about it I've been there*

– The spy's friendships can only be warily professional.

> *cats cosmetics the weather words without meaning polite lies*

– His appetites and weaknesses, even the small ones, must be rigidly self controlled.

> *choke yourself with your own hands that's what you do you have cash you can't spend shoes you can't wear*

– He must be capable of living for long periods under exceptional nervous strain without cracking.

> *you don't know you won't break till it's over*

– He is, indeed, a very special type of civil servant.

> *every job has a downside a girl has to earn a living somehow unless you get lucky Mr Right a man with a packet I didn't*

When a spy is discovered, he is hanged immediately.

> *one evening I was coming out of Tom's room in the Adelphi I'd been copying appointments from his bedside diary*

– Is it me you're looking for?

Mosley's voice triggers physical reactions with enough variety and intensity to pack a thriller, cover to cover. She falls from his cliff rends to his knife stanches her wound thrashes water spinning, knocked from her feet by Tomfire. Her brow weeps, alar creases flood a philtrum flush salts her lip her tongue bloats, a ball gag ballooning her cheeks. Icebergs collapse her spine. Her hair gluts with an infestation of deadly viruses.

– Me you're looking for?

Tom's voice flutters in the lampshade.

Joan snaps to armour, her lips liquesce.

– Oh Tom I was just.

I come no spy with purpose to explore the secrets of your realm.

I'd been well trained I pointed at the bottle I'd put by the bed

– Vino for we oh how marvellous Joannie yes I'd like that you and I, I want to dearest, of course, sweet Joan, we will but Cissie's here. She'll be here any minute. Let's tryst tomorrow my dear. Tonight I'll dream about you.

you misunderstand O M I say it's a gift from the local branch there's a card attached

– Of course you did, how clever of you, you're a smart one Joannie, we're a kind you and I.

He takes Joan's hand, the hand pointing at the bottle. Tom draws her close.

We all went to bed with him, Georgia says. Afterwards we were rather ashamed.

he strokes my hair touches my cheek he pets me like you won't but he's torn he's listening for Cissie sleeping alone that didn't happen much to Tom he never booked a single bed in his life it's Lady This at the Dorchester Lady That at the Grand Lady That's daughter at the Randolph Miss So and So at the Crillon her sister at Monte Carlo it makes Willy furious not the passes not the affairs he envies those what makes Willy angry is Tom going awol cruising beds never at his post a part time leader it was tricky keeping tabs on Tom

– They never catch on?

Willy saw me with a B5b in the King's Road twice who's your new catch he asks he doesn't cotton on it makes him jealous more ardent I was even more secure

– Who was that chap? The undertaker with the bouquet?

I let him stew in his juice for a week I'll see who I want I say a previous employer I lie a chance meeting he stamps about a bit they do then he suggests a weekend in Tonbridge

I won't describe the meetings in dark reeking alleys, in basements without lampshades, however atmospheric they may have been.

after that we use side streets for contact

– What difference did she make?

Joan's service file lists her duties. From 1934 she organised Mosley's diary and travel arrangements. She minuted meetings and managed the expenditure of the leader's office. Germans and Italians, including contacts at the embassies, went through Joan to get to Tom.

A case of readies arrives from Rome. Specials raid the treasurer's home. They've had a tip-off. Six thousand lire disappears. Nothing was found, say the officers. No record of a seizure in the file. No charges laid. Joan's furious. Sticky bloody fingers, she rages. Mosley suspects a leak, lays off staff. Hard man Henry Vernier shouts at Joan in a basement.

He pulls a cosh from his fly. He slams it on the table.

– You're a snitch Cade are you Jewish too you commie bitch?

He sputs his nose a nod from hers.

– I'll strip you down we'll sell you as parts.

he yells he farts he's foul he thumps the table with both hands he stamps he flicks my ear and yanks my hair he doesn't frighten me nor any of us girls we'd all of us fathers brothers husbands just like him I cared no more than if a pig had grunted they never found me out

During the test of the set no fault was detected.

– You're in the clear girl.

yes a hard flick to the ear you sound a little disappointed would you prefer a maimed and tortured me a rugged 007 to the rescue

The walnut set flamencos. Invisible heels hammer the carpet. Joan turns to me. She holds a golden fan. Her eyes sparkle at the brink.

or Mata Cadi dancing in Tom's office my breasts chafing in carved brass plates studded with pearls plates held in place by golden chains on my shoulders gaudy bracelets cuff my wrists my arms my ankles I'm wearing a headdress feathers flutter I'm magnificently exposed from the nails on my fingers to the nails of my toes but Tom and Willy don't look up they're planning a tour of the north I do the Salome baloney I slither I moan but still they don't look up I get between them and lay on the map Tom kisses me one cheek Willy the other that's the story you want to hear isn't it Joan Cade seductress for the state cloak and dagger totty well wise up I could dance like that for you would you like that ha ha

Ideas of spying and being spied upon touch fantasy systems at deep and sensitive levels of the mind.

– We'll say no more about it.

I'm a hollow woman pleasing everyone I admit I enjoy the excitement but no I was never a fascist

– Was she or not?

– It's hard to tell. I'm not sure she knew.

Anybody can be antifascist. It's being pro something that's difficult.

– What are we dealing with here?

– A tellable slice of national history.

– A theme that plays well with listeners.

– A bit of a twister too.

it's hard to be matey with neanderthals I stay out of Shoreditch keep arms length well away from the knuckle-draggers but the service tells me to mix with members win their trust laugh at their jokes call a yid a rat whatever's needed we want to know what they'll do next I do what I'm told I sip sour ale sow seeds of confusion give feuds a stir and just like that the fools are toms in a sack

I hope this is still interesting for you, she says, I know it's not what you came for.

I turn a page she hears.

what's that you're reading let me see hand it here

Only this I say I give her this.

it looks like a script of some kind what is it

I'm not sure I say it's work in progress.

I see what you're trying to do will it work do you think

Before I can respond, in butt the sets.

– Art offers stability over flux.

– It masters confusion.

– Restores order from chaos.

The highway to greatness, the walnut receiver solemnly tolls, is imitation of the Greeks.

Expressionism, jingles the tran, is a pathological symptom of decline.

Modernism, the pockset screeches, is the crime of a diseased imagination!

– Oh do shut up all three of you.

we argue about Ulysses in the Union most people say it's dirty indecent they haven't read it but we're against censorship people forget that Willy read Finnegan's Wake aloud in the Rundfunkhaus Jimmy Clarke hears him Tom says Ulysses should be published but not read not by everyone ha

All the highbrows see, old faithless explains, is the chaos springing from the welter of conflicting thoughts and emotions of the day. They fail, says the tran, to reduce their experiences to any kind of order. They fling back into the teeth of chaos a still more reckless chaos, the walnut adds. Their products, the pockset declares, are the denial and negation of art.

that's Kenny speaking mister A K Chesterton to you Willy was writing a book on Bloomsbury along the same lines a spiritual pox he spat at the Woolfs a quack's diagnosis I spit back he was clueless sometimes so out of touch the trash he wrote when he was a student let me think for a minute

Away with livid plays of modern sex.

Eradicate, destroy, efface 'complex'.

She gives me back the printout.

you know exactly what he'd think about our little pas de deux don't you dear he'd burn this in a public square you too

It's dark when I leave.

Joan's paling in the starlight, a funerary monument. Sleep holds in its grasp all living things upon the earth. Except me. Thoughts popcorn my lid.

– The crumbling of the moon.

– Raven wings a rustle.

I pass below the mill I hurry down the hill.

I live on a high place because I was an eagle in my youth

Two men, alternating, flap leather coats against a hide cushion. Pumping, a large umbrella spreads then shuts and spreading, shuts, spreads.

– The swan has leaped into the desolate heaven.

Joyce steps back from the studio mic. He flips his script silently, expertly.

Cry of an owl, owl cry and beating coats.

High above the sleeping town she circles, a caryatid airborne, immense. Aerolon wings of stone from nape to heels. Riding the air she comes, lur'd with the smell of infant blood. Engraved she screams, jaw skeletal, hands clutching cockpit head. Her elbows shovel shade. The night hag's marble plaits thrash the billowing caenstone. She's vultural, flint for feathers, shoulders plucked. There's no way this sarsen can fly but she does, every second threatening a fall.

– I know the beating of your wings the sound of death.

Half woman, half bird of prey. Volume which flies in the silence of night, lost.

– There's a story a man not a man saw and didn't see a bird not bird.

She tears me with her beak she blinds me.

Dover and Folkestone have been destroyed Willy says on the

The elements melt, the stars do fall. The umbrella pumps. Ice on my nape, I cower beneath a tree not far from the Watchers.

– Cade's on her rounds again.

– 'Mazing at 'er age s'all I ken say.

He calls in the egress.

– Twenty-two-ten Jack airborne outward over.

A vintage fan, panting. I lift it away from the mic. The curved blades slow. She's calmer.

I sleep right through the night raids I know he's coming

Wings with memory of wings.

– The soul remembering its loneliness.

Matisse lays in wait for homing Joan, flat on his back in the glebe. Bronze Joan hovers, a wedge, eyes incised, throat exposed, nose coning to a lancet lip. Henri cuts poppy from her ribcage. Empty arms close on the fuselage, fleshy flaps trail her feet.

– Touchdown Jack twenty-two-thirty over.

The clamshell opens. Paparazzi flashbulbs pap and razz, strobing. Joan descends the airstair. A nurse attends with a wheelchair. The ladybird takes such possession of the scene all politics goes out of it.

The Watchers step from shadow, applauding.

I join them.

I'm putting my eggs in one basket, she says.

that basket is you I go to the Black House every day I shave their locks they never know

What kind of thing do you get your hands on, I ask.

Willy wrote a report for the Germans the Union is going to capture parliamentary power by means of the ballot box he says hardly a secret and not at all likely but the dog walker's delighted not long after Hitler sends a Scot to meet Tom it's a stressful time Tom's looking for help wherever he can get it membership was falling he can hardly tell anyone that can he it's not the way to raise more funds

– All's going well in the districts, that's what we tell him.

– We knew better!

the Daily Mail dumps us the Public Order Act bans marches and uniforms everything starts to slide money was still coming in from Italy but it's cut right back cash gets tight we leave the Black House for a smaller place on Great Smith Street Tom puts family money in a lot bucketfuls a hundred thousand pounds he can afford it he looks at radio as a way of raising funds a station outside Britain but for Britons like Radio Luxembourg we get Eckersley the BBC's top engineer involved to set up transmitters in Ireland and Sark and Scandinavia for the advertising not so much the politics but put Tom near a microphone it's obvious what will happen next we run out of time the sackings start so many laid off me and Willy too

– Why do you think Joyce went to Germany in thirty-nine?

he can't fight his heroes can he the only nation standing up to bolshevism and Judah Willy wants to prevent war with anywhere but Russia then the Bleeder sacks him he knows they'll jail him if he stays maybe Margaret too I wave him off at Dover no tears not many there's no way of staying in touch once he's gone but I recognise his voice on Hamburg I know it's Willy straightaway he's Jane Fonda reporting from Vietnam

There's no way there's no comparison you can't say that I say to Joan.

I can say what I want dear isn't that what the war was all about no he shouldn't have gone we always said we'd never turn against the Crown but Willy did

– Why does he make that choice?

I don't suppose he had a choice in Berlin a beggar with a wife to feed he'd have done the right thing by Margaret I

doubt she put him first she never did she had an appetite for
men Berlin was a cake stall

– Can we go back to the goodbye. Was anyone else with the Joyces?

I'm not sure it's not easy to say I think so the dog walkers
were pushing him to move to Germany to work for us they'll
never say so but August would have been the last chance to
get him there he speaks with the squirrels after the sackings
I know that they knew he was leaving get out fast one of them
said where else would he go I hope he was on our team if he
was nothing good comes of it they know he'll go to Berlin so
one hand is keeping secrets from the other isn't it I'm sure he
was I don't suppose we'll ever know for certain

Interference.

– They are accusing you of making up quotes.

– That's ridiculous. They're taped interviews!

– Your transcripts are contentious. Your cuts and links are suspect. Your punctuation is described as heavily biased towards an unsubstantiated minority view.

– Censorship disguised as subbing!

– Joan Cade is vague about detail at key moments.

– Her memory wasn't perfect. She was describing things that are traumatic to look back on.

– She manipulated you to erase her support for fascism, it's being suggested.

– So she's not a vulnerable old lady after all? Who's inconsistent now?

– She was a senior administrator in a fascist organisation. The confidante and lover of a spokesman for genocide. She was active in right wing publishing and public meetings, a drummer at intimidatory marches, a go-between for Nazis, a defender of Joyce a convicted traitor. There's no record of her speaking out against fascism before she joined British Union. No dissent during her time with Mosley. Not much after. No one will confirm she worked for MI5. There's not a peep or suggestion of this unlikely story until you come along.

– That's why her disclosures matter. She's been kept under wraps to protect the intelligence services. The spooks don't want to admit Haw Haw worked for them in Berlin. At first at least. Imagine the reaction.

– There's no evidence he did. None.

– The call telling him to go.

– A favour from a friend. Wasn't she just a lonely old lady stringing you along?

– You've heard the tapes. Does it sound like that?

– She tells you what you want to hear.

– Someone's got at you.

– Take the possibility seriously.

– I press her constantly for detail, I search for inconsistencies. Yes, they're there. But I check everything that can be checked. I ask everyone that can be asked. She was plausible. More than plausible. I believed her then and listening again today I believe her now. Can't you hear the relief in her voice? The weight lifting as she shares?

– It sounds like she herself's not sure what happened.

– Joan was used and pushed around. She's trying to make sense of her past.

– Or it simply isn't true. She wasn't a mole. She's covering her tracks, selling you a pup.

– That's bollocks. She told me this would happen.

No reflection from the moon.

An hour after blackout, Joan shades in the garden darkness. She finds the spot – the soil is still soft – where spuds were lifted yesterday. She digs two shallow pits. She works quietly. There are night patrols, rooftop watchers on the High Street, armed men alert in nearby bunkers.

177

A neighbour hears the spade hack.

– I thought she's emptying her lav pail's what I thought.

– Did you look out?

– What were the need?

Joan crams the pits with coked coal. Groping, she backfills most of the topsoil. She lays in mats of copper gauze. On top, more earth. With the back of the spade she pats the pits flat.

There are two copper cones in her wicker basket. She lifts them one at a time, fearing a clink, fearing the chime. They're cold. She holds them close. Ridges and glass insets dimp her forearms. They're breastplates, Turkish dancers wear them. A copper lead is soldered to each cup. She attaches the wires to terminals on the back of a wooden amplifier, spinning wingnuts with her thumbs, touch trained touch sure.

A scrape, frost to her nape, a slam. Back door that's all, a back door pulled to. Who? Squat she pauses. Squat she waits.

– Setting up a transmitter.

– That's back to the slammer for her.

– It's not what she's up to.

Cutlery, squeal of hinges, drop of a latch. Steps recede the lane. Joan remains motionless, crouching woman, compact bush, a blur in the shadow.

One of the leads has a spur. She slides a pinch along the rubber, finding the join. A zinc spike tips the shoot. She stabs it in a pit. A bronze peg is wired to the box. She thrusts it in the twin. Soil falling on a drum. Fingers poking rolled oats. Both together. Here it's silent.

The battery stays in the basket. She connects it to the amplifier. She hides the kit with buckets.

– No need, it's pitch.

– Don't interrupt.

There's one more lead, coiled and lengthy, four linked strands with two loops. She goes to the back wall of the house. Fingering the brick, she finds the hook. She loops one spoke to it. Feeling the way with her feet, listening for cinders, she follows the garden path to a wash pole. That hook is just above her head. She plucks the line. It's taut, no need for a prop. She stoops to the amp. Another earth. She socks the jack, completing the circuit.

- A wishing machine.

- That's kill or cure!

- But why? A diagram, a description, is just as effective.

She flicks the kit on, adjusting the settings. She draws a snap of Willy from a pocket. Cradling the photograph in her hands, she kisses his image twice.

> *I hoped I'd got it the right way up it was dark I couldn't be sure*

- She's playing with fire.

- She knows.

Joan lifts a bucket. She places the image inside the two breast cones. For thirty minutes she sits in the dark on the doorstep.

- Nothing happens till someone wills it.

A warden stalks the lane. He checks the unlit terrace. No light, no longer, or somebody made a false report. He stamps off.

So she slops her pail after dark, says the neighbour. Nowt odd about that.

No sign of a signal, the warden says, it's land of nod out there.

Occult Joan rocks to rocks fro.

> *I wanted to heal Willy not harm him it was me my doing mine*

Ariel looks me in the eye.

- It's definite. Someone's trying to block the programme.

- I bloody knew it.

He slaps a report on the desk. I reach. He snatches it back.

- Obstruction upstairs. First degree with thumbscrews. We've been referred to Editorial Policy and Standards. I'm to explain the circumstances in which the recordings were made. Is or was Joan Cade a vulnerable woman, was she a reliable witness, is she being led, was she being challenged? It doesn't help that no-one can hear your questions clearly. I've got to speak with the family, deal with any concerns they raise. Assemble an appropriately wide range of significant views. There's a budget review too.

– Bastards.

– We'll get it through.

– You're sure?

– It's about principle now. I'm up for the fight.

The fist smoothes long strips of packing tape onto Joan's window. On the sill a sparkler smoulders in a plastic beaker on its side. The fist tugs tape krik krick krrrrrrrrrik again krickrrrrrrrrik the sparker fizzles sputs and stuts.

Correcting faults, the elimination of extraneous noises, the tracing of radio interference. There are a hundred and one factors to consider in order to ensure that a receiver functions satisfactorily and economically.

A holed and hollow plastic shell tied to a piece of string. Whirl it fast whirl slow faster slower wheeeeeeeeeee-oooooooooooooooooo-wheeeeeeeeeeeeee-oooooooooo-eeeeeeeeee routine broadcast whistle.

– Fix that racket or turn it off.

– I'm trying.

The snapping of a stick one hundred times. Pull crackers ten cracks ten more stragglers. A screamer, running. Mix them. The best method of avoiding interference is nearly always to suppress it at the source by connecting suitable suppressors to the apparatus causing the interference.

– Appoint a new producer.

– Use the material in another programme.

If tactfully approached, few will object to the necessary suppressors being installed. In cases where nothing can be done to eliminate the interference at its source it is necessary to consider alternative methods.

– Don't pussyfoot just pull it.

In extremely bad cases of interference it may prove necessary to supplement a suppressor with choke coils.

– Downsize the budget.

Good salaries are paid to capable engineers able to diagnose faults rapidly and apply the necessary remedies.

– Wireless must be managed.

In 1933, in Eaton Terrace in Chelsea, BBC executive Colonel Alan Dawnay holds his first meeting with head of MI5 Vernon Kell. There's a two-item agenda: vetting and vetoes.

– We censor ourselves, we know the national interest.

– We take particular care to achieve due impartiality when a 'controversial subject' may be considered a major matter.

– Our guidelines are robust.

When dealing with 'major matters', or when the issues involved are highly controversial and a decisive moment in the controversy is expected, it will normally be necessary to ensure that an appropriately wide range of significant views are reflected in a clearly linked series of programmes, a single programme or sometimes even a single item.

Cade is a historical hate crime, says Ariel.

– It's going to be a marathon isn't it, uphill with a headwind all the way.

– It's worse than that.

– How do you mean?

– My bag was stolen yesterday.

– Where who took it?

– Someone in the Ship. Last night. I called in on the way home. Two men, I'd never seen them before, they started talking about a village I once lived in.

There's no such thing as coincidence. It's a rule of the genre.

– They named names, knew local stories, the vicar who drank the takings from the fete, who rang the bells at midnight, whose tools changed hands on the turn of a card. I couldn't help joining in. They were pros, I see that now. Ken Brenning and Stephen something. Librarians, that's what they claimed to be. Ken had a war archive so I told them about the series. I thought he'd be useful. I go to the toilet and when I get back they've gone. So has my bag.

When the programme on Cade was commissioned by Canticum, officers interviewed friends and family of the producer and presenter. For a BBC newsletter, they say. A colleague trawled databases.

– We need leverage, anything to influence the station.

– Or interviewees or Cade's family.

– Members of the production team.

– The producer as the last resort.

– Crime, drugs, dishonesty, extreme opinions, sticky fingers weak spots.

– Everything.

They mug up on broken windows, teenage pregnancies, pirate broadcasts, employment histories, forty years of incident and rumour. Rehearsals for the conversation with the target take four days.

– Who was it, the vicar said he'd bank the cash but necked it?

– The fete takings?

– Yeah.

– Oames. What year?

– Sixty-five wasn't it.

– Paid it in at the Rose and Crown!

– Hahahahaha

– Liked a drink. Continued communion on the way home

– Tossed empties in the rectory pond.

– Is that Polstock you're talking about?

Manmade static, jamming and blocking and calming the waves.

Interference is a fact of life. Some hiss is inevitable. The hiss of history. Hiss sets a limit to the amplification it is worthwhile to use.

- Every station has it. Every receiver introduces it.

- There is always some present on the carrier of the transmitter itself.

Evidence log JC599/KWTST/36: audio files, production meeting re interviews conducted with retired operative Joan Cade (11OM/31) relating to her service period with the British Union of Fascists.

- I let my guard down. I knew it would happen. I feel such a fool.

- What do you mean, you knew?

- I've known since the British Library. Donkeys back, the old one, researching Joan. I'd fill out a request for a book. There was always a man in a leather jacket. He'd look up at every sound – the catalogue slamming, coughs, pencils dropping. When I went back to my desk, he'd always be next up. There'd be whispers and glances. Then the trolley wouldn't deliver my item. It's in use or missing, they'd say. Once I tried to stare him down. He didn't blink. He didn't have eyelids. He laughed at me.

- Some of what you used was special access. I don't see how it has anything to do with yesterday.

- Notebooks went missing.

- Like they do. You lose things now. Your pass, your ticket, the end of your sentences.

- That's different, you know it. Nearly every day a blue car would park below Joan's window. No one got out. The rear window opened. Joan's nurse would leave the building and speak to the passenger. Then the car would reverse and leave.

- Is that all? Did Cade notice? Did she say anything?

- My protectors, she called them. They look out for me.

Receiver hiss is a normal characteristic of radio, a fact of modern life.

Sunday afternoon, *Brains Trust*.

Serious in intention, states the Director of Variety. Light in character, adds the wireless. Spontaneous answers to questions you send in, the transistor explains.

– The next question comes from Albert Acton, an oyster fisherman from Kent. When you say fascism, he asks, what exactly do you mean?

– That's the subject of a huge debate.

– What you understand by the term?

– Well, to keep it simple, using force to regenerate unify and purify the nation, seeing one's race as one's nation, violent racialised nationalism, the socialism of nationalists, the socialism of soldiers, antidemocratic paramilitary nationalism, capitalism threatened and defending itself, one of those methods adopted when the threat of the working class to the stability of the capitalist class becomes acute, a terrorist dictatorship generated by capitalism in extreme decay, a political bad smell, the rule of monopoly capitalism in its purest untrammelled form, the stage reached after communism has proved an illusion

From Squadrismo to Guernica, White Terror to Auschwitz. From Operation Condor to Bologna railway station. History's bloody punctuation.

– Open terroristic dictatorship on behalf of the most reactionary most chauvinistic and most imperialist elements of finance capital, a parodic messianism, the discipline required since the Fall, the Chosen People flipped as Volk and Reich, a middle-class juggernaut, political rococo bourgeois bolshevism, an independent and revolutionary third force, an extra-parliamentary mass movement of the right

– Thankyou, that's plenty for us to think about.

– A mass paramilitary movement using the state to abolish politics, the tools of the padrone, ferocious reaction against democracy and the constitution especially egalitarianism trade unionism and socialism, a scar on democracy, a great humourless evil routine, responsibility to those above and unbending authority over those below, the collapse of morality and liberal values, a new religion and transcendence, a resistance to transcendence, genocidal annihilation of other races of rootless loansharks cosmopolitans with no patriotism, an integrated surge of pathological xenophobic and authoritarian psychologies, a movement of cultural despair in which aesthetics replaces rational liberal democratic politics, Wagner in uniform, authoritarian personalities acting in concert on the state, the artist-hero man of action saving the spiritual nation, facilitated by radio, by radio fasci-nation, the hysterical hero unashamed of his antics, lies, false tones and clowning, the masses unchained but

184

misled, everything for the state nothing outside it nothing above it, regimented economic efficiency, an alternative to politics

– OK, let's take a breath to consider

– A counter-revolutionary kick back at Bolshevism, a middle-class hissy fit, the despotic rule of the educated classes as an end to our troubles, revolution against a revolution of untermenschen, true Tudor revivalism, resistance to modernisation, modernisation overcoming resistance

– I wonder, what does the rest of the panel think?

– The petty bourgeois imposing order with an iron hand, spivs leading lumpen chavs, the Italian corporate state, the Italian corporate state perverted by German race theory antisemitism and holocaust, national pride plus the delirium of race, a palingenetic form of populist ultranationalism, a politics done and defeated dead and buried, a movement whose time has passed, a movement which will come again has never gone away, a reflex always reawakening, meat porter mood swing, skinhead gutter politics, white power fantasies, neo-fascists neo-Nazis neo-meta-post-ultras, Great Britain First, a recurring feature of modern globalised capitalism, a network of relationships without a fixed essence, all or some or one of these I think that sums it up.

– I see.

– And then there's Arendt.

– Who?

– The ideal subject of totalitarian rule is not the convinced Nazi or the convinced communist, but people for whom the distinction between fact and fiction and the distinction between true and false no longer exist.

– Oh my goodness that one's scarily up to date.

– As is laugh a minute leadership, the stand-up comic drowning truth with play and insincerity.

– I'm afraid we're out of time.

Select the material.

Desert in sun. Song that's speech. Atonal scrape.

- I am not a German, not a European, perhaps scarcely a human being. The Europeans prefer the worst of their race to me.

A klezmer band with sleigh bells. Funereal trumpet, trudging.

- I am an intruder everywhere, welcome nowhere.

Select a pretext.

At night, on their side of the border, Germans dressed as Poles attack a wooden radio tower, Sender Gleiwitz. Retribution by the German army follows.

- My grandmother was killed.

Poland, brown ink street. An elderly woman face down, hands pinned beneath her gut, toes turned inwards. Her right calf pillows the head of her dead son. Gaunt, expressionless, his arms are crossed and twisted on his chest, hooks for hands. The son's feet tread the side of an aged man with a wispy beard. His father, on his back, dumped parallel to ma.

Resting on the son, the boots of his own boy. The cadaver has been dropped to his right, neatly aligned with the grandparents. This father this son, the grandson, the heaviest contours of the household.

Arm wedged under his back, the head of the son's son rests on the rump of a pale girl with plaits. Face to slab the sister swims the paving, stiff arms scurfing past grandad.

Beneath the peak of boots, below the twisted arms and spine, the shins of a woman, calves of the son's wife, mother to boots. On its back, her carcass branches left, gravid seven months.

At her shoulder, heels to her breast, the corpse of a toddler, hand cold above its head, as if about to throw a ball.

Seen from above, a family swastika morte.

The females were dragged out first. Mother, daughter, mother in law. Next the son, perpendicular, from mother to wife, her knees in his back. Then his son, feet to his midriff, head on his sister. The bearded patriarch last, dumped at the base? Or the tot the final touch.

Maybe not. Head of the family his daughter his wife, three staggered horizontals. Son across them all. Line up the granddaughter, bridge with the grandson, drop the toddler.

Seven lifts seven drops. Or six, free hand sweeping up the mite to save a trip.

– They're lighter than bodies tend to be.

– We get used to it.

Two soldats hoist and heft, the ober steers design.

– Curve the girl at the hips, yah that's it. Now separate the plaits, follow the vake of her arms, that's good and close the eyes.

Street art on yellow card.

– Not pleasing to the eye.

– Cut it?

– No.

– Should art shield our eyes?

– It mustn't.

Max opens a chain of wireless shops in the 1930s. He knocks out People's Receivers on the cheap. Cut rate two-band citizenship.

– Our sets stifle Slav channels. They're the very latest. Our sets don't pick up negro signals. They bypass Judeo-bolshevik stations. German wireless sets at German prices for the German people.

After the war, he finds a loophole in the controls on wireless production. Heinzelman, a valveless radio, squeezes through. Heinzelman fathers the Weltklang. She's legit and mother to the Grundig Boy. He's portable. In ten short years the family is the biggest begetter of radio in Europe. Fruitful they multiply. Television, tape recorders, dictation machines, typewriters, cassette players, colour sets, car radios, video recorders, quadrophonics, talking clocks, satellite TV, the cordless phone, internet TV, voice recognition, connected white goods.

– Mahler playing from a food mixer.

– Free jazz toasters.

– It's a miracle.

Wireless receiver on a coastal shelf.

A cupboard pub with a dial. It's an inn in Kent, the announcer says.

– A quiet after work kind of place early on a Wednesday evening, a good spot for a pint, a smoke, the evening paper on the way home. The kind of place you might relax for half an hour while the pans bubble and your wife sets the table. The Old Neptune a wooden alehouse on Whitstable beach.

Willy is hunched at the counter, cupping a tumbler. The barman towels a tankard. Willy croons a patriotic anthem to his glass.

– Hark the sound of many voices echoes through the vale of ages.

One of the pump handles has been replaced with a mic, a lozenge-shaped ear on a stick.

Willy pushes the brim of his hat to the crown of his head. He places both hands on the bar. He straightens his arms, he stiffens his back, he sings more loudly.

– Britain listens and rejoices gazing on tradition's pages.

Behind him, couples and pals and loners listen to the song. As Willy pauses to sip from his glass, pensioners at a window table whisper the chorus. Keep the flag forever high. Families on neighbouring tables join in. The volume of the song rises. A brass section bucks rhythm in the corner, a guitar swingles into view. From an alcove drums ratchet up the tempo.

Willy pitches the next verse boldly, sliding from his stool.

– Patriots your cry is heeded heroes death was not in vain.

A trumpet toots exuberantly, chased by a snare. Everyone in the bar turns to face the band, everyone except Willy. He returns to his seat, setting his elbows on the bar. The music continues. He props his chin with a hand. He seals his empty glass with the other. He uncovers the glass. The barman pours.

A couple rise from a table, hand in hand. They dance. She spins, his arms winch, she kicks, his palm hovers over head, their feet dab, hips gyre in hip sync. Willy sighs into his drink. Jazz swings and swirls and flaps behind him. He takes no notice. The walnut receiver resumes its report.

– A waiter in a white jacket is spinning a plate on his finger on the edge of the dancefloor. It's getting rather lively in here now.

A clarinet sprees. Willy raises his head, canting.

– We to your place have succeeded Britain shall be great again.

Now we will hear a short drum solo, the announcer says softly.

– Notice how the rhythm changes pace and direction, taking unexpected turns, interrupted with pauses and unusual taps and tempos. That's the wireless loudspeaker he's striking now.

A seated man, elderly in a suit, scowls shaking his head. Short horn bursts, a breaking tempo. Rising he shouts:

– Bars require licenses for this kind of thing!

He pulls on white gloves. He rolls up a newspaper. Bending to pick up an umbrella, he turns, grins, and tapdances through the bar. He thrusts his chest forward, brolly ticking, his heels flicking at tables.

Applause erupts from the seats.

– Captain Keam has taken to the floor and it's turning into quite a night here at the Old Neptune!

Smiles split mugs, cheers pop the length of the bar. More tapping, from where, heads turn. Tapping at the door which edges open.

Joan enters in a broad hat and kinema cosmetics, her cheeks planing with tilt lines, a sharp nasal shadow skewing her jaw. She flounces through the crowd and parting dancers. The captain returns to his seat. As Joan approaches Willy's back he spins an empty glass. She stands behind him. She swivels her hips, bumping the stool with her butt. She jabs her elbow in his back. He turns to object. He grins and slides off his perch, taking her hand. Palm to palm, forearm to forearm, they sidestep onto the dancefloor, his ear to her breast, her cheek to his crown.

Beach bar ballroom bliss the barbarous clanging of a gong last orders please.

They dance into a recess. I glimpse them spinning in a bright chink between a chimney breast and the neck of the man standing in front of me. I squint through the living keyhole, brick and nape soft with down.

As they return to the centre of the bar the jig switches. Willy's right hand rests on Joan's handbag. He's thumbing the catch. Two of his fingers steal into silk. A pound note rises between them.

The wireless, masked by a sleeve. Rose nails pinch the dial. That's all we've time for here on the coast tonight, says the host. He wanes, the plates of the capacitor yawn, electrons thin to shiss.

- Join us for another BBC surprise party in a town near you tomor-rowsshh.

It's late. Joan's tired. It's time to go. I pack and whisper gnight. As I leave the room I sense someone else withdrawing.

Smoke, sour coat, scotch breath. A listener's lighter tread.

Letter from America.

So many gaps to fill, asides to consider, years to check. What was Joan doing in the United States in the fifties? Her answers – radio, I told you, radio my father and advertising – had been evasive. On whose payroll, doing what?

I pick up pointers here and there.

- Off the record, Ms Cade was placed Stateside. She'd been treated badly after the war, no fault of her own. She kept tabs on persons of interest, Americans that Mosley had met, Coughlin's followers.

Nine months it took to get that interview. Was it the truth?

Astra, the daughter, wouldn't comment.

- It would be really helpful. Anything you can tell me would.

- Leave me alone.

I gleaned a few pointers.

- Radio the Motown sound. I hadn't a clue what it meant.

- Did a flit with a wireless engineer dint she. Cross the pond. Griddance I thought, Nazis ain't welcome here.

- Joannie used to boast about the stars she'd met, Little Richard the Supremes.

She was hard to piece together.

> *Washington the windy I loved Memphis race music they called it the sound which became rhythm and blues life it was new life fifty wasn't so old I sold radio slots*

The crown of her head is a vortex, spinning floss across her scalp.

jazz clubs that's the only place I'd seen blacks before you didn't see many outside London not unless you were looking to sometimes one or two from off the barges but nothing like later or the states

The thirties were the peak of white supremacy, spurts the crown. We've had racial recession ever since, adds the nape. You have to give everyone a chance pleads the crown, fair goes for all. Loss of prestige, towns, jobs continues the nape, schools a babel, surgeries full. That's all we can expect now, they nod. The transition to a more equal society will be convoluted, says the crown. There will be resistance, says the nape, new openings for fascism. They both nod vigorously.

– What were you up to in America Joan?

ad sales I learned a lot in America white business wanted black customers not like here in the states radio chased the black dollar that opened the door to rhythm and blues to civil rights to rock and the sixties we chased down sales and sponsorship took what we could get purchasing power is a great equaliser in this world Tan Coffee House that show was the game changer the direction sponsors point that's the way you go we were called race traitors race music takes over radio everything else is squeezed to give it room current affairs religion talks other kinds of music

Two decades it took she says, I saw most of it through. Music and markets drive change, she says, politics doesn't.

– Pop doesn't change laws. It can't.

it changed everything if you were over the age of twenty you didn't exist as far as the controllers and deejays and sales teams and sponsors were concerned no playlists for past-its every other kind of music and programming was pushed aside radio was youth and nothing else America wasn't a country for older women the young in one another's arms dodos like me looking on enviously I was young once but too soon phuh so I come back

I met her doctor in a beach cafe. Cat out of a bag she was, then tight as a clam.

- Joan was never there it's all fantasy she's never even been to the States not Joan.

- She says she had a job in radio.

- I know but she didn't.

- She met a real father there?

- After the war there was a period of, let's say, difficulty in Joan's life for a number of years. I think that's generally known. She found it hard to cope. I believe she had some residential treatment during that time.

- What kind of treatment?

- The notes don't really say. I shouldn't be telling you this. I don't know why I am. I'd like to help.

- But people remember her going to America.

- That's not possible.

- So why would they say that?

- I don't know. Ask them. She was here all the time.

- Was it a breakdown, in a mental hospital? I mean mental health support. How ill was Joan who put her there?

- I really can't say. I've said more than I ought.

- Why so long. Ten years?

- I have to go.

After that I didn't know what to think.

Gangsters and thugs.

That's what the fash were, says 94-year-old Reuben Reznick, when I join him in the garden of the care home.

- Gangsters and thugs, failed businessmen, maladjusted soldiers, small shop keepers, Jew haters all of them. If there'd been an invasion they'd have built camps and ovens. We knew it. We had sources. Ears on the inside. They had the same murderous fantasies. Take no notice of what the Cade bitch says, she has our blood on her hands, Jewish blood and British blood. She wants her past made over, that's the only reason she's speaking to you. I bet she's not confessing is she. I bet she isn't and I'm no gambler.

I'm trying to understand, I say, why people like Joan supported British Union.

– Understanding is the wrong approach. They were murderous anti-semites. We have to confront fascism without flinching, not give it airtime. Giving them a hearing is collaboration. Forgiveness is not for her kind. I'll withhold forgiveness to the end. I'm looking forward to Lilith Cade's end, I'll hold a party. I'll splash out for marshmellows. I'll play the trombone. We'll dance in the corridor and burn her mattress here in the garden.

Mrs Resai is a cleaner at the home. We talk in a storeroom during her coffee break.

– You listen too much to this lady Mrs Cade. She is very confused. Don't believing her. My husband is from Rajastan, we are from Rajastan. She says a man, Professor Joyce, will be the Viceroy of all India when I am a girl. He would stop the independence. Who is this Professor Joyce? My husband studied history in Delhi. He is not in the books. He is not an important man. Mrs Cade she is not honest, not at all. She uses bad language. She says bad words about Tom Owem. Who is Tom Owem please? She is sad, looking at the window, her children do not visit.

I have one more exchange with Astra, the daughter. She doesn't want to meet me. She doesn't want to talk to me. I record her over the phone.

– With permission?

– Well, she knew I was making a programme.

– In other words?

– No.

A television vexes in the background. Astra's voice is all but lost in comical music and laughter, a children's programme. The recording is unusable.

– The old mother and me hehooeeuhuhuh aren't close you know. Never nor will be.

An overblown horn, drum slam.

- Mother kept me on a tight leash. Sometimes she'd leave me with neighbours, I didn't mind that, she'd be razzing it up with actors and musicians, putting on airs. I met a few. She'd stink of drink when she got in. Next morning she wouldn't get up. She'd shout me my breakfast and off to school from her bed. I married as fast as I could, got out. She's a stranger to me, always was.

- Nanny the elephant fell over nanny nanny look.

- Not now Cosmee I'm on the phone. Look she has some demons that's her it's how she is it's what she is. She lives in a world of her own, she goes on and on about stuff I don't want to know I've my own life.

A hooter hoots, the young girl yays.

- It's a long way up that hill I have grandchildren to look after that's all I've got to say so I'm putting the phone down.

I ask Emeritus Professor Howard-Dunne for background on the Black House, the fascist headquarters in which Joan worked. Mosley's office leaked like a sieve, he told me.

- There was endless gossip, many blackshirts sold stories on the side, making them up at times, easy pickings for journalists. The trade unions put a spy in there, more than one I expect. The senior ranks were at each other's throats most of the time. Joan Cade was promoted from the typing pool. She mixed with the leadership socially. She was Mosley's Girl Friday on the inside track. She may have had affairs. There's nothing definitive on that. Mosley doesn't mention her by name but that's hardly surprising. She joined at the off in thirty-two and left her post in thirty-eight. She's interned during the war. Later on there was speculation about what she had really been up to, an undercover snoop for the left, sand in the works, something covert, mostly put about by her I suspect. That water's very muddy. Generally speaking, she wasn't believed. No value to scholars.

The morning after we speak I bump into him on the steps of the care home. He's on the way out, carrying a clutch of files. He nods but doesn't speak. Hi I say bye to the seam on the back of his jacket. He raises a hand to the Watchers and doesn't look back.

- Warning her off.

- Stealing your thunder. He'll get to print before you.

Beyond the beeb.

From Joan's window we could see abandoned metal forts standing in the estuary. It annoys me to see them today. They remind me of someone I failed to interview, a household name who would have upped our ear count.

> *such fun on the old sea fort Sutch Radio on Shivering Sands David Lord Sutch was a breath of fresh air oh lordy flawed Sutch that's what I called him he understood radio he gives the new gang hell never lets up ha the fogeys splutter over their radiograms he used to read Fanny Hill and Lady Chatterley over the air the fishing boats circled to listen their catches go down hahaha*

Cream of The Pops. Swing with Those Chicks. Vote for insanity, you know it makes sense! The Savage Teenage Party. Every part of me was open, and exposed to the licentious courses of her hands which like a lambent fire ran all over. Truth! Stark naked truth is the word. Radio Sutch, the first teenage radio station. It's a pity the cannon have gone!

> *David wires a record player up with lorry batteries he lets the best albums play themselves over and over just like you would at home there was no soundproofing you could hear engineers and visitors coughing doors slamming he'd shout he screamed it was a holiday in your head not audible wallpaper the BBC but radio reinvented Dave Berry The Outlaws Max Miller The Fortunes over and over*

Anyone who thinks that the pirates prove a demand for local radio of that kind is deceiving himself. That is the official view of the postmaster general.

– For a little bit of heaven tune to 197.

The BBC has exposed itself to pirate competition through a policy of refusing to provide what most people want, concedes the postmaster general.

– We have an announcement to make. This is not the BBC.

Yellow on black, a skull and femur party hat. DON'T BE A PIRATE! glares the eyepatch. That's the official view of the postmaster general.

– You need a license to look or listen. TV four pounds, radio one pound, a pound for car radios too.

Pirates have given radio a new image, says the head of advertising. He has

195

an eyepatch and a parrot feathered with dollars on his shoulder. Advertise, the parrot squawks. New image on the air on the air a ton a minute ton a minute.

– For the man in the car, driving alone, and for the lonely housewife, these stations provide instant companionship. To the teenage audience they mean instant beat presented in a happy package of pops, plugs and pleasantries.

> *transistor radios weren't much use if you wanted to listen to pirate radio the signals were faint tranny aerials were too small they couldn't pick them up properly*

– Weak as foam on sands.

– As wavering as Hamlet.

– They're broadcasting to an audience of seagulls.

> *that's why I keep old faithless going David and the pirates one of the reasons I wanted to hear the newness of it all the Tom and Willy and David of it all the breakthrough commercial radio arriving here the American now*

The estuary is calm and clear today, the tran crackles, perfect weather for the authorities to deal with the pirate broadcasters. Fanny tonight on 197! squeaks the portable. A little bit of heaven on one nine seven bellylaughs the walnut.

– From the helicopter I can see Whitstable over on my right, Southend to my left, and the river Thames spilling gently towards the North Sea below me. We're circling one of the sea forts at Shivering Sands, looking down on it. It's noisy up here, so I do apologise for having to shout into the microphone as we loop.

The fort is a group of iron strongboxes on concrete stilts, rusting cells with windows. They are linked by walkways. On one there's a banner attached to the railings, RADIO SUTCH it shouts in capitals SONGS FROM FANNY HILL.

– That's a reference to the obscene novel they have been reading on the air illegally. I can see the pirates who have taken over the fort very clearly. They are a motley bunch, dressed in leopard skins with long shaggy hair, cartoon cavemen. One of them is waving a flag at us, a skull and crossbones of course. Another is shaking what looks like a cutlass. There's an army helicopter sitting empty on the airdeck. A shocking scene is unfolding right below us. The pirates have bound the arms of the pilot, who appears to be an officer, to his sides. They are making him walk a plank which extends from one side of the fort. Their victim must be at least fifty feet above the water, perhaps higher than that. The leader of the pirates, Screaming Lord Sutch as he is called, is prodding the officer with a large and extremely dangerous-looking blade. Sutch is in leopard skin as are his followers. He is distinguishable by the enormous pair of horns which are attached to his helmet. There's a woman in a cocktail dress down there too and oh my word I think she's carrying a gun. They're freeing his hands. My goodness the officer now has only one foot on the plank the other is poised above the drop he appears to be shouting at his captors surely they are not going to force him oh my goodness no this is horrendous he's in the water.

On the transistor Joan and I listen in to hoopla from the fort.

– The crocodile and the ghost, Mr Punch, that's British politics. First they frighten us. If that doesn't work they use the stick. Vote for the National Teenage Party! More sausage less mash with panache.

> *old mains sets multivalve receivers with attic aerials or outdoor aerials they gave the best reception people have forgotten that I always said if you want to hear the sixties clearly listen on a nineteen-forties set I stand by that*

The helicopter fades. The footboard receiver pouts Sutch vaudeville.

> *The monster's the most I'm his number one fan*
> *Yes I've fallen in love with this monster man!*
> *She's fallen in love with a monster man*

> *everything was a game to David I called him Lord Haha make of that what you will a lovely man Sutch a lovely he was David was a true friend he made me laugh*

– I carry a swordstick. To protect myself from folk fanatics! End licensing laws! Cut hospital waiting lists! For broken legs get plastered at the pub.

> *hahahahahahaaa*

The zista issues bulletins on the flotsam pilot.

– It's peeing down here on Shivering Sands, so this morning Uncle Harold kindly sent me a raincoat, a Gannex. It was special delivery from number ten, a whirlicopter dropped it off. We're keeping that too. And guess what, my deary earies. We discovered our postie's amphibious! He's swimming for Herne Bay pier right now. Midday ETA. Finest job in the world they say. SOS save old sausages! BBC Boring the Bloody Country.

Work and play all over the globe. Go to war on an egg.

– I was a kid in the blitz. I taped kitchen knives to the wheels of my tricycle. I fought Roman tablelegs. I sieged a Roman sofa. Radio Sutch the four Rs, reading writing rock and roll. Britain fools the waves!

David knew Reg who took the station over Reg used to be his promoter that ended badly Radio Sutch was a hoot while it lasted Radio City came next there was Radio Invicta and King and 390 and such an argy bargy between them Reg was murdered his killer got off

Offshore gangsters are stealing copyright, endangering the livelihood of musicians, taking wavelength illegally, interfering with other stations and endangering shipping! The pop pirates are a national menace! States the postmaster general.

– I couldn't believe the whole government machine and the establishment would stop something not causing any harm to anyone and giving such a great deal of pleasure. I hoped it would go on forever.

Commercial pirate citizens band! It's time to stop the rot from the top!

– I think we have to seriously consider the enormous disadvantages of having a vast army of people who can communicate with each other very easily.

– Thankyou for joining us, Lord Wells-Pestell.

if radio wasn't controlled by governments and corporates we'd be able to hear what's going on around us properly we'd hear the other side of things radio pushback we'd say the other side of things new points of view broadcasting's not conversation but it's a start

– The lifeboat is a few yards from the officer. He's been fighting the waves for nearly nine minutes. They're throwing him a line now and yes he's in safe hands at last. They're hauling him in, he's almost on board.

*I so wanted a job in radio an announcer deejay secretary
any job it's why I cross the Atlantic I try out with David he
does his best for me Dee Cade he was going to call me the
Dee Cade Decade was the name for the show joining bits of
songs from different times together montage my voice was
too grey for the station I never made it don't let that happen
to you dear don't be deflected where have you got to getting
our chats on the radio*

I'm getting nowhere I admit. The casters aren't biting. She turns the wireless up at that. Loud, far too loud for us to continue. It's her way of saying leave.

– I'm sorry Joan I haven't given up.

I don't mind the early finish. I've things to get on with. The continual search for evidence. Confirmations. Corroboration. I need to know more about Radio Sutch. I seek out out memory Ed. He's in the bar on the beach. I ask him about Shivering Sands.

– You remember it?

– Ooooh yeah. Sutch. Reg Calvert. Smedley. Pine. Yeah coursadoo.

– You listened?

– Oooooh yeah. Little bit of heaven. But who wants to know about that these days.

He rolls a smoke in a rip from a library history book. On one wrist he sports a torc, on the other a pocket watch hanging from a bracelet. The ring's roman, lion intaglio. His clothes reek. We step outside so he can suck a cough by the sea wall.

– What did they play? What were their links with the town?

– Four tunes and lotsa stuff. Hoarragkhich! Pth-tha. They used the basement café of the record shop for business. Heuck. Ptha! Loads of visitors from London they had, loads. If you want to try out as a deejay you go there, a record to plug you go there, just for a gander you go. I used to go there, now and again I went coursadid. Oooh yeah cream of the pop the Krays were in it of course this is not the beebysea ooh yeah the twins yesso.

– They came and went by boat from here?

- What the twins?

- No the staff. The team that worked on Shivering Sands.

- The Harvester took stuff out a couple of times a week. Provisions food you know, tins and beer. It was a tragedy.

- What was?

- Tom Pepper drowned didn't he. Woke up one morning dead on the beach. Fred Downes, the Harvester was his. His waders fill by the harbour, he dies in the mud. That was later. Drops a piece of wood in the drink walks out to fetch it and goodbye. And Reg the guvnor he was shot.

- Pepper was Red Sands wasn't he? A different station.

- Scold out here innit.

We return inside. A Watcher in a white coat enters. She orders a spritzer. I touch Ed on the shoulder, mouth a silent thanks and nod to the publican. He bolts the door behind the new arrival. I slip behind the bar and leave by the kitchen. The lock clunks behind me. As I jog along the beach the white coat flaps from window to window. I pause in a gateway. I crouch behind bushes. I'm not being followed. I circle home slowly. Forty minutes later I walk into a toyshop. I leave by a backdoor, climb a gate and drop through the skylight into my kitchen. I thumb the radio on, keeping the volume low. Hishfuzzen-click coastal storm then:

- This is not the BBC.

I roll the dial.

- To be uninformed is to be unarmed.

That's more like it leave it there.

- A microphone in one hand and a gun in the other.

A freedom signal, broadcasting from deep in El Salvador. Air journos firing news bullets, accompanying the people step by step in the march to victory.

- Listen to Radio Venceremos! Where the mortar blasts are real.

They search for a microphone stand. All they can find is a crucifix. They lash a microphone to it.

- A thousand campesinos murdered in El Mozote

- People joined up because of Santiago's voice

I nudge the dial again.

- The walkie-talkie of the riots!

A crossroads in the air, twenty hours of free speech daily, information from listener-callers, analysis by listening groups, a station without walls.

- Any comrade who knows anything, give us a call.

- No censorship, political or aesthetic. Listen to Radio Alice!

- Radio for participants.

- Radio of the uncanny.

I sit at my desk at my keyboard.

Mao-Dada! the set calls up the stairs.

- Towards a network of guerrilla radio stations!

Interrupt the language of machines, of the work ethic, of productivity. The practice of happiness is subversive only as it becomes collective. After a while you stop hearing it.

Hummmmn hmnnn hums Joan.

there's a photograph I want you to see it belongs to Major Thurlow it will set your mind at rest we'll have to go there

Hmoooon hmhm hmnoooowwwm.

- I could collect it.

no I have to go in person John won't open the door to anyone else we'll have to go ourselves an outside broadcast

- No problem. There's a car I can borrow.

oh goody a spin speak to the desk for permission they won't say no I've told them already hmmmnnnoooon

- When do you want to go?

today of course this afternoon I'm ready now you fetch the

car they'll bring me down HMMMnuuuu

When obstinate causes of modulation hum are found it is always worth while to try operating the receiver somewhere else.

– I'll be back in half an hour. Are you sure?

when aren't I am I sure of course I am or I wouldn't be asking off you go what's keeping you

When Joan is wheeled to the car her face is swathed in silk, a pink wave which sweeps over her head, across the chin, back over the shoulder. She's wearing panda shades. Only her lipstick, the nose and a finger of forehead are visible. She's encased in a mauve leather coat and knee high boots. There's a multicoloured ribbon on her chest. She's eyecatching, a head turner incognito. In her lap she clutches a battered jewellery box.

Eyes front she says and put the radio on.

Caroli the sound of the nationnnnnn Caroli the sound of the lannnnnd Carohmmm grrrrzzz. Joan's humming the station's zuffing the car radio growls quietly as the engine pounds.

– What's in the box Joan?

on the need to know list are we

– Ok.

The nurse whumps the car door and steps back. She gives us both a hertzy wave.

– Have her back by four. Call if there's a problem.

– Will do. Belted in?

drive along the coast first I need to check for a tail don't stop at any lights when did you last do a sweep of the car

– You think I'm bugged?

no it's dusty back here

– Where to Joan?

Church Road

Boss radio your all day station we're on the air in a safety harness spinning the hits, around and aground we go.

She unbuttons her coat. The lining is silk, a brilliant orange embroidered with ears and eyes.

– That's beautiful Joan.

> *it was a gift I know it's lovely Gheeraerts for special occasions Johnnie Major Thurlow he's special*

The streets are empty we're there in a trice. But finding the right house, parking, waiting for Thurlow to get to the door, waiting as he coaxes a dog into the garden, explaining my mission, returning to the car, getting Joan back into the wheelchair, manouevring the chair to the front room of the house, that takes the best part of fifteen minutes. Wait in the car she says.

– How long will you be?

> *come back in an hour exactly knock three times loud then count to five knock three times softer three five three ok?*

I sit in the car reading *An Elementary Wireless Course*. The wiring associated with circuits forms a sort of network. There is an appreciable capacity effect between them. Any current which wants to leak, leaks to this screen. There must be no stray couplings, no danger of interaction. The hour passes. I close the gate behind me. The dog erupts. I knuck-uck-uck hard, I count and sock three.

– Yes?

– I've come back for Joan.

– Who?

– Joan.

– Who is it you want?

– I brought her here an hour ago?

– Oh, you mean Mata, come in

It was my nickname, she says from the sofa.

Her lipstick is smudged, lopsiding her smile. The pink scarf is smeared. As we leave she says:

> *take a different route back always vary the route be*

unpredictable you'll stay alive longer

– You're the boss.

Wonderful Radio London!

Roadside lights by the old toll gate stare red. A generator guns nearby. A labourer leans against a wall flicking through a redtop. He glances our way then tosses the paper aside. He whistles.

I don't like the look of this it's a trap go go reverse get away from here

– Don't get alarmed Joan, it's just road works.

there's control with the radio running the op go go

– What radio?

A cottar in a trench has a mobile to his ear. Faces reflect in the windscreen, headphones to their ears. High visibility jackets approach.

get us out of here move

She's frantic.

– The light's green Joan, here we go.

don't stop not for any reason don't stop

The labourer climbs from the trench, stepping into the road. He slices his throat with the side of a hand. A studio door opens.

run him down the fascist

As I swing around him he bends and looks in the rear side window. What's going on? It's Mark, my producer. He thumps the boot twice. Joan screams.

Boss radio, hit on hit.

they're on to us they're closing in it won't be long

– Who is they Joan? Who are those people?

floor it bloody floor it

She thumps the back of my seat. In the mirror I can see the labourers shouting, running after us. They give up and jab at phones.

I drop the hammer. The tyres wail nonchannel frequencies.

Charlie Alpha Delta Echo, breathless Ariel barks.

– Eyes on.

– What's your twenty?

– Ask the scripty.

go past my road go up to the roundabout come back down

– Sure, of course. I can do that.

I blast the car up the hill. Burning oil we centrifug the pond of grass and exit. I catch a blue to the rear, listing in our wake. Another blue oncoming, hustling to the rounder. Blue at the side window, blue wing and rear, the screen green as a car launches into our lane from a side road. I swing right and brake to avoid a smash. Straightening I see a pink scarf in its rear window, Joan's hand beating the driver's seat, my own mess of hair. The green car horseshoes to the other side of the road, shrinks in the mirror.

Traffic news on the hour.

I slam down a gear, and stamp. The engine hollers as we pull away from our pursuers. The seatbelt bites my shoulder as I brake for another car joining the hill.

he's boxing us hit it go go break out

A van breasts the brow ahead of us it hootootoooooooooots the driver is leaning to the screen pumping her palm towards the roundabout, pressing us to turn around. She's wearing headphones.

do a youeee do it now now

I plunge the wheel right, and tug the brake. The teeth of a metal comb rake a steel plate. The car rocks up the kerb and drops. Two kicks at a cardboard box.

Receding bursts of blue. Counterclock the rounder Joan yells, go right! Spank a plastic cushion. A medley of engines, rapid heartbeat, clomping pedals, deep sucks of breath.

The lights of the van wink left, wink right and left. A pen, click it. One and. Two and. Three and. My mirrors void, the road behind is empty. The road in front, all the lanes converging on the rounder, are empty.

not a word to the nurse not a hint nothing happened now get

When we're back in her room, she hands me a photograph. In the picture, Joan's middle-aged and standing with a group of black musicians. One holds a guitar, another a saxophone. They're wearing yellow sequin jackets with dark lapels and stage grins. Joan has a microphone in her hand, a salt shaker. It's pointed at a young woman, a face I almost recognise a name I ought to know but don't.

  – It looks like you, Joan, in a broadcast?

> *from my time in Memphis the Supremes I told you all about it sieve brain there's your proof*

  – Why does Major Thurlow have it?

It's his, the nape explains, he took it.

Pages from Europe's bloodiest chapter.

Let's talk about something else today she says.

> *did you know Peter Cushing lived in Whitstable we used to spend wonderful days together he was a gentle man*

  – Are you there Peter?

A film poster commands the entrance hall. Explosions flame on pink, a vampire stalker, Sherlock SS black, whip primed about to crack. SAVAGE JACKBOOT, tanks and gunfire, HAMMER corpse and cleavage.

I'm here, Cushing calls out of shot, I'm here he shouts from the upper landing. Joan looks up the sinuous stair. I am near but also far he hams, the camera shifting up a floor. And there he is, eagle beak above red flag, swastika branding on white. Cheery Holmes van Helsing, doctor Franken Who himself, hand flapping.

  – Come on up Joannie. Park your pony and pour one.

The stairs are lit like a movie set. Her silhouette grotesques the well.

  – Mum palled up with Peter Cushing the actor. He's dead now. They made an odd pair, people used to point and stare. It was like seeing a trailer for one of his films.

Soon after the friendship with Joan commences, Cushing paints a self portrait, a watercolour of himself as a Nazi general with a brutal scar carved chin to temple.

– If you step back a little, you'll see it better.

> *Peter was a dear a rock he asked about the blackshirts too tell me about yourself Joannie you and the traitor the voice of Berlin explain that to me please Peter was arrested during the war making Nazi flags in his room ha for a film he says your secret's safe with me I tell him he laughs at that he was fascinated by all the regalia he had model armies he was sound of course I saw him in Watch on the Rhine playing a German funding the antifascists I went with B5b a pleasant chap he's marvellous in Hitler's Son an old commander rebuilding the reich round the Fuhrer's boy that was my Peter they didn't release that movie he's SS in Shock Waves too perfectly cast Peter was made for those roles a retired Nazi a beach recluse Savage Jackboot would have been the peak of his career we both said so oh we had wonderful times together Willy spoke to me through Peter helped me to my feet*

– How do you mean, spoke?

An elderly man with a facial scar sits on a bench on the beach. He takes in the estuary. Is that a seal looking back? No. An aryan head, a blonde soldier in goggles, rises from the tide. The figure registers the watcher on the shore. Another head rises to his left. To his right another. The seals stand and multiply, statuesque. I'm here, Commander Cushing calls to his mermaid kamerads.

I'm here, he calls down to Joan.

The amphibious squad slops towards the shore, converging on the seat on which I sit my notebook open.

I'm here, Joan replies, how are you this morning Peter. She walks into the lounge.

– Reading is not an end in itself but a means to an end.

Peter Heinrich Hassner is reading Mein Kampf to a young man wearing leather shorts. He puts a finger to his lips, tip to the root of his scar.

   – I'm a gentle fellow, never harmed a fly.

Peter suggests they go to Paris together.

   – Let's hop a hovercraft Joannie, we'll be there and back in a shake.

They sightsee in a sedan. Paris Opera Champs-Elysees Arc de Triomphe. Posing by the captured Eiffel, a shot of Peter in a cap a tie a trenchcoat, clasping gloves.

   – The lift cables are cut. There's no way up.

   – We'll do Napoleon's tomb instead.

15 Rue Miromesnil, the rented apartment. Joan's head is framed by a red lampshade. She's writing in a red notebook, writing with a red pen, consulting a pamphlet with a red jacket, each red a match to the shade. A controlled palette. Behind Joan, on a shelf to her left, there's a short wave radio. Its splayed antennae double in a mirror. She could tune the set with her near hand, the left, but she doesn't. Twisting towards Peter, Joan reaches over her right shoulder, leaning back, arching and bubbing.

   – Johnson giggles and me I wiggle Mao Mao

Light opium of uninterrupted rhythm.

Peter kisses her nape.

   – What's the book Joannie.

> *I was never a student girls didn't not then no you're lucky*
> *grants is it loans a library encouragement no I never enter*
> *the academy no such luck I study alone autodidit my way*
> *don't waste the chance you've got*

Radio the Russians eat and would you like to dance asks Peter. She would she does she dances Mao Mao. It was the dream of my life to be permitted to see Paris. I cannot say how happy I am to have that dream fulfilled today. Treadling, bending, crouching hipping, Radio the Russians eat they dance to Mao Mao. I love that song she says.

> *in the sixties I was sixty I don't look it I'm not past it*
> *dogeared maybe but the pot was still warm Paris with Peter*
> *was a dream I stay for a year*

An elderly lady in spectacles stands in the Sorbonne yard. She masks her face with a paperback, raising a fist in the air. Police shields wing about her, closing on a knot of students hurling cobbles.

All my life, she says, I have had a certain idea of France.

Let's get back to the blackshirts.

– What were they like in Whitstable?

I returned to Whitstable for meetings a few times before I move back women were the spearhead here the men had fought each other to a standstill fallen out and failed there had been arson in the town timber yards boatyards shops up in flames the place was unsettled for months with street patrols at night volunteers ex-servicemen traders working hand in hand the Union tries to build on that but the men stumble the women have a surer footing Olga Shore and I launch a womens branch in Morland Hatch up by the church in Mrs Pullen's drawing room it was standing room only that night her son was a blackshirt her husband died in the war one lady reads Kipling very defiant the women here had plenty of spirit but bound feet no intellect no sensuality I came down with Willy once he spoke in the Foresters Hall I met my husband Joe that night

In May 1936 William Joyce, director of propaganda for the British Union of Fascists, addresses a well attended meeting in Whitstable at which he sets out the programme of the party. There is no protest in the hall. There are no arrests. He wears a dark suit and black jersey.

– War is looming. There is grave danger of an unnecessary war, another European tragedy. We have never conceived it to be our duty to solve the problems of any other country. We can achieve peace in Europe by uniting with the German people in a friendship which will allow us to resist the two great enemies of civilisation, the Bolshevik and the international financier.

If we must declare a war, a man shouts, make it a war on want! Applause and chanting, Union Union Union. Joan joins the cantillation. When they arrived the hall was full, so she's standing towards the back. A burly man hears her shout and offers his chair. As Joyce resumes, she smiles and sits.

– We are being led and exploited by international finance. It is a waste of time to elect members to the House of Commons until we have rid ourselves of that control. Financial democracy is failing us. Let us mind Britain's business. We would be thankful if politicians would give attention to our own affairs. Mills are closing in Lancashire, closing because of imports from India. Poverty and unemployment can be alleviated with controls on international trade and credit for British businesses. Jewish cut-price shops should not be permitted to undermine local traders.

Will you close their chain stores, a woman calls from the second row. Only if you cut your prices Hetty shouts the man who gave Joan his seat. Laughter fills the hall.

– A stronger state, a corporate state will provide the necessary solution. Every trade and profession will have a voice. British retailers will agree fair prices. The farmer should control farming, the fishermen the fishing, not Whitehall. For goods to sell there must be money to buy them. Wages and salaries should be higher. British credit must be mobilised for production, not used for loans to foreign powers which flood our markets with cheap produce that can be made here better.

The audience rises, slamming hands. At the back men stamp their feet. Put Britain First! the man behind Joan shouts. She turns and nods. Put Britain First! she shouts to Joyce. The donor of the seat admires her nape.

– The control of money must be taken out of the hands of international financiers. We will introduce a shorter working day. We will give representation to women. They should receive equal pay with men for doing the same work. Planning and control are the only alternative to ruin. Our people lack strong leadership but give them that, and the inspiration of our National Socialist creed, and they will prove themselves once again the greatest people in the world.

God Save the King, the cheering and the clapping end. I'm Joe the man without a chair says, Joseph Foad. What did you think of that, tell me over tea how do you take it?

Willy sounded radical he sounded reasonable right wing and left wing too that was Willy all over Willy tells Joe in the Albert afterwards if you love your country you're a national if you love her people you're a socialist be a national socialist like me it's a turn of phrase that's all it had a ring to it

Joe couldn't run to a drink, she says, he was looking for work so I buy.

— Sir Oswald, you've met him, what makes him tick?

Tom has sacrificed his career I tell Joe turned on his own class to be a socialist now he has to fight Labour too Joe gives me a long look then he says Mosley is a secret agent well the shock I went white as a frozen bottle of milk he puts his hand on mine you're cold as a ghost he says well that thaws me what do you mean I ask him and Joe says Oswald Mosley is an agent of the secret discontent of his class the discontent of his class with its own rule well I laugh what's funny he says you've gone red as a wireless valve well I couldn't explain so I say let's drink to Mosley to Mosley Joe says the cause of our meeting then Willy comes back

Falling backards down the stairs.

— Come again?

that's what it felt like being back here one day Tempelhof airport next a salt marsh but Joe was a good provider he worked the coastal steamers he leaves the Union after Munich we know what's coming which side we're on my Joe was a grafter perfect clockwork precision-tooled a man of the new race I lose him in forty-one on the convoys he was gone two years after Astra's born a torpedo life is tragic you only begin to live to hear things properly when you realise that

You'll learn it too, she says.

Willy stays over he takes speaking engagements in Kent so we can meet Joe was more away than not Willy he'd stay for a while then storm off it wasn't his sister he stayed with another Joan the little wolf he's not at hers he's at mine an easy mistake to make ha pyah I can assure you he wouldn't think so and before you ask again if Willy or Joe is her dad I'll tell you my last word on the matter I never knew how

could I I loved her just the same

Someone draws a knife through a sharpener. Chair legs drag against the wall. The bedside portrait of Willy revolves towards me, its silver frame catching and scratching the grain of the cupboard, pushing a spoon to one side.

– Just to be clear Joan.

– Back off Red.

– Astra could be the daughter of William Joyce?

Don't ignore me, he says, speaking too low for Joan to hear.

what did I just say she may be and just as maybe not Azzy was born on Tom's birthday fancy that slap in the middle of a Union knees up at the internment camp

Leave while you can Willy growls softly.

– You've never wanted to know? She's never wanted to?

you said it yourself Lord Haw Haw was the most hated man in Britain he wasn't the nation's favourite dad

Last warning Joyce says. The words mist the glaze, cloud his face.

– He wasn't hated by you.

no not by me of course not never by me

I lay the portrait on its face, on top of the spoon. Joan won't know she never looks this way.

– I'm sorry. I had to ask.

give me a moment dear

The nape sniffs, beak in tissue. It sighs.

there shall come forth a star they said and there was Astra

I rest my elbow on the back of the picture frame. It squirms.

– Get your hands off me!

she's my daughter but she don't visit never does how do these dry bones live I'm on my own every night I ache for a fellah to make me laugh and feel wanted and hold me as I sleep

- I'll stay a while longer.

will you dear that's very good of you I do try my best to entertain you

I grind William Joyce into the spoon. I hear him crack.

Shadow on the page.

- See what you're reading, that house on the way to Herne Bay he lived there.

I'm in the Ship again, with a biography of Lord Haw Haw. I tap my pockets. Phone, wallet, keys. Strap of my bag round my ankle. All secure. A mongrel truffles pork scratching under the table. Goulash pricks my nasals.

- Villa or bungalow it is.
- You mean the one called Joycelyn?

Football on the high screen stains his scalp moss green.

- Yeah it had swastikas over the fireplace Joycelyn did.
- The bungalow with the fancy fretwork?
- That's right the one named after Hee Haw.
- I don't think so. It was called Joycelyn before the nineteen-thirties.
- Never referee no way!

His right ear rouges blushing yellow as the chequer flag waves. The mutt takes its leave, nuzz swabbing the carpet, sashaying past bar stools.

- An' it had a tunnel.
- Sorry but there's no link between Joyce and that house.
- How can you say that, not an English home is it?
- Joyce, Joycelyn. German trim. An easy mistake to make.

Mind if we sit here asks a hip by my shoulder. I swivel I toetouch, I roll in my bag. I cut it with inside under my seat. Fans at the home end applaud.

- They signalled to U boats and Heinkels out there.

- There's no record of that.

- Makes sense though. Swhat you would do backing Hitler over us. He used to go for a wet in the Albert Hee Haw did fore the war on 'is way to the radio shop, pedalling along the slopes, my dad and 'is mates told me and they would know they drink there he was a straight up bloke.

- I don't think so.

- You sayin my old man made it up? You callin me dad a liar?

- Facts have got muddled over the years.

- I'll fucking muddle you mate.

- GGOAAAAAL yeahh hoowoo good strike YES!

- YEEEEAAAAHHH we all love the hammers yes we do.

He swings away head tipping back reaching for the rim of the counter. Claret and turf pool on his face, slopping his neck.

- Ooo got it oo was it?

Ignore him, says a barman clearing tables.

- Fourpenny pieces the blackshirts were. Britain didn't need 'em doesn't now ignore him.

I return to the book.

There's no record of her death.

Mark has received another email from upstairs.

- There must be. Records office. Ask the crematorium.

- I have.

- She had an obit in the *Times*!

- But no death certificate.

- That's not possible.

To cut a long story short, we never find it. Was Joan Cade even her real name? Perhaps not. Is it possible she's still alive? No, too many years have passed. Though I never saw the body. A faked death, that would be dispro-portionate. Don't go there Mark says so I don't.

I do confess I look. I search museums and galleries and stately homes. I squeeze behind sculptures, cheek to the wall, hunting for Joan's nape. I know she's out there but where? For years I follow her laughter.

Sculptors bodge napes. They fumble dips and domes, heap on plaits or cheat with hoods. Most fall short, failing Joan.

- They use collars as screens.
- Decapitate too high
- They've no respect.

The Barbedienne Penelope, sand cast bronze, hints at her.

- It's kin, close kin.
- Too young. Too romantic.

Joan's Canova, she's Chinard. Bernini? Elusive isn't the word. I don't give up the search. I owe her that but centuries of blinkered tradition stand in my way. The face isn't a window to the soul. That's a myth put about by portraitists. Critics and curators swallow it whole. A conspiracy of anterior supremacists prevents us from viewing three-dimensional works properly. Adequate rear access is long overdue.

The frontist establishment also restricts the circulation of posterior repro-ductions. With no images to narrow the sweep of my search, the hunt is a long one. I search between one and four galleries a day. I fly long haul to cities I've never heard of, staying a few hours before moving on. I forego all sightseeing, wasting no time on destination restaurants or any art other than sculptural.

I steal the chair on which I sat to interview Joan. I think a consistent posture will help me to trace her. The seat, alas, is too cumbersome to transport by plane and taxi. I am reduced to borrowing chairs of wildly varying heights to view works varied in size and setting. Some attendants are obliging but the sight lines are often a mockery of what's required. I often have to place the loaned chair at such a distance from a nape it defeats my purpose entirely.

I push my luck. I ignore the restrictions placed upon my view. I step over wires and I stand on benches. I sneak photos, trigger alarms, check spans and vertebrae by hand. Last year I was stuck behind Bathsheba at the Getty for fifteen minutes, my foot caught between the plinth and wall. Three security staff escort me from the premises.

After a week of cat and mouse in the main hall of the Victoria and Albert – I was still impaired from the Getty – the deputy facilities director issues me with a formal warning. A risk to the collection, disturbance to visitors, repeated reminders, the full works. Failure to desist will result in a ban, so I sign a binding undertaking.

At the Borghese in Rome I'm welcomed back after closing time.

I've hopes of a Bernini. The omens were good from both sides. Hopping for a better view – to cushion my swollen foot I was wearing a foam galosh – my fancy of a match grows stronger. My confidence rises when, deploying binoculars from a balcony, I detect the unique irregularity of Joan's left lateral flexion. After a costly negotiation, I am authorised to mount the plinth. A helpful director provides me with a mirror on a telescopic rod. Sadly, the trapeziod is misshapen, the work of an assistant with no talent. The nape is lifeless. I leave, disappointed, after forty minutes. Not long after that, I run out of cash for airfares.

A counsellor suggests my grand tour is a refusal to mourn, a grandiose act of denial. My bank manager is even more judgmental. He cancels my cards. My homies confront me with half-truths. They say I've paid for flights without paying my share of the bills. Since returning, they allege, I've done little but sit in my room listening to radios.

Then I find her. Late in August, at the Metropolitan, in a Rodin cabinet.

She is smaller than I expected. Cast in the first decade of the twentieth century, she has shrivelled to an aged courtesan, a stooped maquette shaped for a Gate to Hell which is never installed. I recall her greeting.

> ***didn't think to hurry did you oh no took your time and every
> year that passes is cruel to women I did tell you that didn't I***

She had indeed, one wintry afternoon. The hill was floured. We watched children building snow fish. It was then, she says, I knew my time was up.

I'm a nape man. I need to hear her, to see her, the way I used to. I press myself against the wall at the rear of the cabinet. The attendant chooses that moment to intervene. As he approaches I begin to explain but he hands me an envelope. It is a note from Joan. I knew you'd find me, it says.

Don't go.

It was a mistake to leave.

– He couldn't stay.

> *Willy was wrong to think we'd bend to Berlin let England*
> *go he took that road spending the war in chokey wasn't an*
> *option for Willy clink wasn't cosy it didn't come with telly*
> *tutors tabletennis he couldn't take arms against his Caesar*
> *which way would he shoot a right loose cannon he'd have*
> *been would he rat on the Reich open a door I think the*
> *service hoped he would it's why they tell him to run I should*
> *have known he'd go he said he would he gave us notice read*
> *National Socialism Now anyone surprised was faking it*

– If war breaks out, I will fight for Hitler since such a war would be against Jewry.

> *couldn't have been clearer they could have stopped him if*
> *they'd wanted to they didn't win-win-win it was Willy gone a*
> *win Willy showing his true colours a win Willy as a contact*
> *there that would be the biggest win of all*

– I wept as I left the shore of my native land.

– In B5(b) we had very much a free hand to recruit anyone we thought might be useful.

– I was an exile taking to the high seas.

– The air felt cleaner with him gone.

> *war was Willy's birthmark his mother bears him for misfor-*
> *tune soldiers hew him from bog oak a Galway neighbour is*
> *shot in the head teenage Willy finds him fingers rebels for*
> *the Tans a Fenian here a communist there he's always at the*
> *barracks by the trucks and ready to ride*

– Weapons, murder, warfare at a tender age.

- They're no excuse.

- I served with the irregular forces of the Crown in an intelligence capacity against the Irish guerrillas. In command of a squad of subagents I was subordinate to the late Captain P W Keating , 2nd R.U.R.

- He was just a kid fifteen and easily led.

- Joyce said where, Tans burnt it down, he said who, they pulled the trigger. He wasn't a child victim don't even go there.

> *the Ra tries to rub him out the family comes to England and after the treaty one broadcast runs in Willy's head just one he picks up its signal wherever he turns empire crumbling Europe on the brink feeble government the Bolshevik threat perfidious Jews a Jesuit shaveling catechised him so Germany's his hero Jews want action against Hitler action to defend Jews well Willy joins up the dots the Willy way any other way is Hebrew but the Union can't stop war the wirepullers are formidable the parasites in Mayfair follow their lead the legislators fall into step the BBC too but Willy didn't quit*

Again and again there rush into her mind thoughts of the great valour of the man and the high glories of his line. Her neck shines with a rosy light. Her hair breathes the divine odour of ambrosia.

The weather is turning.

It's colder. The pavements are empty. The bay is grey. The nape is muffled in wool, a cardy with a collar.

> *funds were running low some weeks we're paid short paid late the bungs from Rome and Berlin aren't enough Tom tops them up he's lost his way wants to go home to the Tories he's surrounded by flatterers hears his own echo empty pockets are an excuse to get rid of his critics*

- Tell me about the money from abroad.

> *from Italy five thousand a month for years we used to collect it from the Paris embassy the Germans from thirty-six cash*

> *in a mix of currencies through Ireland and Switzerland*
> *couriers to contacts some direct to Tom but not enough*

– She's right. And if she knew it, five knew too.

– Indeed.

– We'll get more flak for that.

> *the Bleeder sacked Willy and Beckett in thirty-seven I'm out*
> *too ha a hundred of us are told to walk the plank I stay as a*
> *volunteer that's what Tom wants the dogwalkers too they're*
> *all in agreement stay put Joan the country needs you Max*
> *gives me a rise*

That night we had a bottle party, she recalls, a bender letting off steam.

– It's a power grab, the accounts are a smokescreen.

– Someone's got to him. Who?

– Oily oriental blackmail.

– I ain't volunteering, need a job me.

– Funds are scarce you know, Tom borrows.

– True National Socialists are being driven out!

– Cos we tell him woss 'appening.

– He's keeping the yes men.

– Mosley's not the man I thought he was. He invited me in to discuss things. I refused. The conceited popinjay.

– What the muck we do now?

> *Willy keeps his plans close he knows there are informers in*
> *the room he and me and Mag we leave with Beckett Willy*
> *was furious funny too the drink talking*

– We'll set up our own shop. We'll confront the Jewish Conspiracy head on with no holds barred. We'll stand shoulder to shoulder with Germany without wavering. National Socialism, no Bleeder veto!

On Westminster Bridge Joyce and Beckett yell at the river.

– WAR ON WANT IS THE ONLY WAR WE WANT.

- War on Moscow's the war I want prof.

- March on Moscow and want!

- March on Moscow and bloody freeze.

- Melt Moscow!

- All in good time prof.

In Great Smith Street Joyce hammers on the door of the Union HQ.

- DOWN WITH MOSLEY.

In Parliament Square Joyce unpins his badge. He hurls lightning at the moon.

Bouncy shoulders jig the nape, she's laughing.

> *you won't believe this but we ran up Whitehall all four of us holding hands in a line shouting Mosley and Pollitt what are they for thuggery buggery hunger and war we ran all the way past number ten to the square it was a scream ha*

Four pairs of feet doppler the street. Panting and laughter, what are they for. Fifteen minutes later, in the Embankment Gardens, William Joyce weeps.

- It's over. The yids won.

He calls Mag a tart. He knocks her down.

- You heartless glory chaser. Parasitic ball and chain.

> *I wasn't in the mood but I take him back to my place he sings to himself as we walk the Strand his mind is somewhere else in bed he turns his back on me his tail is down it wouldn't wag Jewish devastation I hear him say then over the eggs I do for us they have penetrated our ranks someone in the office is a rat he tells me to keep working for Tom I was going to anyway keep us in the know he says*

- We'll cover your rent, your spending, a little more.

- We, Willy? Who's we?

A rattle of cutlery, kettle whistling.

- Real national socialists.

- With Scrimgeour's money?

- Tom must believe you've put him first. We'd better not meet for a while.

Cup click to saucer. Scrape of a chair.

- Don't go.

> *that's a constant they all think Joan'll keep going no need for a hug you're no better party comes first I tell Tom not Joyce the movement's what matters face the traitor down I said he's over with he's done*

Joyce and MacNab launch the National Socialist League.

> *I thought I'd be told to join Willy's bunch we'll wait and see they said then no decision was taken I knew diddly all would come of the League the diehards of the Union were angry no doubting that tugging at Tom's leash but they stick by him they're not deserters Willy's outfit dead the moment it's born Ches got Willy right*

- Ches?

> *Kenny A K*

- A nasty piece of work.

> *I do agree but listen*

She turns up the murmuring transistor.

- Something has happened to Joyce's clarity of vision. Despite his frequent assertion that his National Socialist League is entirely British, his emotional identification with Germany increases as the months speed past. When Hitler marches into Prague, most of us who sympathise with his work, uniting purely Germanic peoples, recoil in dismay. Not so Joyce.

BRITISH FASCIST SPLIT, the walnut wireless interrupts. NEW MOVEMENT FORMED.

- Dissensions in the ranks of the British Union of Fascists have led to the formation of a rival organisation led by two of Sir Oswald Mosley's former lieutenants. The leaders of the new organisation, the National Socialist League, are Mr John Beckett and Mr William Joyce.

- The HQ was a single room on the top floor, no carpet.

- Piles of leaflets. A bottle or two.

- I saw them working a street corner. One spoke the other heckled, an old game to draw a crowd.

- A terrible comedown it was.

A sheet of paper on my seat.

A letter, typed on yellowing stock.

I'll wait while you read it she says.

In the event of war with Germany

SIS on Joyce, William, to Home Office undated

He has identified himself unreservedly with the Nazi cause, maintains close contact with Nazi officials and has shown that he would be quite willing to take action inimical to this country in order to further the campaign against the supposed 'world Jewish conspiracy'. He has on several occasions shown that he favours violent methods and through his whole career has shown himself to be a man of unbridled fanaticism.

RECOMMEND DETENTION.

It's a carbon. I've seen the original. It's genuine.

- How did she get hold of it?

- And when exactly?

She won't say. We all know what followed.

- I was driven out of my native country by a dreadful sound that was in mine ears, to wit, that unavoidable destruction did attend me, if I abode in the place where I was.

Was it Joan? Did she tip Joyce the wink?

> *Willy knew arrest was imminent we all did when that we don't know it could have happened any time*

He phones her from a call box. He's out of breath. He has walked a mile to avoid a tap. If there is a war, they will imprison us, he tells Joan.

– To avoid that Margaret and I, we may have to leave the country.

– Back to Ireland?

– Mag would rather go to Germany.

– Oh! Willy.

– We've friends in Berlin, Bauer he'll help. There's a risk the Germans will lock us up. I'll look for work as a teacher, perhaps as an interpreter. Or do better, helping further the cause. I hope so. Joan, I want to see you before we leave.

> *they'd been tapping my phone since thirty-eight they hear that for sure so they know they do know*

Why you speak treason, Joan says. Fluently, he replies.

He announces his departure to a gathering of the League.

> *the watchers were there too half the members were paid by the service and special branch of course they knew*

A porter helps Willy and Margaret stow trunks on the train.

– Berlin! That's a rum place to be going right now.

Who is the man who joins them in the carriage? He claims to be a courier for a contract broker. Margaret fears every shadow from the corridor. It will slide the door open, and bundle them off the train. They'll get us at Sevenoaks at Ashford in Folkestone. Where will they take us Willy she whispers. Are they officers in the next carriage? I don't like his look. Willy will we be stopped? Joyce is untroubled. The broker dozes.

> *I'm at Dover the day they switch to the packet for Ostend oh when I see him I fall as though dead at his feet*

– She fainted briefly. Grazed her knees that's all.

– On one tape she says the Joyces are accompanied.

– Does she say by who?

> *no dear there's nobody with him except Mag and she was decent she gave us a moment*

He hands Joan a book. Inside the book there is a letter and some photographs. They part with a kiss. And in that show how stay they would, yet forced they are to go.

– Now I grieve, for I foresee the fall which threatens you.

my sap turned to dust as I watched him go

As Willy sails, the police are watching his basement flat. They wonder where he's sleeping.

– No sign of either of them, sir. They didn't come back.

– Find them! Get on it!

– It was one of those beautiful later summer days on which the sun, to have full meaning, must pierce the mists hanging over the azure sea. We kept our eyes fixed on the Dover cliffs until the haze drew over them that impenetrable veil which, for us, was the end of the old life and the beginning of the new.

– Dinner is served deck two dining room call for dinner call for dinner deck two dinner is served.

Stewards herd gullet to sittings. Waiters count and price the catch.

– When we could see no more of the land which we had loved and tried to serve I said to my wife – curtly enough – let's go to lunch. So we did.

Six officers break down the door to the basement. They find unpaid bills. They find leaflets. They do not find William and Margaret Joyce.

– The Nazi bastard's flown the coop sir.

From that day forth they consulted together, to put him to death.

Whitstable readies for war.

Gas masks swing from shoulders. Necks crane to notices. Troop trucks fug the high street with shipments of men, rifles for masts. A commissionaire locks the cinema gate. Road signs are removed from the foot of the hill. To the jangle of spanner, villages vanish, lanes lead nowhere and a city takes cover.

At the care home tins are stacked in the foyer, tins of meat, fish and milk.

The cook goes room to room collecting coupons from ration books. Shipping churns the bay, planes ply overhead.

The nurse drags the wireless and table aside. She borrows my chair. Stand for me Joan, she says, pushing the foot of the bed from the wall. She sets the chair in the rift. Up she steps her stretch a spire.

— What's that?

— Blast tape. Thousands will be killed by glass shards.

She masks the window with kisses, the faux leading of war.

— Will it hold?

— Wait and see.

> *the news was never cheerful as I recall evacuees arrive*
> *names on labels round their necks we're paid an allowance*
> *they leave the money stops evil prices shops shutting men all*
> *gone a camp fills the holt gun emplacements checkpoints all*
> *the improbables actual in an instant*

A palisade is planted in the bay, scaffold bristling spiken. Dragon teeth stub the harbour gum. Roads serrate. Slotted hives, concrete fungi, speckle the hilltops, blooming by gates and forks and lanes which have no names.

> *there's honey on the moon tonight that's what we call a*
> *bomber's moon up there won't wear a hood*

Entrust us with the darkening of your windows! Lamp proof cloth by the yard. The black rain is caused by smoke from Dunkirk. Though envelopes are practically unobtainable, Cox is still offering threepenny packets of twenty-five, the pre-war price. Mr and Mrs Allen of 37 Sydenham Street have been informed that their son Pte E V Allen of the Buffs is a prisoner of war. At bakers the present price of bread should be eightpence halfpenny per quartern loaf, a halfpenny above London prices. Mrs Reed of Corinza, Church Road, has received official notification that her husband CQMS Royston H Reed the Buffs is missing. Council dismiss a Conchie. The Rink Hockey and Skating Club will carry on despite the war. Why Every Family Should Grow Their Own Food. Knit for the Forces at the Gas Show Rooms every other Tuesday.

> *dreary days I was interned in 1940 springtime ha a change is*
> *as good as a rest a local constable we went to school together*

him and a truckload of Tommies lam the door at Gladstone
Street it's the dogbox for me they found parachutes at Blean
so it was bound to happen they see I'm carrying it makes no
difference lots of others are snatched up too I say hullo to
Holloway for a few months Hollo is hard after that two years
in a boarding house the Isle of Man where Astra's born no
visits Joe and I weren't hitched

Tis impossible to describe the terror of my mind, when I was first brought in, and when I looked round on all the horrors of that dismal place. I looked upon myself as lost. The hellish noise, the roaring, swearing, and clamour, the stench and nastiness, and all the dreadful crowd of afflicting things that I saw there, joined together to make the place seem an emblem of hell itself, and a kind of entrance into it.

there were dozens of us lifted Diana was too the huntress
Tom's second wife Lady Ladedah I'd never come across one
like her before how you rhyme horse with loss beats me that's
how she speaks like her jaw is too loorrnng she's fluent
in toff calls us gells we do admire her though a fair few
worship her she's a vase my bunkie said an alabaster vase
lit from within today she's still a rose so elegant not like me
with grey hairs on my nips every tuft has a name you know
Hitler Stalin Hirohito but you run out of dictators I wish I
was with Willy no one has ever admired me as he did

– What was it like in Holloway?

a dump it smells it's cold the cells are unlocked we mix we
move around at night no shelters for us blasts the walls
shaking but the fun we have to start with anyway women no
men every girl should do a bit of time live that Diana was our
queen a personal friend of the fuhrer if bombs come through
our roof she says Hitler himself will grieve the Germans are
our friends she said friends who attack our capital because
our government gives them no choice it didn't ring true but
Hollo wasn't the place to speak out Diana was Helen Adolf
was coming to rescue her it made the girls feel safe

A beekeeper jots a question in her diary. Remove English queen, replace with an Italian? The authorities lock her up.

— They keep her in two year!

> ***the ignorance of people the spite of petty officials mind you
> they were only twenty miles away the Nazis if they'd landed
> the Union would have resisted Tom said so here in Action
> people forget they don't like the truth***

As she turns the browning newsprint the pages crack and split, freckling
the duvet.

— Got any more of those?

The nape ignores my question. It searches a page, finger trembling the text.
Mosley taunts me from the cover, speaking from the fold.

— No war for Jewish finance.

He stares me down.

> ***here we go here it is in the event of war every member of
> British Union will be at the disposal of the nation***

Joan's voice, Tom's words. Then Mosley again.

— Every one of us would resist the foreign invader with all that is in us.

— Why the conditional tense?

— Period style?

— He thinks the war won't happen.

> ***however rotten the existing government and however much
> we detest its policies we would throw ourselves into the effort
> of a united nation until the foreigner is driven from our soil***

There, says the nape, tapping the text, the Bleeder in his own words.

— You think he meant it?

> ***dow you must be joking he was covering his back Tom was
> banged up too within a week***

Let me explain, the Mosley covershot drawls, face up on the duvet. It takes
a deep breath, rippling his pages. I am not offering to fight in the quarrel of
Jewish finance, in a war from which Britain could withdraw at any moment
she likes with her Empire intact and her people safe. The explanation fans
from the bed. Rusted flakes of decayed newsprint dust the air. They settle

on the microphone, on my notes, on Joan.

Can I chip in chirps the tran.

- An item I picked up it might help.

- Home secretary Sir John Anderson tells the Cabinet Sir Oswald Mosley is too clever to put himself in the wrong by giving treasonable orders.

> *true but Tom said if you weren't serving you had to carry on with the work of the Union take every opportunity to awaken the people demand peace that's what he says in his message to members join civilian units air raid precautions the special constables explain it's not our war*

- And did they?

> *a few not for long not after the bombing starts in Douglas they keep the faith speeches on Tom's birthday wonderful parties songs speeches to keep our spirits up they were good times safe too do I dig my way out with a spoon it never crosses my mind does Willy send me a file did he heck*

Joan Cade is not considered to pose a danger to Her Majesty's Government.

> *it was B5b got me out I can't say much they turn up one morning with a master key three men and a boat waiting off the coast they lower me and Azzy down the wall in a basket hide us in a hay wain stow me in an attic out felt good even if a third of the earth was burnt a third of the trees terrible times just as we'd warned a consuming fire and Willy sneering on the wireless promising more of the same but it was Willy by me in my bed Willy in my ear his meanings concealed for me the pectoral and fundamental aspects of women he knew I'd know so clever he was*

She turns on the walnut. We wait as the five valves warm.

- Use the time to compose yourself.

- Prepare yourself to receive.

- Jairmany calling Jairmany

> *I've a date with a dream dear time for you to go*

No beach access.

Obstacle Z, a trellis of wired scaffold, cages the bay. At upper windows of the Old Neptune armed lookouts rick their necks tracking estuary traffic. The wave trap blocks their view.

Joan slips through, plashing silt. Gulls swoop and strafe the breach yau yau yau she paddles on through beak flak.

I'd planned my flit I'd picked the spot

– I'm where you raised me Willy.

Shin deep she was and sinking. He crouches at her shins, uproots her.

up up I go leaving my shoes behind

Over his shoulder, butt to the sky, his cheek at her thigh, Joan breasts the small of Willy's back she grabs the hem of his coat his heels sprelch.

we slop to the Neptune his arm clamped behind my knees.

That's where she digs, out by the drool.

I guddle for shoes long gone scooping sludge

– Oi you down there!

Startled shouts from the tardy pub window.

– On yer feet let's see yer!

– Dint move a bliddy inch.

The guards clatter downstairs blusting whistles. They shake the scaffold, kick poles. Clamped tubes glock and ohm. Spiked wire zings. Farside they fret. She wades the wash thigh high she bellies and rolls.

Monstrous crying of the wind.

Bob feet awash in radial waves etheric hours suspending.

I channel Berlin steer north tuning to the Elbe Havel Spree signal swamping bombers buzz in grids a fighter pinwheels whistling ploosh it's off the air heavy rollers sub scopes circling

– Were we only white birds, my beloved, buoyed on the foam of the sea.

Serpent coils snake the swell, Soe Orm drifting, tow of seventy yards.

– Hairs two feet in length hang from its neck, flaming eyes.

I'm weary slowly sinking by degrees

Porker seals in whiskers bottle by. She upskirts cloud, plates in electrolyte, lays in wait for stars. Joan sings, venting from her blowhole. Keep smiling throughooo, she whales, you always dooowu.

whatever I do remember I'm true

– You never enjoy the world aright till the sea itself flows in your veins, till you are clothed with the heavens and crowned with the stars.

Willy I'm coming I'm on my way

Spiracled benthic Joan glides the seabed ventral-eyed. Her crinoline inflates. It floats her gracefully ashore.

I find her in a shell which harbours echoes.

I'm too easy to track.

My house has one door, I tell her. It opens on to a yard with a high fence and two gates to the same road. I could climb the stockades of my neighbours and emerge further along the street, I say, but that won't get me past the Watchers. The kitchen has a skylight. I could leave by that. But I don't know next door well enough to pass through her house to the back street.

– What can I do?

> ### *rent another place with two ways in and out spread the Watchers thin two homes three doors more windows force their hand burn a hole in the surveillance budget stretch them till they break that's what I'd do*

Two vacant buildings flank my place. To the left there's an outhouse used for storage, to the right an abandoned factory. All my windows but one face left. There's a shop round the back and a derelict warehouse over the road.

– What do you think?

> ### *there will be Watchers Trackers maybe Hunters too in any or*

all of those buildings they'll be to the side with windows for sure a shop's too public the warehouse lacks sight lines I'd choose the outhouse perfect for audio camera eyes on and follow don't you even think of going in to have a gander I'd miss you I've got used to you

If the source of interference is outside the house it will generally be necessary to call in the assistance of the Post Office. An experienced wireless engineer will continue the search.

If I'm at home they know. If I go out, they know. And I'm due to report.

don't kid yourself you'll give them the slip you won't

It's harbour day, a festival.

I wake in the early hours, the darkest and earliest hour I can. I pull on a wetsuit. I know every inch of the house, no need to turn on a light. Hooking flippers to my waist, I footsy into water shoes. I open the front door. I step into the night. I inch the outer lock. I burst from the gate straight into the path of a speeding van.

– Fuck that was close.

– Not close enough!

I sprint for the beach. A door slams. Pursuers drum behind me. I race up the alley, they're still in the road. I roll the sea wall and scramble the shingle. I rush the wet I wade I squat below the surface. I creep deep, a knight's move, another, taking wary sips of air. I kick my slips and flipper up. Swimming east I roll on my back and breathe. Keep smiling through, I whale.

The Watchers are on the beach, raking the water with torches and making calls.

– A portly bunch.

– Watchers not Trackers, no Hunters.

not a flattering turnout it looks like you're clear why didn't you say you could swim you're a natural

A launch spumes from the harbour. I've already passed the arm. It chases its spotlight, retracing my path. I'm away.

- Motor boating is a form of instability which manifests itself in a receiver with a noise not unlike that of a petrol engine.

it's self-oscillation at very low frequency

I beach at Tankerton. I pull a towel, clothes and a weapon from beneath a beach hut. I've three kits at separate locations. I put the catapult back. I unchain a bicycle that's locked to the leg of the hut. Ten minutes later I'm in a lane on the edge of the town. No lights no sound or passing vehicles. I wait in a ditch. A familiar face comes off shift. He walks from the petrol station to his car. He's right on time. We get in and I'm gone.

A tiger chews an umbrella.

The late owner's topper survives, his teeth are scattered nearby. The umbrella is labelled. His name was appeasement. The snack's Edwardian, recently Eton. Hitler and Stalin gorge on zapiekanka stolen from Poland.

- The scum of the earth I believe?

- Ahmnn umnn bloody assassin of the workers, I presume?

- Hmmn mn.

Give that pizza back!

- I have to tell you now that no such undertaking has been received and that consequently this country is

AT WAR WITH GERMANY

Report for work carry out your duties God save the King. Wailing from air raid sirens, a scurry for shelters, take care descending basement stairs. At Tower Gate beefeaters gag Booh! from gas masks. London stockpiles children in the countryside. School assemblies truck by train. Files of children trail behind banners, placards at their necks.

Full blackout from sunset. No news on the Home Service. Cinemas, sports venues, theatres are

CLOSED UNTIL FURTHER NOTICE

Exodus of men. Advent of ladies in trousers.

LET THE PEOPLE SING

THE HOME FRONT

UP IN THE MORNING EARLY

Roads, trees, and rain. The endless beat of marching feet. Rain and trees and roads.

– Keep mum abaht the wevver chum!

WHO IS THIS MAN WHO LOOKS LIKE CHARLIE CHAPLIN?

ADOLF IN BLUNDERLAND

– The only way to strengthen the morale of the people is to tell them the truth, and nothing but the truth, even if the truth is horrible.

Now imagine me in the Maginot Line
Sitting on a mine in the Maginot Line
To my old tin hat I cling
I have to use it now for everything

– It might have been a pink ribbon across Europe for all the good it was.

Young lovers embrace in a car by a wood. Dad's Army sneaks a peek. Sneaking behind them unseen, German parachutists. Three months later, England's ready. The parachutists are descending into a zoo, about to touch down in a lion's den.

– Dunkirk runkirk run run run bang goes the farmer's gun gun gone.

The little holiday steamers made an excursion to hell and came back victorious.

VICTORY THROUGH HARMONY

THE WHITE COONS CONCERT PARTY

MUSIC WHILE YOU WORK

IT'S THAT MAN AGAIN

Churchill takes charge!

– We have differed and quarrelled in the past, but now one bond unites us all: to wage war until victory is won and never to surrender.

Paris has fallen but we shall never surrender.

A lonely figure on a rooftop at night. Falling towards him are three bombs with the eyes, moustache and floppy fringe of Hitler. Four mines of matching mien drop alongside them, shells and incendiaries too. The spotter is spied on by three chimneys. They also have the fuhrer's hair, his eyes and moustache.

– There is no depression in this house and we are not interested in the possibilities of defeat. They do not exist.

> *the beeb buttons its lip plays organ music people hear about ships sinking learn the loss of their sons from Willy aunty has a deal with the press delay the news keep print in business Willy unveils Churchill's cabinet not our tongue tied BBC we hear the raid on Narvik fails from Willy's lips the Admiralty wouldn't let on*

In public houses people stop ordering drinks she says they huddle to the end of the bar where the loudspeaker is.

High on the cliffs of Dover a sentry stands alone. The grass at his feet is the mane of a lion carved in the chalk, watchful eyes on France. Its hefty paws hold the beach.

Angels and devils clash in mid air. Brazen swords clang brazen helms.

– Upon this battle depends the survival of Christian civilisation. Upon it depends our British life.

Joan unwraps chips in the blackout. Vinegar spats fighters storming bombers crossing France. The Seine sours, the Meuse malts, news pages drip. On page five, the rear gunner of a Lancaster puts up his feet. He's firing with one hand, a pad of pickled paper in his lap. Dear Mum, he scribs on the damp, I'm sorry to hear our Billy has measles.

A second vera drops a string of high explosives on a factory. The pilot shouts that makes us quits for the hole you made in my garden.

They weighed so lightly what they gave but let them be they're dead and gone.

Jairmany summons Joan to her set.

> *it was Willy I knew it would be*

– The dreary blunderer of Downing Street is a drunk.

Humbug from Hamburg.

Joan stillettos down the steps.

She has a pillow under each arm and a blanket over her shoulder. Tillery tumps and warnings sireeen. Spots rake the up there.

Deeper she goes. The echo of her step mutes. Sleepers mat the platform.

>*when I go down the tube at Aldgate not that I do I look along the platform I look at the tiles and steps and the rails to think I used to sleep here of night*

She places the pillows end to end, putting her handbag between them. She covers the roost with the blanket then rolls herself up. Facedown she listens in to the late station.

– Do you ever hear that bloke from Hamburg they call Haw-Haw?

– I never tire of him.

– He's opened my eyes.

Doom thuds from the stairwell.

– He's a bloody good speaker.

– You ought to have heard him the other night, skitting about Churchill.

– On the nail!

– He tells lies. He says we're starving. What bunk!

Snoring, a tub dragged along the rails. Gropes, slaps, late feet tromping.

– We aren't educated enough to understand all the words he uses but he's very interesting.

– I feel inclined to smash the set, what he says about England.

Millions give an ear to Willy nine fifteen behind the evening news. Misleading ministers, misled members, captains of torpedoed commerce, Brits at wits end dazzled sleepless through the blackout.

- I learn some things from Hamburg before our people tell us.

- The man in the street is asking if we've anything to hide.

Voices, add layers of echo, in basement gloom.

- They are wondering why news is so scarce, why it's out of date when it arrives, why facts they know are not released.

- We always have it on at home.

- The black-out, the novelty of hearing the enemy, the desire to hear both sides, an insatiable appetite for news and the desire to be in the swim all play their part in building up Hamburg's audience. The entertainment value of the broadcasts, their concentration on undeniable evils in this country, their shrewd news sense and their presentation is better than ours.

- Fight back for God's sake. Tell the truth!

- I am not sure that the constant reiteration of Lord Haw Haw as the topic of discussion is not having a bad effect.

- Some listen to him with a passive fascination which reminds one of the snake's prey.

- Morale and rumour are a serious business. Haw Haw and his kind are undermining public morale.

- In Germany it is a penal offence to listen to foreign radio broadcasts. We have been remiss.

- Tonight our bombers will be coming over Stamford Hill and Stoke Newington so you have that pleasure to look forward to.

- Jam him and ban him!

I go into a house. I decide who's alive who's dead. I tot up the number of victims and work out what is necessary in the way of fire services, ambulances and demolition. I'm quite used to seeing dead people. I've got hardened to it.

Blood, blood toil, blood toil and tears, blood toil and tears and sweat.

- England will become a land of skeletons by the wayside.

   I knew it was Willy a mixed blessing yes but Willy

With this instrument you can make public opinion. Mental confusion, contradictions of feeling, indecision, panic, these are our weapons. Confusion of voices, as from several transmitters. Broken phrases and many birds singing in counterpoint.

Trust the common sense of the British public. It will see us through.

> *I used to listen no one knew to J B Priestley such a warm homely voice he talks about the people's war on Sundays our community pulling down fences us the people fighting back I'd go up early keep the volume low I always thought of Priestley as a whisperer the homeless heart we all possess he says pillow talk intimate moments between us was I cheating on Willy yes I was no no Willy had left me he'd gone in my line of work listening to Priestley was frowned on he challenged Churchill I hold him close beneath the blankets*

– She's lying.

– Priestley's broadcasts start in June 1940. She's in Holloway then.

– Hollo didn't allow radio?

– I'll check.

Heavy enemy raids were directed upon the capital and sections of the coast last night. A blast behind the church at Wateringbury has stripped the fruit from apple trees. The farmer says it's been the quickest picking ever.

Flames plummeting. Cauliflowers blossom in blue. Silk mushrooms spread on the Downs.

A broken window. A handwritten notice. My pane has gone be one in Hitler's neck.

– The town clock in Lewisham is three minutes slow.

> *it was obviously Willy he knew those places*

– If you don't want to miss a Haw Haw broadcast buy a Smiths clock!

We shall defend every village, every town and every city. The vast mass of London, fought street by street, could easily devour an entire hostile army.

We would rather see London laid in ruins and ashes than it should be tamely and abjectly enslaved.

Dornier drone and jeery Junkers. Pareidolia of the ears.

– I'm looking at you I'm looking at you I'm looking at you I'm looking

On the step of ten Winnie waves his fist at lofty wafers.

Goofing is watching a dogfight in the sky instead of taking shelter. Who's afraid of Winnie the goof?

In the event of an air raid staff are to go to the wood and lie down, preferably in pairs.

Goebbled accounts for trip wireless.

Snores, grunts, whistles, moans and occasionally deep sobs were mingled with sad sighs, and snatches of song. Sleepers are stepped on by newcomers.

I had a terrible bruise on my hip once I could hardly get back up to daylight I limped for a week

– We've just hit a Messerschmitt! The pilot's not getting out of that one. Pump it into him pop-pop-pop boyohboy he's going down an absolute nosedive. That was beautiful.

Hitler is on the French coast. He's wearing laurel, a toga and jackboots.

– I have conquered all Gaul. How long will it take to conquer Britain?

One moment my Leader, says the seer in sandals, I will consult the omens of the air. Geman bombers corkscrew from the sky.

Today a bomb was severely damaged in Wigmore Street.

– A programme for the Forces makes sense. A man sitting quietly by his own fireside can concentrate on a Beethoven string quartet or a Shaw play. No soldier, however intelligent, can listen in the same concentrated way in a crowded canteen with people calling for drinks, playing darts and keeping up a crossfire of talk.

Sutherland remembers the silence. The absolute dead silence, except every now and again, a thin tinkle of falling glass. Now, now, again.

– A noise which reminds me of the music of Debussy.

– Europe callin'. Pound speakin'. Ezry Pound speakin'.

Willy wasn't the only one there was Baillie Stewart Margaret Bothamley both the Eckersleys the actor Jack Trevor Amery

Bowlby Baden-Powell more than forty in all

What fortitude he showed inside the wooden horse.

NEW BRITISH BROADCASTING STATION

CHRISTIAN PEACE MOVEMENT

WORKERS CHALLENGE

RADIO CALEDONIA

The Germans train men to impersonate BBC broadcasters.

– The Nazis use Received Pronunciation to fake the news.

To al' Northerners wheriver you may be good neet says Pickles.

– On trains late I'll be!

Eyes waiting to ear from my spies. When I get mice pies I'll mince my words.

– England will have her neck wrung like a chicken.

it was obviously Willy who couldn't know by then

Hong Kong, fall of the garrison. Surrender of Singapore.

Byrd, Purcell, Gibbons, all that jazz. Helgar, Villiams, Valton and such volk.

KITCHEN FRONT

THE RADIO ALLOTMENT

WOMEN AT WAR

BEATING THE COUPON

Eat potatoes as a substitute for bread.

– Beefeaters? We ain't beef eaters. We live on spam like everyone else.

My missus sees a queue. She joins it. After fifteen minutes she taps the woman in front on the shoulder and asks what she's queuing for. And the woman replies The Canterbury Tales. You've got to eat anything these days.

ACK-ACK BEER-BEER

Hitler storms Russia, Japan Pearl Harbour.

> I love the Bolshevikis, the lovely Bolshevikis
> I'm telling you Ducky, they're very nice.
> I'm going Bolsheiviki, let's all go Bolsheviki,
> they're lovely people Ducky, take my advice.
> Mayfair goes Bolsheviki, the King goes Bolsheviki –
> Don't be a fool Ducky, why don't you try?
> I'll make you an English Bolsheviki,
> a gentlemen Bolsheviki with an Eton tie!

I went to bed says Churchill. I slept the sleep of the saved and thankful.

In place of the young men, urns and ashes are carried to the houses of the fighters.

What economy is it to go to bed, to save candlelight, if the result be twins?

 – This is the last day of the year in which Hitler promised you final victory.

V for Victory, Vinnie's vees, three dots a dash, Beethoven. Chantez le V, sifflez le V, for Victory in Muscovy.

LENINGRAD SYMPHONY

AMERICA CALLING EUROPE

IN HONOUR OF RUSSIA

ATLANTIC SPOTLIGHT

Miller dies in a plane flop. Don't know where don't know when. The cater-wauling of an inebriated cockatoo, says the governing board. Popularity noted but deplored. Vera says she's reminding the boys what they're fighting for.

– The precious permanent things rather than the ideologies and theories.

HMS WATERLOGGED

THE FOURTH CHRISTMAS

AUS DER FREIEN WELT

Whoever finds this will know who won the war.

> Let's go bombing
> Oh let's go bombing,
> Let's go shelling
> Where they're dwelling!
> Let's shell Churchill's women, children too!
> Let's go to it! Let's do it! Let us bomb neutrals too!
> Let's go bombing! It's becoming quite the thing to do!

Tobruk changes hands five times.

– I have ordered that all plans and instructions dealing with further withdrawal are to be burnt. We are going to finish with this chap Rommel once and for all.

Monty wins by radio. At Stalingrad the Germans surrender.

Ajax lies dead and there lies Achilles my son too.

Who can account so so many losses?

> *Run Adolf run Adolf run run run here comes*

Joan opens *Reynold's News*. Nazis raise their hands in the air. At El Alamein Axis soldiers surrender to a Tommy in a lorry. He's annoyed.

– 'Op it some of yer. I ain't capturing more than a 'undred at a time.

Shortages of batteries, of valves, of radio repair men, of working sets.

Hitler salutes a parade of skeletons returning from the front. They bone in snow in their thousands, banners aloft. The army which was to have taken Cairo. The army which was to have taken the Grozny Oilfields. To have taken Moscow. To have taken Leningrad.

IM NAMEN DES DEITSCHEN VOLKES VERLEIHE ICH dem Hauptkommentator William Joyce in Berlin-Charlottenberg DAS KRIEGSVERDIENSTKREUZ 1. KLASSE Fuhrer Hauptquartier 1 September 1944 DER FUHRER. Black fruit salad pinned to Joyce.

every night after putting Astra to bed I sit down to the wireless I don't listen in to Willy anymore I am too worried for him

COMBAT DIARY

WE ARE ADVANCING

HOME IS ON THE AIR

– In Rome my jeep is half full of roses.

Drones inna rubble rockets reeling an a-rolling in da Little Blitz.

– Sorry to have bombed the Cock Tavern at Highbury for I have had many a pleasant drink there. It was meant for Cossors, the radio factory. I will get it yet.

everyone knows it's Willy they announce his name before each broadcast best horse in my stable Goebbels calls him

With half-lighting, in the dim-out, windows start to glow again.

– I'm going to get lit up when the lights go up in London.

JOBS FOR ALL

FULL EMPLOYMENT

– This is the day and this is the hour.

Two million men on the move, ten thousand trucks, three thousand heavy guns, one-and-a-half thousand tanks. Ninety-three destroyers set sail, twenty-two cruisers, six battleships, four thousand assault craft. Ten thousand planes take off carrying three airborne divisions and six thousand tons of explosive.

– Jairmany falling! Jairmany falling!

Shake hands with Ivan at the Elbe with De Gaulle in Notre-Dame with Dimbleby in Belsen.

– She was a living skeleton impossible to gauge her age for she had practically no hair left on her head and her face was a yellow parchment sheet with two holes in it for eyes. She was stretching out her stick of an arm and gasping something. Medicine. Medicine.

– This is Germany calling. Tonight you will not hear Views on the News by William Joyce. I'm seated in front of Lord Haw-Haw's own microphone, or rather the microphone he used in the last three weeks of his somewhat chequered career. And I wonder what Lord Haw-Haw's views on the news are now? For Hamburg, the city he made notorious, is this evening under the control of the British forces.

C	C	C	C
o	o	o	o
l	n	l	l
u	v	u	u
m	o	m	m
n	y	n	n
s	s	s	s
o	o	o	o
f	f	f	f
t	s	p	r
r	u	r	e
o	p	i	f
o	p	s	u
p	l	o	g
s	i	n	e
	e	e	e
	s	r	s
		s	

Hostilities will end at one minute after midnight tonight.

Japan, with all her treachery and greed, remains unsubdued.

243

PEOPLE MATTER

MAKE A DATE

The force from which the sun draws its power is loosed.

LIFT UP YOUR HEARTS

–   The W-W-war well it is O-O-O-over.

The day peace broke out I looked at the missus. I say you don't look happy. She says there's nothing to look forward to no more. What do you mean I say.

there was always the all-clear before ha ha

New York City twenty-five years later.

The gig's a twelve bar outing with the mums. Three names – Frank Len Nono – are expected on stage. Joan's in her sixties. She's a fan. She listens on the pocket set.

At the window her elbow skips fingers dancing. Go, go, go Joannie be good spurts the tranny. Joggling shoulders shimmy her hair.

the crackling is awful I press the radio hard against my ear to make out what they're saying haha the plastic grille puts stripes on my cheek like warpaint

The stage floats in from the bay filling the view. The special guest waves. He's wearing a white suit. He takes hold of an ask Charlie what kind of guitar it is. The woman's in black, empty handed. Frank quietens the audience down, he says hey sit down cool it for a minute so we can hear what we're gonna do. He shouts instructions to the band.

–   Cinnamon or blues.

Not the standard changes, he tells them, but it's close.

–   A song I sang in the pool in a cave I haven't done it since.

Am ease heaven diem two-three-four!

– You know I love you baby please don't go well baby please don't go.

oh I love this song I always have I sing it to myself here by the window you know I love you baby please don't go my song for Willy our song but it's black music I doubt he'd like it

Kite Joan loops and bobs at the window.

– You know I love you baby please don't go well baby please don't go.

– Is he singing honeychile or honey child?

honey child of course he's English pipe down let me enjoy the song

I listen to my recording of her listening. The playback's sand in a tin, lo-fi spectral grit. Joan's squealing, high pitched, a cattish mewing wail of pain. It's babylike but laughter too, playful, intense. A frail don't go, a roar, a bumping metrical growl.

– Nothing that I wouldn't do for you right now.

Deafer are the hearts of men than the hardest rock.

Primal screams, squawks, a jazz march moan, keyboard noodling. Axe impro, chants of scum bag scum bag scum bag. A siren sounds from a sack then it's all over. Fans depart from the window sill, drifting across the beach. The crew wades out for takedown.

she couldn't sing it was drive time conceptual they were a lovely couple growing close through politics and art like Willy and me like me and Peter too and David she was screamier than Sutch I was shocked when he got shot it was a terrible day brought it all back for me John gone he'd never be back I couldn't believe it in a way she was lucky his death was unexpected it was quick Willy's wasn't I used to lay in bed worried sick night after night what's going to happen to Willy will he escape survive be shot what will they do to him

– Listen to me Joan. If there is war with Germany I will be shot rather than take any part in it on behalf of Britain

Don't go honeychile pleads Joan, please don't go. Willy Walnut brays basso from the bedfoot boombox.

- I do not so much regard it as a war between nations as a war between opposing political faiths.

He falsettos from the zista.

- England is a colony of Palestine.

Twin Willy duets in stereocast.

- I will-ill not fyite for Jewree.

Baby please don't go Joan purrs, lips teasing my mic.

- Victory with a perpetuation of the old system would be an incomparably greater evil for England than defeat coupled with a possibility of building something new, something really nationalist, something truly socialist.

Well I know I want you baby, Joan gruffs.

- The newspapers say I am an ex-actor, and a former shipping clerk, an embezzler, a gangster, a sadist in family life, an unscrupulous mercenary. I have dishonestly eloped with a girl from Manchester, namely my wife. I was born in several different countries. I cannot speak English, I am illiterate, I am insane.

Nothin' I wouldn't do f'you right now husks Joan. Willy ignores her.

- I am almost permanently in a state of intoxication. I write my scripts well in advance so I have something I can read on air when I am completely plastered. I live with my wife in a well appointed flat in Kaiserdam. She has affairs. I beat her. She leaves me for a while. We divorce. We remarry.

Twenty-four chairs are placed in an arc on the window sill. The performers sit, half of them holding radios. The conductor bows. The sets are switched on. They are tuned to different frequencies at varying volumes, some inaudible. News sports reports interstellar phone-in Mozart chantry western. The radiolists perform in pairs, following notation charts. One surfs frequencies the other fingers tone and volume.

- Will relinquished. Order abandoned.

- Could one get any further from Bayreuth?

Performer five ups the volume on radio three.

- This is probably my last broadcast. Germany will live. No coercion, no oppression, no measures of tyranny that any foreign foe can introduce will shatter Germany. The people of Germany have in them the secret of life, endurance and will of purpose. Heil Hitler and farewell.

I love you honey child, Joan sings to herself.

– It's over. I am spent. I wish I could go out like a man, with plenty to drink and good cigars.

I love you baby please don't go.

– I still love England and hate to think that I am to be regarded as a traitor to her. I am not.

Radio seven soft and barely audible.

– On this tragic day, the death of Adolf Hitler was reported. I have to drink wine for breakfast as nothing else is available. How we are going to reap the whirlwind. But, thank God, the burgundy was very good today.

Performer thirteen stands, she steps to the edge of the sill. She hurls her radio at the bedroom wall. It shatters to dozens of pieces. Casing frag circuit boards batteries buttons strew the room.

This piece by Cage works, the nape tells me, it incarnates our structure of listening. I saw it performed in London many years ago she says.

England means so much to me and I am old.

Haw Haw's voice rises from the severed speaker at my feet. So much to me and I am old it wheezes. The diaphragm splits. I miss the wireless very much indeed it gasps.

We've got Haw Haw!

I quarrel with him, Mag recalls.

It was in Flensburg near the Danish border, she tells Joan, William takes off in a huff.

– I went for a walk. Two soldiers were gathering wood. I point more out with a stick. I speak to them, in French. They thank me in German. Then I say in English, here are a few more pieces.

Vowel and semivowel sounds are musical. Their distribution matches the first ten harmonics of the speaker's vocal chords.

— You wouldn't happen to be William Joyce would you?

— I reach in my pocket for a passport. One of them shoots me in the thigh.

— My name is Hansen I tell them, I'm not armed.

— He doesn't have a weapon sir.

— They take both of my passports. They give me first aid and take me to a hospital. My wife is arrested too. They steal her jewellery. When I'm interviewed I point out I'm American.

— Hoho Haw Haw you're no Yank.

Cellos sound at the foot of the bed.

— You're a captive now. Fast in my fetters. Just as you wanted the world to be.

Chirrup from the tran.

— Pity they didn't aim higher

Our enemy is delivered into our hands, the one who has lain waste our land and multiplied our slain.

— How did you feel when you heard the news?

> *you idiot Willy first rule of politics don't get caught why was he still in Germany there were places he could have got to laws he could have used everyone wanted him dead I knew what was coming I prayed they'd let me see him they surely owed me that I begged them to*

CELL READY FOR LORD HAW HAW AT THE TOWER

REPORT OF TRAITOR'S CAPTURE

HIS DATE WITH THE HANGMAN DRAWS NEAR

When he arrives at the prison counter, Joyce is carrying two cases. In one are clothes and toiletries. In the other, books: Horace, Armies of the Revolution, Dr Faustus.

He is bound in bronze shackles. His head is shaved. In the prison they set him to work grinding grain. The hair on his head begins to grow again.

My wife is innocent he says.

Irrelevant to the case.

I understand the resentment that my broadcasts have, in many quarters, aroused.

This has no bearing.

It is not a mitigation of his actions

Final judgement cannot be passed on me until it is seen whether the country can win the peace.

This has no bearing.

Irrelevant to the case.

I know that I have been denounced as a traitor. I resent the accusation. I have been guilty of no underhand or deceitful act against Britain.

The substance of the case denied.

I'm an American. As such I could not have committed treason against Britain.

Is this true?

Why didn't we know?

Clarification required, urgently

We won't look favourably on you hanging one of us, warns the worried face from Washington.

– We being your allies and us settling your bills. Haw Haw has rights.

The polished teak table mirrors the director general's face. Neither he nor his service exist. I avert my eyes.

– He may argue he's technically not a traitor but

The minister's fist rattles the wood.

– The British People know the answer to that!

The Attorney General doesn't reply. The minister mops tea with a handkerchief. Westminster is in two minds.

- I hesitate to think what Moscow will say if it should so happen that the House of Lords should take a view favourable to Joyce. They will regard it as an intervention by Reaction.

  the defeat of Germany strengthens the Soviets Willy was right on that his warnings about Moscow are repeated by Churchill a few months later they were on the same song sheet Willy and Winnie there's a Russian dimension to every decision after the fighting stops

The Attorney General's mahoganny table is heaped with documents.

- We've one witness ready to state he heard Joyce speak before the war and that he heard that voice again during a broadcast by Haw Haw.

- One? Is that all?

- He'll suffice.

- It's essential to prove that Joyce is not an American.

- But he is. Sam says so.

- If that is so I fear we have no case.

- Indeed.

- May I? In a passport application in 1938 Joyce claimed to be British, not for the first time. He renewed that passport in August 1939. He did not become a naturalised German until some time in 1940.

- Tell me something I don't know.

- Well you might say that even though he lied about his nationality, the passport placed him under our protection.

- Misrepresentation? That's a two-pound fine.

- When he started broadcasting he was under the protection of the Crown?

- He owed allegiance.

- Got him!

Central Criminal Court, Old Bailey EC4.

- Are you guilty or not guilty?

- Not guilty.

– Gouge his eyes! Lop his ears!

No alcohol for Joyce, no tobacco, very little food. He debates eternal life with McNab. Mag the wife blubs for the press.

– It were a fit up.

– Nazi's a Nazi snuff for me.

– But he was a Yank!

They twist the rules to trine him.

– One could wish he were condemned on something more solid than a falsehood.

Bring out Samson to entertain us! Haw Haw leaves the cell in Brixton shackled in chains of adamantine. Joyce walks the yard at Bow Street burning in penal fire. Scarface stands in the dock tongue stilled the world is ours.

The last unpublished interview.

– I have sad and haunting memories.

– We all do. So shut it.

– I yield nothing of my political opinions.

– Bloody ought to. Your lot'll never be forgiven.

– I did not act wrongly.

– Yer most definitely did. Guilty as charged, Goebbels.

– I was once regarded as an ardent patriot.

– By half a dozen Quisling loonies!

– I hate the idea of dying as England's enemy.

– Hate's your thing Joyce. Glad to oblige.

– Hitlerite scum he was. He held his chin high. Really high.

– His nose where the top of his head should a bin.

After the last supper his cell smells of spam and dripping.

– I am proud to die for my ideals.

- We'll bury them with you.

- My work has not been in vain.

- Course it has, loser. Never again.

- After I have died I will resume.

- Nutter.

Here shall thy proud waves be stayed.

- I'll say goodnight then.

Drums as spotlights play on monumental capitals BRITISH MOVIETONE NEWS edited by Gerald Sanger presented by Sir Gordon Craig.

- This is Movietone, Leslie Mitchell reporting. THE VOICE OF JOYCE IS SILENT. William Joyce has been executed and to millions of Britons that must have seemed his obvious destiny once captured.

Joyce, older but recognisable by his scar, steps from a car onto a country road between a meadow and a ploughed field. Hands in his jacket pockets, he strolls from the right of the screen, and is cut, then back to the right, to be cut again, smiling and nodding to the camera. He is flanked by an armed guard in uniform.

- Pictures of him are rare. This picture shows him at exercise during his captivity before being brought to trial in London. Convicted as a traitor, he carried his appeal to the House of Lords. No man could have had a fairer hearing but in Wandsworth Gaol on January first his life was forfeit.

Grey prison gates, high grey walls, the prison's blue clock in grey.

- Crowds gather outside as crowds always will, to read the notice of the forthcoming execution.

A shaky shot of a form being filled by hand. Screws pin a notice to a board. Berets, a hooped school cap, headscarves, trilbies. They read. Nobody takes off their hat.

- Doubtless few had not listened to, and detested, the voice of Lord Haw Haw.

It is surely time for the English people to reflect, whines overdub Joyce, that if it is Paris today, it can be London in the very near future.

– Yes they've heard that voice, they've wished the man dead, and they'd waited, almost as they waited now. The notice has been posted proclaiming that Joyce has been hanged. That is the only end that traitors to the country can expect.

After his death there was a quarrel over the disposition of certain mantelpiece ornaments of no value.

The Union Movement British Empire Party League of Empire Loyalists White Defence League British National Party National Socialist Movement Greater Britain Movement British Movement Racial Preservation Society Action Party British Defence League National Democratic Party National Socialist British Workers' Party Candour Spearhead National Front Flag Group Official National Front League of St George Our Nation Britannia Party National Assembly Anti-Communist Commando White Nationalist Crusade British National Party National Socialist Group National Independence Party National Party National Action Party November 9th Society National Socialist Workers' Initiative UK Patriotic Front National Socialist Action Party English Solidarity British Democratic Party Constitutional Movement National Party of St George National Democrats National Socialist Movement British Resistance White Nationalist Party England First National Democratic Freedom Movement Nationalist Alliance British People's Party Redwatch New Nationalist Party International Third Position National Action Britannica Party English Defence League Britain First British Democratic Party.

– None can see me, though he may seek; everywhere am I, though hidden from sight.

he's waiting and watching he knows his time will come

– In death, as in life, I defy the Jews.

The pillars don't budge. The temple doesn't fall.

The dead which he slew at his death were none.

Judenmord he yells.

The nape flinches. Her voice wavers.

my brother he confronted me rolled up his Manchester

*Guardian clubs me with it shouting Judenmord Judenmord
it's your damn doing woman he was furious he didn't speak
to me for months it was horror on the wireless it wasn't my
doing I couldn't tell him could I*

– This day at Belsen was the most horrible of my life. I saw it all – furnaces
where thousands have been burnt alive. .. The pit – 15 feet deep – as big
as a tennis court, piled to the top at one end with naked bodies… The
British bulldozers, digging a new pit for the hundreds of bodies lying all
over the camp.

*Dimbleby on old faithless my life shatters when I hear him
had I done enough what had I done I couldn't breathe I
resolve to be lower than the grass quieter than the water I
burn in shame*

– Dark huts piled with human filth in which the dead and dying are lying
together. You must step over them to avoid the sticks of arms that are
thrust imploringly towards you.

*our windows are broken and smashed again more than once
I leave cardboard in they nettle Astra's face rub horse shit in
her hair how can they do that to a girl a child animals they
won't serve me in the shops I stand at the counter they look
past me as if I'm not there hand bread and meat to women
either side of me pretend not to hear me I'd be polite then I'd
be angry but it's not long before I realise invisible is good*

At this point there is a silence on the tape. Nothing is said for more than a
minute. No sounds of any movement by Joan, or interruption by a nurse, or
my own presence. The nape is still and I'm shtum. Was she gathering her
thoughts? Necking water? She picks up the glass silently sips inaudibly
puts it back down without a sound lifts it again sighs noiselessly.

– It must have been hard.

*on the tip of every tongue the toe of every boot that was me
dear ha they wanted to shave my head parade me naked
in the streets like France I would have welcomed shears
hewing at my hair being attacked gives you someone to hate
a scapegoat for yourself they didn't have the guts*

On a tyme, as this creatur was at Cawntyrbery in the church among the monkys, sche was gretly despised and reprvyd.

- Thow shalt be brent! Her is a cartful of thornys redy for the, and a tonne to bren the wyth!

- Tak and bren her!

John Bullies, she says, Tommy bulldogs, young boars they all take a run at me she says, a ravening roaring lion confronts me on the hill.

At the railway bridge whaaabhaaarrrpp carriages archover archover arch overhead, human stench sent by train to feed a furnace on the saltmarsh.

Sallow fingernails ghetto a shower at the baths. Swarms of claws scaling tile. Sussurating scratchers gang to fists of clip, fling at Joan, husks tamping the sprayheads, clogging pipes. The infest showls and wails lamenting in the tox shar-la-ma I lift my eyes to the mountains.

> *in the camp on the marsh they watch me through the wire silent I turn away I hurry away I will not be part of it I go to the harbour out on the arm to the drop but I don't I'd come a bit unglued I see a ship a Hebrew prayer on the sail eyes trawling the coast it comes and goes with the tide I scut inland the huts are Auschwitz snow falls ash they snatch me on the high street drag me in a van*

The curs came all around. A pack of evil encircled me. They cast lots for my clothes. They count out my bones.

- You're worm not woman. A disgrace.

- Mosley's slut.

- Haw Haw's whore.

> *thumbs in my eyes I couldn't get my breath they grip my wrists clamp my ankles filthy fingers in my mouth laughter and ripping they came about me like bees*

The bed a gulf between us grows.

> *all who see me mock me curl their lips and shake their heads*

Hiss of the tape deck. Reels belittle and enlarge.

> *I gave my back to the smiters I set my face like flint*

A butcher in his apron, blade raised.

– You'd be Joan Cade?

– I am.

– There's the door.

Cleaver hacking, splinters pitting chop.

She pays for the loaf. The baker keeps the change. He stabs his fingers into the underside, spits on the crust, then wraps it. The wives behind Joan laugh. She bags the bread and leaves.

The bus swerves, sluicing a puddle. Joan's slopped. The passengers stand to see her, kids' noses flat to the glass. The driver gave notice. A chorister kicks her basket over, strewing rations in the road.

– Evil trollop. Trull!

> *my heart longs for a bullet my throat itches for a razor blade*
> *so I go to the railway crossing*

Stains and scratches on my desk. I wait.

> *to give way to sorrow unfits us for everything*

Dust and hair foul my keyboard.

> *there was many a throe and pinches of the purse*

Blocks, a bar, staggered junctions, dark estate of letters.

> *nobody would employ me*

Have I nothing to say?

The echo profile changes.

It's livelier, the reverb's more pronounced.

> *Willy like our Lord suffered hard strokes bitter scourging*
> *shameful death*

There's a thudding sound. The back of her hand I think, beating a pillow.

> *the fatal tree that's how it ends but it doesn't does it though*

– How do you mean?

death isn't death he gets that from McNab the Catholic in him bouncing back tug of the Jesuits the end's the end I always thought then I see him feel him with my own hand

I was frighted to death, I never was in such a consternation in my life, I thought I should have sunk into the ground, my blood ran chill in my veins, and I trembled as if I had been in a cold fit of an ague, I say there was no room to question the truth of it, I knew his clothes, I knew his horse, and I knew his face.

As I listen I see her. Nape framed by the bay, diaphragm quaking, a mole, a fine chain. She raises a hand. It points at the town.

he's still there between this hill and the waterline caught in the shiftings I know I used to see him when I could get out

A crowd will gather, and not know it walks the very street whereon a thing once walked that seemed a burning cloud.

Once, a Bank Holiday, the bell dozened noon. The air bit shrewdly. He sought Joan out.

hold hold my heart he calls crossing the road towards me do not be afraid Joan he says hold hold my heart I tell myself

Fear not, nor think it is a phantom which thou seest. The grave walks.

we stand two fools saying hold hold my heart looking at each other in wonder I look into his eyes touch the wound it was in Red Lion Alley doubting Joan he calls me when I touch his cheek I was but not for long it's Willy I hold him I will not let him go people turn to look at us

Joan my love from the best of days, he says. Wonderful times, he exclaims, the union, our plots, the parades, Hoxton, Joannie, remember Hoxton? She does. And Hastings and Munich and here in Gladstone Road. How's Joe?

– Joe's gone.

– I'm sorry.

– Willy how could I ever forget.

– You and I Joan my love.

She fingers the scar.

was I loved Willy was I lovable really did you love me I ask I was fearful too of course I thought by then he'd know

A joy to see you Joan he says.

– I've missed you.

– Together again, us.

– Why did you go Willy? To Berlin.

He'd sworn an oath to Menelaus. Was obliged to fight the Trojans. The command came from Athena. Mercury arrived with orders from Jupiter.

– I thought life would be better in Corinth.

– With Margaret?

then he kissed me Willy kissed me gently kissed me here

She keeks my way. Joan raises her right hand, touching the cheek nearest the window. The nape's quiet for a while. The eye closes. I give her some time. I can hear the trundling of the tape. Joan raises both hands to her face. She lowers them.

there was in a dazzling light I'm lit on a stage I'm rising in the air a perv looks up my skirt Willy's lifting with me he points to a window lovers on a bed in the Albert we laugh smut soots my mouth we're up by the chimney pots my eyes sting I cough we climb higher skywards far too high for me

– In our proper motion we ascend.

– You've got it.

I open my arms wide I feel like a kite the road tilts a gull lunges at us scrawking its beak smears soot on my blouse there's a light breeze the chunter of a bus gusts of music the sea opens before us littered with sails the high street curls left a crane in Sea Street masts in the harbour smoke and steam straps biting my armpits

I photograph the undersides of their feet. They are wearing curious shoes. The soles have heels beneath the toes and toes for heels.

– Throwing Trackers off the track.

I study their reflection in the window of a stable. Inside a disembodied hand scratches on the glass with a nail.

nam dlo dab

se'h wonk tn'seod

Dead how's this happening?

> *it's breathtaking high above the town but quite a drop I'm safe so's Willy no hood no cuffs no bag on his head I won't let them take you I tell him people are kneeling removing their hats neighbours strangers passers by sharing in the miracle sieg heilers in the car park little sods throwing stones as well there's no cover up there they crack my knee bruise a breast everyone's looking up faces freckling the junction the Union always drew a crowd at the Horsebridge I must rally their racial spirit Willy says I'm going down to speak to them we mustn't waste this moment wait I say but down he goes don't go I call they haven't forgotten his hat catches on my foot and falls I clutch my bag close don't go but he's gone leaving me and the gulls Willy's mobbed I hear cheers and catcalls boos hang Haw Haw laughter I feel exposed ridiculous even I can see the yard of the Duke porters and kitchen staff I may as well be smoke for all the notice they take after an age they rise towards me I taste soot I smell leaves rotting in gutters the couple in the bedroom have gone the alley gets wider it closes about me*

Fortitude, Joyce shouts up at her shoes, fortitude and loyalty will see us through. Joan's toes point behind her, to me. I hear his question.

– Have you upheld the cause Joan, new Britain, our nation unpolluted? Where do you meet, is the turnout good why aren't you wearing a badge?

> *times have changed I call down to him there's nothing anymore we don't that future's past it's over*

– You're a deserter? You too, perfidious Joan!

She's frightened. How will he be when he knows it all?

> *adieu he said remember me he marches off in a huff down the*

259

alley to Harbour Street he was hair trigger always flaring
up don't go I call I reach down between my feet towards him
I paddle the air one minute Willy's beside me then he's gone
he hadn't changed a bit

Here she burst into uncontrollable grief, and the remainder of her words were inarticulate.

– She's having a bit of a turn.

– You were right to ring the alarm. We've seen this before.

– Very like, perchance 'twill walk again.

– Whatever she's got you've caught it.

The nurse pinches Joan's cheeks, forcing a shaft for pills and water.

– Go now she needs to sleep.

I climb the hill with foreboding.

I've had a call. Someone at the station leaked the rough cut to the news team. The hacks have dubbed Joan the Nazi Nanny. They've been calling our critics for soundbites. They're doorstepping staff.

– The station is the news.

– It's reporting on itself.

– Narcissus on air.

The sky is field grey and rumbling like a tank.

Joan's not well.

– I'm cluck today.

She's slipping away, slowly.

We listen to the rough cut with a radio on for local news.

we're over Germany it's like mid-Kent all chequered with
orchard acre after acre of rosebush and medieval market
towns home with mountains

- Residents in Whitstable are outraged that a ninety-year-old former fascist is being interviewed about her past for a broadcast that is scheduled to go on the air in six weeks time.

I helped launch a womens branch in Morland Hatch up by the church it was standing room only in Mrs Pullen's drawing room that night

- We spoke to campaign spokesman Reuben Reznick earlier today.

- I do not want a lying fascist voice in my sitting room a Nazi from the past invading my home. What does the BBC think it's doing? In Europe today, the fascist threat is real. Radio Canticum is complacent, it's deaf to victims of antisemitism who once again live in fear. The BBC mustn't normalise fascism.

they joined to get rid of the Old Gang unemployment the threat of war that's what fired them up some said the Old Gang was run for the Jews others said by the Jews yes but that wasn't the spark

- Organisers say a protest march will take place later today, setting out from the car park, passing along the High Street and ending near Century Close on Borstall Hill where the elderly woman now lives.

- On Older and Wiser later this morning Dr Jeffrey Senez will reveal how ageing involves a journey back through our lives, a living in reverse which prepares us for what W B Yeats called the shiftings that await us after death. That's Jeffrey Senez, Older and Wiser, after Sports Talk.

he never owned a radio shop here he didn't work in one either it's a myth I know people say he did but they're remembering another shop two other chaps in the Union

- Remarkable pictures have been taken of what appears to be a winged figure high in the night sky over the coastal town of Whitstable in Kent. Local artist Ceri Swanson-Nolde, who took the shots, will be talking about them here at ten pm on Monday.

- At first I thought it was a very large gull but it got bigger and bigger it was circling then it disappeared behind the mill.

I'm tired, says the nape, my batteries are flat. Keeling slowly to the head board it sinks into a pillow. Counterweights, white with blue veins, pop up at the foot of the bed.

turn the radios off will you

A sudden boom, prolonged and deep, shakes the window. It comes from the direction of the harbour. There's a curl of smoke above the horizon, like a question mark. The explosion triggers a harsh buzz like a drill piercing a wall.I see smoke thinning over waves recoiling from the beach. Alarms sound in the distance.

I think we're running out of time

Joan's left elbow pivots, raising a forearm. A rumpled palm distends towards me, fingers raking, hold my hand she asks.

be sure to tell them that Willy's American his British passport's bogus he wasn't entitled he wasn't here he couldn't commit treason get this over clearly Willy should not have been hanged it was murder lock him up for fourteen years he deserves that the noose no it wasn't legal it was retribution

Her hand is cold, she has no grip. I bed it in mine.

I went to the trial it was like being at a very bad play dreary and wooden a ritual you knew exactly what was going to happen next

Then went the jury out, whose names were Mr Blind Man, Mr No-Good, Mr Malice and the others, hanging is too good for him said Mr Cruelty they therefore bought him out to do with him according to their law and first they scourged him, then they buffeted him, then they lanced his flesh with knives after that they stoned him with stones, then pricked him with their swords and last of all they burned him to ashes at the stake.

More rattles. Two yellow bursts, almost simultaneous, near the town centre. Twin rings of smoke hang above the bay. Eyes drawn by a sky cartoonist, they turn our way.

Watchers step from the trees. There are three of them. One climbs onto the bonnet of a car. She stands, shading her eyes, scanning the town. They confer.

we had a petition calling for Willy's reprieve but no one signs Tom turns his back so do members who'd been interned oh oh what heart were so hard it could let a man burn

The smoke swells like a fungus, smudging the bay, sealing the eyes.

that morning the morning they take him from me I go to the old church at Seasalter its quiet there I like it

– It's been standing for a thousand years.

I take Astra with me she plays with lead soldiers on a pew pyoo pyoo she makes shooting noises I hear her now pyoo pyoo I look up at the son of whoever I see a political prisoner hanging there I hear something many will come in but I can't not properly I shout stop at Astra hush I frighten her she points a soldier back at me pyoo pyoo

She stood, a crimson rose weeping, watching him bear a criminal's death, who was guilty of no crime. And while she stood there with full heart the crowds cried out loudly: crucify him, crucify him.

Willy's execution was a sacrifice a thanksgiving his blood for the end of the war it was necessary the price I see that now he took our sin against the Jewish people with him

Smoke drifts towards us, staining the foot of the hill. It's swept aside by a haystack levelling wind. Trees bow in its blast. Sheep and cattle are rounded up and quickly herded into trucks. Stubble blazes, the burn advances slowly, rinsing the hillside with streams of smoke. Children scream through the cul de sac, seeking their mothers and fathers. The mill sheds a sail. It slams into a house and cartwheels over fences.

Crouching by the car, the Watchers dispute among themselves.

The mob is climbing the hill with pitchforks to stick in our vitals.

The wind breaks. It sighs, ceasing. All is still. Then Louis Armstrong swings blue from the walnut. Wynton Marsalis allegros the tran. Hugh Masekela mbaqangas on the pocket set. A lorry appears at the foot of the hill. In its wake excavators, vans, cement mixers. Boles advance in columns hoisting cables. Hard hat scaffolders assault the slope. Arials sprout from rooves, watered by a rising lap of asphalt. Approach roads branch and twig, webbing the slope. Trees thin, the green deflection dims. A barbican rises and rots. Shrills, aggressive dissonance, corroding timbres grate the air. Posters – This is Your Hour! – ride invading lampposts. Flyers – The Hour of Darkness! – seize doormats.

- I heard the voice of the great multitude, as the voice of many waters, as the voice of many thunderings.

- All the creatures of the sea rise to the surface bellowing. Dogfish, swordfish, gurners. The bay burns east to west.

Heads weapons shoulders, the forward edge, men of action, men on stilts, lion ox and eagle. Stormzone static, demon whistling, scream harmonics, the insurgent cacophony of radio.

Grinders produce a continuous rattle with occasionally heavier crashes. They are most prevalent in summer on the warmest days in the afternoon.

Antifascist chanting loops, tax averse grumbling, censor whoops.

- A vast vanity fair of shouting indulgences.

The spine of language cracking.

Post-punk pensioners egglobbers stoner bluds mums in mumodium broad-casters of first stones gleegionaires gladyhaters spookbusters popuppies Peachers Boseites Cushingclubs showerdenying rabbi-rousers antispyonists nonSutch ravers Tarka the otter and Toad Hall inter-onanists sighbores saltcons takeback controllers herstry profs of uncreative writing Maxtonites levellers landscapers twotskyists skypeers Friends of Oswald Mosley Taxbail Alliance Searchlight windmill preservation truss Sivanandanistas counter-facturers primes. Rising scree. The very rocks and stones wrangle.

Concept implosion concept once oe .

They will sweep out thy house and burn thy belongings, the beams and roof shall lie on thy chin.

- Nothing is now possible but some movement or birth from above preceded by some violent annunciation.

they're coming for me see he's coming too

Deeply disturbing echoes sose ose.

- Do quickly what you are going to do.

As a wireless engineer, the author has come across many cases of noisy reception, howling and intermittent changes of volume being due to nothing more than a down lead wire rubbing against a gutter.

A blinding flash, twenty yards away. A rough hand scoops up the care home, shaking us like cupped dice. The transistor pitches across the bed. It shatters on the wireless. Fuses frack.

– A sound which is like no other a streamline train rushing towards you.

– Inter-atomic bonds stretching, stress cavities fracturing.

Tensing, crinkling, rifting, the window shards into the room. Jags gouge walnut wall and plastic, lancing books scoring Joan slo-mo. Arc voltaic scythers volley vivid sparks.

– The wrath to come is here.

– Axe to the root.

Shattered glass jewels the bed, frosting the recorder.

> *he is risen who was long asleep he crushes the moon huge he stands he cannot be silenced by his light nations shall walk dust and ashes this his story I pass it to you*

– No!

My knuckles crack. Her grasp chokes my fingers.

Smoke fists the room, wadding my nose and throat. Optic scorch, I can't see. Walls shudder, men slam and shout at a distant door.

Three FX interns beat the wall with timber. A fourth churns the wind machine, slinging scrap at a zinc tub with her free hand. Sheet tin shake waves. They all yell at the top of their voices.

– Anyone here can you walk this way towards me hurry.

I will never forget the crackle of the radios, the call signs.

– Charlie Alpha Delta Echo third floor up go up.

A rescue mission? The ceiling drops. Slabs of plaster hole the smoke. Dust spirals, helicose jiving.

During a Raid Keep Calm. Don't Panic. If you are at home, close all doors and windows. Take the necessary extras into your Refuge Room. Turn off gas at the meter, put out all fires. Call the roll of those who should be present, see that each has a Respirator. Seal the room. Don't lock the door. Rest and keep quiet. Twice as much air is used walking about as in sitting still. Don't go out until the All Clear signal sounds.

- Take a wireless set to the Refuge Room to hear official information.

- Turn on music during a raid to drown the sound of explosions.

An abyss opens under our feet. Inherited convictions, presuppositions of thought, fall into it. The walnut wireless follows. Smoke and smoulder coil upwards through the holed ceiling, dust a contrapernal cone descends. The cataclysm barrels down the backslope.

Joan, caked with stucco, hangs head down from the bed. I raise her back to the mattress. Her words are a slow puncture.

- Hurry, find a sibilatori

death flashes of fire a raging

- Joan are you alright Joan?

She turns to me. I see her full on for the first time, caked with gypsum.

I desire you would use all your skill to paint my picture truly like me and not flatter me at all

She brushes crust from her forehead.

remark all these roughnesses pimples warts and everything as you see me otherwise I will never pay a farthing for it

She scours her sockets. She spits in cupped palms. She rubs, she sputs, she mops her dial.

What has disfigured the face that was once so serene? What wounds are these I see?

A badge of love. The scarred cheek from lip to lobe. A sag toward the jaw.

I used a razor in the scullery after they topped Willy I took out the photo I stripped I washed my face I used a mirror to lippy the line I stood on a fresh towel I puffed out my cheek and I cut it right through

- Good god a narrative arc.

- Shoosh.

it was solidarity I love Willy love resists I won't let him die

The rut drains.

You can't be sitting here, says the cop.

- You need to move away sir.

Flashing lights, clip radios croaking. The cul de sac is busy. Police cars are bluesing, a van of flatfoots idles white, yellow tape droops between the trees.

A private ambulance swings past the demo. A hand painted banner says NO PLATFORM, a megaphone horns BBC BIAS, protesters chant BAN THE BROADCAST.

Three care home windows have been smashed, says a Radio Canticum reporter live from the steps, the doors to the foyer have been wrenched from their frames.

- The damage was done before the arrival of protesters opposed to the radio series being made about Mrs Cade, an elderly former member of Oswald Mosley's Blackshirts and a supporter of Hitler before the second world war. The demonstration is noisy but many of those taking part are now beginning to drift away, shocked by the scene of violence and vandalism which has greeted their arrival. It is believed that large explosive fireworks were set off around the Canterbury Close care home during the attack. The building was almost empty at the time as many of the residents had joined the protest and there appear to be no eye witnesses.

The microphone siphons reassurance from the Super.

- It's too early to establish exactly what has happened here but we will spare no effort in finding and bringing to justice whoever is responsible for this appalling attack.

We do not condone acts of vandalism, says a PR for the protest. Ban the broadcast ban the broadcast bias bias ban it! The mic trowels her voice from the roadside chantry. We were not involved. Bias bias burn it!

- The BBC encouraged this attack by giving a platform to fascists. We call on the local station to suspend work on the programme immediately.

Don't go, swans Joan as she's lifted into the ambulance. I can't hear her as she's wearing a gas mask. He's not going nowhere answers a Watcher from inside the ribbon. His colleagues nod. One's on the phone. No passengers, says the medic, not even fam.

— Where will they take you? Where are you taking her?

The doors close like curtains.

Four weeks later.

I churn the handle of the dispenser. Budgie seed drops on waxed paper. Bacon sizzles in a pan, I can smell it. I roil a coffee grinder. The beans splinter magnificently, like cannon. Dispenser and grinder and pan pelt rain to the motorway.

— Inside the Whale is a documentary series in which Joan Cade, a former secretary to Fascist leader Oswald Mosley, describes the activities of Hitler's British followers between the wars, the street clashes which took place up and down the country, and the tensions which developed at the movement's headquarters. She discloses details of the funding provided by Mussolini from Rome and Hitler from Berlin. She also reveals the tensions which grew between Oswald Mosley and his deputy William Joyce, differences of opinion about antisemitism, the German threat and how to replace Parliament with a corporate state. As street violence and the looming war with Germany erode public support for fascism in Britain they take separate paths. Mosley spends much of the war in prison but Joyce escapes to Berlin in mysterious circumstances. That's Inside the Whale with Mosley's secretary, Mondays at seven ten on BBC Canticum during April.

Drivers returning late from London thwoc thwoc thwoc through a docudrama downpour.

> *I think Willy was working for the watchers for secret intelligence Toad Hall squirrels I'm sure of it they'll never confirm it no not the service but they did telephone him they warn Willy he's listed for arrest they do say he should leave the country agents accompany him to Dover where I see him off it was the very last chance to insert Willy in Berlin it was a bold move and possibly a desperate one but clearly in the national interest*